ECHO CHASER

A COMING OF AGE FANTASY

NOT ENOUGH BOOK 2

EDEN WOLFE
CRAIG MARTELLE

CRAIG MARTELLE, INC

To those who support any author by buying and reading their books, I salute you. I couldn't keep telling these stories if it weren't for you and for the support team surrounding me. No one works alone in this business.

*The team includes
Beta Readers and Proofreaders –
with our deepest gratitude!*

*Micky Cocker
James Caplan
Kelly O'Donnell
John Ashmore
Christine Ginestet
Latisha Rich*

ECHO CHASER

1

Waves crashed with thundering menace against the rocky coast, but for Ravlen there was no turning back. The boat was already gone.

Ravlen observed her breathing, the beating of her heart, the cold sand between her toes. But most of all, she felt a tingling across her skin, a reaction she couldn't control.

The sensation of echoes all around her.

"Welcome to the mainland." Dina's gravelly voice pulled Ravlen back to the present. "We've been waiting for you." She wore a long black dress, which ended at the tops of her thick, black leather boots. Her white-blonde hair contrasted with her deep-set brown eyes, their piercing gaze pinning Ravlen to the spot.

Even Binner stared at her, head cocked, eyes wide.

"Waiting for us?" Ravlen ventured carefully. She hadn't yet gotten a good read on their new mentor. "Marriel and I came as soon as we could." Ravlen looked at Marriel, but she just shrugged.

"What I mean," Dina continued, "is that we've been waiting for someone like you, and for a long time."

Ravlen gulped. While she didn't know exactly what Dina meant, the waves of sensation over her arms told her that the situation was bad.

Very bad.

Dina tilted her head, as though studying the girls who had been sent to save the mainland. "You've got your work cut out for you. The proliferation of echoes has overtaken the number of us here."

"Proliferation?"

"In other words," Dina's voice stretched and her eyebrows rose as if she was losing patience, "there are many echoes around here. As in, a *whole lot* of echoes popping up all over the place, all of the stinking time."

Dina turned her back to Marriel and Ravlen, her hand on her forehead. Ravlen felt her disbelief.

I've got to do something to convince her that we can do this. Right now, we need her as much as she needs us.

"I know, and you're right. I can feel the echoes." Ravlen ran her hands over her arms. She had goose bumps.

Dina looked back. "You can? You can feel them from here?"

Ravlen nodded.

Dina paused, considering. "This is the landing place from the island specifically because we check it thoroughly for echoes. There aren't any within at least ten miles. This place is clear. And you're having a physiological reaction?"

Ravlen didn't know what 'physiological' meant, but she could feel Dina's disdain swiftly transforming into awe.

Dina turned to Marriel, tilting her head in Ravlen's direction. "Is she always this sensitive?"

"Pretty much." Marriel leaned in. "And if you think *that's* incredible, you should see what she can do *inside* an echo. It's unbelievable."

"I've heard." Dina put her hands on her hips and straightened her spine. "Miss Ravlen, you've built up quite a reputation for yourself, and quickly. I just hope you're able to withstand the many distractions that the mainland will throw at you. You won't be any good to anyone if you let yourself get sucked into the plethora of new and shiny things here."

"Plethora?" Ravlen was trying to keep up, but Dina was so different from Janna. She had a hard edge. It showed in her voice, the turned-down corners of her mouth, and the tattoos covering her arms that Ravlen found both stunning and frightening.

"Plethora means 'many'."

Proliferation, plethora... I wish they'd taught us a little bit more about mainland terms back on the island...

Ravlen scrunched up her nose. It was possible that all this had been covered during lessons when Ravlen hadn't paid attention. There had been a time when she'd thought her classes were all as useful as gobbledygook.

But that had been before the echo arrived on the island, before she'd found herself at the center of an adventure to shut it down. And before Janna had selected Ravlen to be her protégé.

So much had changed in so little time.

Dina scratched her arm where a black snake tattoo wrapped around her biceps. On her other arm was a multi-colored tattoo that looked like a series of scribbles. Ravlen tried to make sense of the image, but it didn't appear to be a real shape.

"That?" Dina saw Ravlen inspecting her arm. "It's what I remember of the entry to the echo that took my sister."

Ravlen lowered her voice. "Oh. Did you find her?"

"Ravlen!" Marriel hissed. "That's not polite."

Dina didn't bat an eyelash. "No, I didn't. I was only ten at the time and had no idea what was happening."

"I'm sorry." Ravlen stuffed her hands in her pockets and Marriel bit her lip.

"Don't be. She's still alive, I know it." Dina pressed forward, leading them to the large rocks that bordered the coast. "I spent ages looking for her, but she's lost deep in an old echo, an established one with years behind it. Maybe one day…"

Dina's voice trailed off. Ravlen shifted and rolled the good luck charm in her pocket, the one Marriel had made of shells from the island's coast. She was going to need a lot of luck if she was ever going to understand Dina and others like her on the mainland.

Dina shook her head as if casting off the thought. "Memories are distracting. Let's focus on the two of you. In the first place, we have to get you some new clothes. Those homemade island sacks won't do you any favors when it comes to fitting in here. Follow me."

Dina scrambled up a wall of boulders that separated the beach from the mainland beyond.

Marriel and Ravlen exchanged an uncertain glance, but their choice had already been made.

"The mainland…" Marriel whispered.

Ravlen broke into a wide smile. "Here we come!"

Binner leapt into action and scaled the boulders as though they were mere stepping-stones.

Ravlen and Marriel rushed to catch up with Dina, who was surprisingly adept at climbing despite her long dress and clunky leather boots.

"THAT'S MORE LIKE IT." DINA PURSED HER LIPS, EXAMINING Ravlen like a work of art.

Ravlen looked down at herself. "I find it hard to believe

we're going to fit in dressed like this." The brightly flowered button up shirt was a stark contrast to the dull gray slacks, but they were the only things her size she'd found in the shed.

"Beggars can't be choosers, and besides, this is temporary. We're lucky we can keep anything here at all. This corner of the property is owned by someone who knows someone who was saved from the echo. The shed is a good cover for new arrivals. But enough of the history lesson. Marriel! What is taking you so long?"

"I found this incredible dress! It's just hard to zip up the back… got it!" Marriel slowly revealed herself, her face alight with the thrill of her outfit. "Check this out! Can you imagine if any of the girls back on the island saw this?"

Ravlen had to stifle a laugh. "*That's* what you picked?"

"What's wrong with it?"

Marriel was in a white dress that looked more like it belonged in one of their dress-up trunks on the island than on a school-going mainland teenager. But most notably, it was *big*. With ruffles that burst in every direction, it was long enough to cover Marriel's knees but hung awkwardly above her ankles.

Dina tipped her head. "I think you're too early for the wedding. Go pick something else."

"Why? This is great! I love the way the lace feels on my arms. And the pants in there are all too short."

Dina scratched her head. "Better to wear the too-short pants than that catastrophe."

"Sure, Dina." Marriel's chin fell. "I just wanted it to be something special for our first day."

"Believe me," Dina chuckled. "You'll have plenty of *special*. Within a couple of days you'll have *special* coming out of your ears. Now put on some pants and a t-shirt and let's get going."

"HELLO, GIRLS," A WOMAN AS WIDE AS THE DOORWAY maneuvered her way out of a small bungalow onto a veranda with a finely manicured garden in front. "I'm your first landing pad. You can call me Georgie." She winked.

Ravlen liked her already.

"How about those pancakes, Georgie?" Dina called out, already rushing past Ravlen and Marriel up the single step and into the house.

Georgie dramatically put her hands on her hips in mock annoyance. "I swear, Dina, you only ever come here anymore for my pancakes. If I didn't know better, I'd say that's the only reason you volunteer to meet the new arrivals."

Georgie's eyebrows flicked upward in conspiratorial delight at Marriel and Ravlen. They both stifled giggles as Dina marched back onto the bungalow's wide veranda.

"That's not very nice." Dina pursed her lips, but Ravlen could tell she was just playing along.

"All of you," Georgie gestured grandly, "get your butts in chairs and let's have some pancakes with the best maple syrup you've ever tasted."

"I've never had maple syrup," Ravlen said as she entered the house.

"Never had maple syrup!" Georgie cupped her head in her hands. "And here you're supposed to save us from our own desires! You'd better have a double helping then."

As she headed toward the wonderful smell coming from the dining room, Ravlen decided she was perfectly happy to stay at Georgie's place for as long as necessary.

"Don't get too comfy," Dina called out from the kitchen. "Georgie is your first landing pad but not your last. She spoils the girls too much."

"Hey now!"

"What? It's true!" Dina looked back at Ravlen and Marriel. "Eat up. Enjoy. Your other carers will pay more attention to the food pyramid."

"What is a food pyramid?" Ravlen asked with a mouth full of pancake.

"Something that smart people thought up to make you eat healthy." Georgie's eyes sparkled. "I haven't followed it since I learned how to bake apple crumble."

"Apple crumble!"

"This one's easy to please." Georgie looked at Marriel while pointing a thumb in Ravlen's direction.

"Just don't let her anywhere near almond croissants," Marriel added, her own mouth full.

"What about manners?" Georgie shook her head and looked at Dina. "Can you add that to your list of mainland lessons?"

"Noted."

The sun set and Georgie settled Marriel and Ravlen into their shared bedroom. Ravlen hardly had time to take it in. As soon as her head hit the pillow, she was out.

RAVLEN WOKE IN THE MIDDLE OF THE NIGHT WITH A START. She was covered in sweat despite a crispness in the air.

Where am I?

It took a moment before she recognized the room with its fading flowered wallpaper and brown shag carpet. Marriel was fast asleep across from her in the other single bed, barely visible under a bedspread covered in flowers the same color as the wallpaper. Ravlen hadn't been dreaming and everything was silent around her.

What woke me?

Her skin tingled from head to toe, like a thousand

feathers brushing over her. She pushed back the cotton bedspread and tiptoed toward the kitchen.

Maybe I just need some water.

She was surprised to find Georgie sitting at the kitchen table, dabbing a tear with a handkerchief.

"Ravlen," she whispered and glanced into the living room where Dina was out cold on the sofa. "Is something wrong?"

"Why are you crying?" Ravlen whispered back. At the sight of the kind woman in tears, Ravlen felt her own throat grow tight and she fought back the sensation of crying herself.

"Oh, sweetheart. Don't you worry about this old carer." She smiled but her eyes betrayed her sadness. "Did you know I used to be a carer on the island?"

"No."

"Those were my favorite years. Once my days of echo chasing had passed—"

"*You* were an echo chaser?"

"I may not look it now, but I was a quick one in my youth."

Ravlen tried to imagine it, but she couldn't imagine Georgie either young or fast.

"Was it the tingling that woke you?"

Ravlen nodded.

"It happens to the more sensitive girls, though most sleep right through it. You didn't get to see much of this neighborhood. The people are lovely, but times are tough. No lack of wanting for more, and it's completely understandable. It also means that echoes pop up here regularly, which makes it a perfect training ground for you."

"Have you gone into any of them?" Ravlen asked, careful with her words.

"Goodness, no. I was cut off at age eighteen. I thought I'd be able to do more than that. Almost all echo chasers think it. But when the moment of adulthood hits, it hits like a truck."

Ravlen remembered Janna in the echo, at her very last moments of managing it. She almost hadn't made it out.

"Yes, I gave up echo chasing a long time ago." Georgie took a loud slurp of her tea, then caught herself and looked over at Dina, but Dina remained out for the count. "I loved being a carer on the island, but they have only a limited view of what the echo chasers do. Island carers do their best to prepare the girls, but carers don't see them as they struggle with the challenges they face here. That's why I transferred. I'm not just the arrival lodging, you see. I also house the girls before they head back to the island for their reprieve. So when new girls arrive…"

A tear threatened to escape from Georgie's eye, but she wiped it away in time.

"It makes you sad to see new girls come?" Ravlen was having a hard time making sense of what Georgie was feeling, interesting and helpful as her story was.

Georgie sighed. "Not sad, not exactly. It's a complicated emotion. I see you now, fresh, eager, chomping at the bit… and I know the next time I see you, you will be tired, worn, maybe even disillusioned. Some girls forget why they came. They forget their mission, or worse, their calling."

Georgie took Ravlen's hand, leaving the chair and kneeling before her.

"Try not to forget, Ravlen. I've heard wonderful things about you. I hope you will withstand the challenges better than the others. Don't lose heart. There are so many of us who would trade places with you if we could. But we can't. Next time I see you, let me find you still joyous, curious, and *full* of heart. Can you try? Can you try for me?"

Ravlen knew that she had to give the carer this gift. "Yes, Georgie. I will try."

Georgie stood slowly, leaning against the table for support. "Good girl. I believe in you." She blinked and Ravlen saw the twinkle return to her eye. "Now, young lady, it is the middle of the night, and you need your battle sleep. Tomorrow you'll venture into your first mainland echo, and I will not let you be anything but rested and ready – with a full tummy to boot."

2

Ravlen tapped her foot. "How much longer is she going to be?"

Dina didn't take her eyes off the haze. "She'll take as long as she takes."

"But…"

"No but's. Your time is coming. Be patient. Go hang out in the park."

Ravlen took a deep breath. Who knew how long Marriel would be in the echo, trying to figure out its logic. Dina said this was a quick assignment to start them off, but they'd been waiting an hour already for Marriel to reemerge.

Ravlen kicked at the dirt, reluctant to call where they waited a park. Rusted climbing structures stood crooked on gravel. A swing set with room for three swings was missing one and another was only attached on one side. The remaining swing didn't look far from snapping off either.

Georgie wasn't exaggerating when she said there isn't a lot of money in this neighborhood.

She debated asking Dina about it, but Dina stood with her arms crossed, staring at the haze, and Ravlen didn't want to interrupt her. Dina's white-blonde hair was braided into pigtails, and she wore a black t-shirt with odd-looking lips on them, torn black tights, and fake leather shorts that Ravlen thought looked uncomfortable. But Ravlen was beginning to get a sense of Dina's ways.

For one, Dina didn't like to be interrupted.

Ravlen squinted into the bright morning sun and saw a couple of boys around six or seven years old running to join another boy who was waiting for them on a bench.

Aren't kids supposed to be at school? she thought.

Ravlen wandered in their direction while keeping her distance. She didn't want to attract attention while Marriel was still in the echo.

The boy who'd been waiting pulled a plastic box from his backpack. He lifted the lid and the others looked in, delight exploding across all their faces. The newcomers giggled and jumped up and down.

What's in there? Ravlen craned her neck but couldn't see that far. *A frog? Jewels?*

The boys reached into the box and took out…

Apples?

Each boy held a bright red apple. One turned and ran under the rusted slide, while the other ran behind a tree, but still in Ravlen's line of sight.

The boys each took their time, inspecting the apple, rubbing it, smelling it, and only then taking a tender bite.

They act like they never eat apples.

It struck Ravlen.

Maybe they don't.

Once they'd taken their first tastes, the boys ate hungrily with huge bites, one after the other before they'd even swallowed what was in their mouths. They ate them down to the core.

The boy on the bench wore a satisfied smile.

The others returned and spoke in low tones but the boy on the bench replied, "Sorry, that's all I have. Mom only bought a small bag of apples. I'll try to get more for tomorrow, okay?"

More talking in low tones.

"I'll try. I'll get whatever I can. My mom might not notice if I take a few crackers."

More low tones.

"No, I can't give you anything for lunch. And I'm already late for school."

There were nods and gracious smiles before the two boys ran off in one direction while the boy on the bench watched them go.

His face told Ravlen everything she needed to know.

What a kind boy to give them food. Georgie was right, there are people suffering around here. I never thought it would be kids.

"Made it!" Marriel's voice drove all thoughts of boys and apples from Ravlen's mind. She rushed back to Dina's side as Marriel emerged from the haze.

"So?" Dina began. "Did you figure it out? Don't give it away if you did. Ravlen still has to go by herself."

"It was pretty unexpected, I have to say." Marriel's brow furrowed. "At first it seemed obvious, but I dug deeper, just in case my observations were off-base." She looked at Ravlen. "That's all I'm going to say. Good luck, Ravlen. I bet this will be an easy one for you."

Ravlen's stomach dropped. After the hungry boys she'd just seen, she wasn't sure she wanted to know what was on the other side.

"In you go." Dina nodded toward Ravlen and then to the haze.

"We'll be waiting," Marriel added with a comforting smile. "Don't be afraid."

Ravlen put on a brave face. *I'm not afraid. I'm* dreading *it.*

She took her first step, and the haze took her the rest of the way.

What she saw was far from what she'd expected.

"Rainbows?"

Ravlen twisted left and right, blinking in case she was seeing things. Sure enough, they were everywhere.

Rainbows filled the sky, landing on the ground in far-off places, but not so far that Ravlen couldn't walk there if she wanted. The rainbows shone in colors she couldn't identify. Purple blended into a deep velvet that blended into ocean waves that blended into blues and on they went, each rainbow an individual combination of colors.

"It doesn't make sense," she addressed the rainbows. "This is against everything Carer Raheen taught us in fourth year science."

Ravlen gently tapped her head, reminding herself of the lessons she'd learned on the island.

"I'm in an echo now. It's not real. It doesn't run by our rules."

She moved forward, pushing aside soft, silky grasses, and found herself nearing a village. Bubbles rose into the air, like the soap bubbles children played with, but these were bursting from a giant bubble that enclosed the entire village.

Wild. Now I see why Marriel said it was unexpected. But what's the logic?

Ravlen approached the bubble's edge and watched as the surface swirled with the colors of the rainbows overhead.

She didn't dare enter. She didn't want to know what might happen if she burst the bubble.

A voice reached her ears. It was muffled, but Ravlen focused on it.

That sense training back on the island wasn't for nothing...

"Come in," the voice said. "You are welcome here."

Ravlen recognized the old woman's voice.

I should have guessed she'd be here.

Ravlen looked through the swirling translucence. On the other side, she made out the shape of the elderly, white-haired woman approaching her. With each step the woman took, Ravlen could see her more clearly.

My referent.

"Come, child." Her referent beckoned to her. "Do not be afraid. I'll show you."

Her referent's hand reached through the bubble, a slick layer upon it.

"You see? Come. The weather is beautiful today."

Ravlen took a step, gasping as her foot disappeared into the bubble. She closed her eyes and stepped through, repeating the mantra to calm her nerves:

The echo wants me to be happy here. It wants me to be happy here...

She arrived and the gentle face of her referent tipped sideways in pride. "I told you. The weather is lovely today. Didn't you see all the rainbows? Much to be grateful for. Today will bring in baskets of plenty."

Ravlen wasn't sure what any of that meant, so she smiled and nodded.

"Run along now, join the other children. They might go for a collection soon."

With that, her referent turned and walked away, leaning on her cane.

"Hey, you!"

Ravlen looked around but couldn't see anyone.

"Yes, you! Over here!"

Ravlen turned all the way around but didn't see anyone except her referent walking away and a few adults in animated conversation who clearly weren't talking to her.

"Don't say over here," another voice added. "It's *up* here!"

Ravlen looked up.

Facing her from above were a boy and a girl, both younger than her. "How are you hanging in midair?" Ravlen's face scrunched up.

"We're not, silly!" the girl replied.

"We're on the bubble, of course." The boy looked at the girl and they both shrugged. Their backs were glued to the inside of the bubble's curve, high overhead. "She's new around here, I guess."

"I suppose so, look at what she's wearing."

"Indeed, quite worn out." The boy looked down at Ravlen. "Do you want some new clothes?"

"Okay…" Ravlen was sure there was a catch.

"Don't look so hesitant! Didn't you see the weather?"

"Yeah, the rainbows…" Ravlen wasn't putting it together.

"Come on up, then!"

Ravlen looked around, but there were no ladders or stairs or any other way to get to the top of the bubble.

"She really doesn't know much, does she?" the girl said to the boy.

"You have to come up the *bubble*."

Ravlen rested her hands on her hips, trying to figure it out. "I don't know how."

"Walk to the edge of the bubble, turn around and press your back against it. Then look at us and you'll have no trouble making your way up."

Ravlen checked around the place, but no one was there to stop her, and the few adults in sight didn't seem to take any interest.

She walked over to the bubble, looked around again, then turned, allowing her back to graze the surface. She felt its slickness as it connected with the fabric of her clothes.

"Lean your head against it, too," the girl called down. "Otherwise, you'll be dragged up by your shirt, and that's quite unpleasant."

"Okay…" Ravlen took a nervous breath and leaned her head backward.

"That's it! Now look at us."

She did.

"Whoa!"

Her feet were whisked off the ground like she was in an elevator with no floor. She slid to the top of the bubble with ease, and next thing she knew, she was beside the boy and girl.

"I'm Clara."

"I'm Ollie."

"I'm Ravlen."

"Nice to meet you, Ravlen," they said in unison.

"Shall we get you some new clothes?" Ollie asked.

"Or maybe you're hungry?" Clara added.

"I… uh…"

"Clothes first," Ollie declared.

"Nutrition first," Clara wagged her finger in Ollie's face.

"Good point, sister. You lead the way."

Ravlen blinked and they were gone.

"What? Where did you…"

"Right here, silly."

Ravlen turned her head. Clara and Ollie were on the outside of the bubble.

"How did you get there?"

"The way everyone does." Clara shook her head.

"We have to teach her everything," Ollie whispered loudly. "Turn your body and come through the bubble."

"Uh… okay…"

She did as instructed, and just as they'd said, her body pulled through the bubble's surface and before she knew it, she was sitting on top of it with them. Here the bubble was as strong as a chair, which made no sense since she'd just passed through it as though it were made of nothing more than soapsuds.

This echo is weird. What's its logic? I've got to find it. It can't just be that it defies the rules of science. There must be something more...

"So," Clara squinted into the horizon, "nutrition..."

Ollie looked over the landscape. "What about that one?" He pointed at a rainbow that was particularly shiny.

"No, that one's 'Tenderness'. Can't you see the warmth radiating off it?"

"Oh yes, I see that now."

They continued scanning the sky. Ravlen joined in, but she had no idea what she was looking for. There were at least fifteen rainbows in their immediate area, and Ravlen thought she could make out more in the distance.

"It's hard to pick out just one when the weather is as good as this." Ollie squinted.

"What about that one?" Clara pointed at a rainbow that had yellows as deep as gold and as light as a sun's ray.

"Isn't that one Education?"

"Oh, you're right. But they call it 'Enlightenment'."

"'Enlightenment', yes, that's it. Wait!" Ollie stood on the bubble. "There, right in front of us, of course!"

"Indeed! The red is the red of healthy blood and deep nutrition. Let's go!"

"Go?" Ravlen stood on the bubble, wobbling. She stuck her head between them. "How?"

Clara and Ollie exchanged a glance.

"Just follow us," Clara said.

They slid down the bubble to the ground below. Ravlen followed behind. She thought she was beginning to understand.

"Off to red!" Ollie ran with Clara on his heels.

"Nutrition ahead! Hurry up, Ravlen. Who knows how long the weather will hold!"

Ravlen followed, her curiosity as strong as her desire to understand the echo.

What exactly is going to be in this rainbow of deep red? Is that the key to the logic?

Within a few moments, Clara and Ollie slowed to a walk. Ravlen joined them.

"There you go." Clara pointed. "Help yourself."

The rainbow's red stripe landed in the ground, and at its base was a big black pot. Ravlen stepped closer.

The echo wants me to be happy. I have nothing to fear. This is the nutrition rainbow. I'm likely to find...

Ravlen stopped in her tracks. The pot was full to near overflowing with plump, juicy, bright red...

"Apples." Ravlen swallowed hard. They were the same kind as the ones the boys in the park had eaten, but these were bigger, rounder, and even redder.

She turned to Clara and Ollie. "I've got to go now."

"But you just got here."

"People are waiting for me."

"Where?" Ollie looked around. "There's no one here."

"I'll be back."

"Do come back." Clara's voice lowered. "It seems no one stays here for long. And yet the weather is so wonderful."

Ravlen stopped. "Clara, do all these rainbows have something at the end of them?"

"Of course. Enlightenment, shelter, protection – like clothes – and nutrition."

"Don't forget," Ollie lifted his finger, "there's the grand rainbow. It's greater than all the other rainbows."

"What's at the end of that one?" Ravlen swallowed.

"A pot of gold, of course!"

She didn't wait another moment. She ran back through

the field of soft grasses, slowing just before entering the haze.

Dina was waiting when she arrived on the other side. Marriel rushed over from the single hanging swing.

"So?" Marriel spoke first. "How about that bubble, huh?"

Ravlen tried to catch her breath.

Dina stood in front of Ravlen. "Did you figure it out?"

"Did you see the piles of brand-new clothes? And the books filled with the secrets of history?"

"Apples."

"Apples?" Dina and Marriel asked at once.

"Apples."

Dina nodded. "You figured it out."

"Do I *have* to close it?" Ravlen hated the thought of taking away the simple dreams of the hungry neighborhood boys.

"Yes," Dina said with her hands on her hips and her chin held high. But then she relaxed. Her shoulders dropped and her voice softened in a way Ravlen hadn't heard her speak before. "But don't worry. Another one will take its place within days."

3

Ollie and Clara waved goodbye as the sky turned gray around them.

"That was awfully easy," Marriel said, raising a suspicious eyebrow. "Closing an echo is supposed to be more complicated than that."

Ravlen and Marriel had confronted the echo with the flaw in its logic, starting with the fact that life was not all rainbows and bubbles, and the sky had clouded over.

No originals had wandered into the tiny echo, which encompassed only the bubble and the fields that surrounded it. They shut it down before anyone else found it.

Ravlen waved while the bright sunshine dimmed. It was as if someone was turning down a light, except it was the whole echo going dark.

"Let's go." Marriel tugged on Ravlen's arm, but she wasn't ready to stop waving goodbye to Ollie and Clara.

The process was so much more peaceful than when Ravlen had closed the echo on the island. Back then, the shock of storms and sounds, screeching and flashing of echo people had struck her. This was completely different. The transition was gentle, a slow swaying into eventual non-existence.

Ravlen waved until the light extinguished on Ollie and Clara, leaving only a gray expanse behind.

"That's it, Ravlen! We have to go, NOW!" Marriel seized Ravlen by the wrist and dragged her toward the haze.

Ravlen didn't fight, but she also wasn't convinced that they'd succeeded. "What if the echo isn't actually closing? What if this is just nighttime in the echo and we haven't broken the logic?"

"Then we'll be able to come back in through the haze. *Now*, Ravlen! We're cutting it too close!"

The girls broke into a run as blackness began to descend. They reached the exit with Marriel grabbing Ravlen's hand and pulling her into the haze just as the void consumed everything behind them.

Marriel marched a few steps away from Ravlen once they'd arrived back in the park. She was huffing and puffing with the effort. Her brow was creased and her lips had turned white from clenching her jaw so tightly.

"You've got to be more careful, Ravlen." She looked over at Dina. "She waited until the very last second before leaving, like she thought she was immune to the death of the echo."

"It's not that." Ravlen joined them. "It didn't *seem* like it was closing. Everything was so quiet, no whistling or screeching. It wasn't anything like the last time."

"That doesn't change the fact that the echo was disappearing and would have taken you with it!" Marriel shouted in breathless frustration.

Dina raised her hands to quiet them.

"Back to Georgie's." She looked from one to the other, showing them what calm looked like. "I'll explain it to you there. Each echo ending is as individual as the people who desired it into being in the first place. There are commonalities, sure, just like there are things all of us have in common with each other. But you have to be prepared and adaptable to anything when it comes to closing them." She crossed her arms. "All that will come, but first, lunch. Then I'll take you through some of the lessons which have been handed down along the line of mainland mentors for generations."

Dina advanced with Ravlen and Marriel following close behind. She stopped suddenly, turning and nearly bumping into the two girls.

"Another thing. Don't talk with your mouth full. I don't want to hear about it from Georgie again."

Lunch was waiting for them when they arrived.

Ravlen bit into the thick sandwich of cheese, lettuce, chicken, and mustard. The flavors burst in her mouth, and she was thoroughly enjoying them when a new thought wove its way into her mind.

She looked at Marriel. "We're pretty lucky, aren't we?"

Marriel swallowed before replying. "Because we chase echoes?"

"Because we have everything we ever needed. We always have food, somewhere to sleep, people who look out for us. The boys in the park today… It doesn't seem fair that they have to dream apples into existence when all we have to do is take one from the bowl."

Marriel put her sandwich down. "If I think about it too much, I find it hard to eat."

"How do you explain it?"

"I don't," Marriel replied. "And I find the adults have terrible explanations."

They both looked at their sandwiches but didn't take another bite.

Georgie strutted in, her arms full of sewn fabric bags. "Something wrong with the sandwiches?"

"No, we're just appreciating them."

"Ah." Georgie nodded. "Your manners are swiftly improving. I'm glad they taught you such humility on the island."

"But Georgie," Ravlen swiveled on her chair to face her, "I saw some boys today who didn't have anything to eat. Another boy had swiped food for them."

Georgie's brow furrowed. "Two boys with brown hair? And did they hide under the slide and behind a tree?"

"Yes!" Ravlen grew animated. "Do you know them?"

"Those are the Anderson boys. They've had a hard run." Georgie scratched her cheek, but Ravlen could tell she was buying time to figure out how to say something difficult. It wasn't the first time she'd done it. "They're good boys. They go to school, help their father at his mechanics shop, but... Well, I'm sad to hear that it's come to this. I'll have a chat with a few other ladies in the neighborhood who have helped them out before."

Ravlen stared at her sandwich. She felt like she needed to do more, but she didn't know what.

"Finish your sandwich, dear. You need it. We'll figure something out for the boys. Not keeping up your strength won't help them." Georgie gave Ravlen a reassuring tap on the shoulder.

Marriel and Ravlen sat cross-legged on the grass in Georgie's garden. They studied the large yellowing pieces of paper that Dina unfolded, held up for them to see, then refolded as she explained the variety of echoes on the mainland. Binner ignored the lesson, bounding about, rubbing his back on the freshly-cut green lawn and digging in the way only a terrier mix can dig.

"You have the new and straightforward echoes, like the one you went into this morning," Dina said, pointing to one of the images. "Those are usually based on simple desires for the most basic of wishes. Food, clothes, money—"

"Enlightenment?"

"You saw that in the echo?"

"It was one of the rainbows."

Dina nodded, folding up the paper and replacing it in the pile. "These are the easy ones. It's still important to close them down, as there's an echo master who minds them and he is particularly adept at finding originals to go in. But in the history of the echo chasers I've worked with, we've always been successful at extracting originals from those echoes. They are too bizarre – even an original with big dreams can see through them quickly. You can close those echoes during your lunch break."

Ravlen and Marriel leaned forward. All their attention was on the aged piece of poster paper Dina was unfolding before them.

A complicated sketch of circles and lines filled the page, with the words "echo master," "original," "slip-in," "logic break," "established," and "emerging" scribbled across various parts of the drawing.

"We'll start at the top." Dina pointed. "Echo master."

This lesson was familiar, too familiar for Ravlen.

Where is he now, my echo master father? Absent, just like he always was. Oaken. If that was his real name. He let me believe him, but I don't know what to believe anymore...

"Ravlen?"

"Huh?"

Binner, Marriel, and Dina had all moved close, surrounding her.

Marriel touched her shoulder. "You were gasping."

"I was thinking of... the echo master... the one from the island's echo."

Marriel and Dina exchanged a glance. Marriel squeezed Ravlen's shoulder. "Do you need a break?"

She wouldn't let Oaken get the better of her again. She had come to the mainland to make a difference. She had to push these useless thoughts – thoughts of echo blood running through her veins – out of her mind or else she'd forget all about why she was doing this.

And she'd made Georgie a promise.

"No, no break." She nodded firmly. "I'm ready to go on."

"That's a girl." Dina grinned her approval and turned back to the page.

Marriel mouthed, "You sure?"

"Totally sure." Ravlen straightened her spine and looked at the chart. She was back in control.

"Echo masters don't run the echo. That's a common misconception among new echo chasers." Dina tapped the word 'Original.' "This is their primary goal. Preserve the echo. Bring in new life. Originals prolong the echo world, creating complex environments through their presence, through their new wishes. More of the echo builds upon itself when an original explores into new areas."

"I saw exactly that," Ravlen whispered to Marriel. "Yuna and I walked into an undeveloped area and *bam!* Next thing we knew, there were families living there."

"Wild."

"It went from nothing to something in a matter of minutes."

"Right before your eyes?" Marriel pressed.

"Just about."

Marriel and Ravlen turned back to see Dina holding the page in one hand, the other resting on her hip.

"Do you think I can't hear you?" Dina looked from one girl to the other. "You're going to have to get your heads around the fact that you have to grow up faster than other girls. You have to be more astute, more aware, more in tune with the behavior of others. That's how you'll figure out the echo logic, and that's how you'll save people from dying when you end the echo. So quit the whispering and pay closer attention."

The rest of the afternoon passed quickly as Dina explained the dynamics between echo chasers, originals, echo people, and echo masters. The most interesting part for Ravlen was hearing about established and emerging echoes.

"Established." Dina marched across the yard with her hands behind her back like she was an eighty-year-old professor and not a twenty-year-old former echo chaser. "When you hear the word 'established,' what do you think of, Marriel?"

"Old," Marriel said. When Dina didn't respond, she scratched her ear and continued. "Set in its ways. Well-known."

"That will do." Dina turned her head to her other pupil, her shoulders back and her hands still firmly clasped behind her. Ravlen watched as the professor turned into an army general, her voice staccato and biting. "Ravlen, describe emerging. Go!"

"Emerging..."

Snakes emerge from the bushes. Deer emerge from the forest. Fish emerge from...

"Well?" Dina stood in front of her.

"I'm thinking..." She racked her brain.

Emerging. Popping out. For an echo, popping up. Established is old...

"Emerging is new." Ravlen jumped up from the grass. "Fresh. Undefined and raw."

Dina raised an eyebrow. "'Undefined and raw'. I like that."

Ravlen let out a relieved breath as Marriel gave her a thumbs-up.

"Echo worlds range along a scale from emerging to established. Emerging echoes are rough around the edges – often like the one you closed down this morning. They're nonsense or limited in scope. People might stumble upon them without knowing what happened and attribute it to a dream or a surreal experience. Children are particularly susceptible to emerging echoes as they are based on innocent desires for care, love, food, and a special kind of power over themselves called 'agency'. The echo this morning was much like that, where you had powers beyond what you ever could in real life."

"That's why the bubble could lift me into the sky." Ravlen looked at Marriel.

Marriel nodded. "And why the pots at the end of the rainbows were filled with food, clothes, and education."

Dina picked up from there. "Which is how we can be certain that this echo was produced from the desires of the children from this very neighborhood. Despite their simplicity, these echoes have their dangers. Remember, the human body does not change in the echo."

Janna told me about it. Like if I ate almond croissants in the echo all day every day, I'd still get fat and grow to hate them. But there's a lot more to it than that.

"The established echoes... They are something different." Dina's eyes glazed over.

Ravlen waited for her to continue, and when she didn't, she stole a glance at Marriel. The older girl just shrugged and leaned forward.

Dina's lip curled when she finally spoke.

"The established echoes are the ones that build from humanity's longest standing desires. They are entrenched, and have multiple entries. Very difficult to close. Their logic is hidden under thousands of years of history and humankind's constant striving for more. They live in parallel to our own world."

Ravlen imagined an echo that looked so much like their own world, that people thought and acted as though they were originals, even though they weren't. How could they ever find the faulty logic in such a place?

"These echoes," Dina continued, looking the girls straight in the eyes, "are dangerous. Not only do they bring originals in, but they also let slip-ins out. Do you know about slip-ins?"

"We learned that on the island," Marriel piped up. "Echo people who find their way through the haze and take an interest in our world."

"That's right. But these slip-ins, from the established echoes, often aren't content to just hang around with us original folks. No, they're looking for more. They seek to make the original world more like the echo."

"Is that bad?" Ravlen shrugged. "I mean, echoes are based on all kinds of wishes and desires. Wouldn't we *want* to make the real world more like that?"

"Oh, Ravlen," Dina sighed. "Twelve years old…"

"Almost thirteen."

"Almost thirteen years old, and you still think all people wish for things that are good and wholesome and kind." Dina knelt, coming nose to nose with Ravlen. "You'll soon see that this isn't the case."

Rising, she swiftly refolded the papers, stacking them on the ground. "Get ready, girls. You're going into an established echo. You won't be able to shut it down, not yet. A few of us former chasers are surveying the entry points. No echo chaser so far has been able to figure out the logic flaw. That will eventually be your mission. For now, just go in and try not to be overwhelmed."

THE AIR WAS DENSE. RAVLEN COUGHED. "IT'S HARD TO breathe."

"I can't see anything in this fog." Marriel waved her arms trying to clear it, but that only swirled it around. "Take my hand. I'll lead us."

Ravlen did as she was told. Dina had been right, this echo was different. Ravlen felt a sense of doom swaying over their heads like a pendulum.

"Do you hear that ticking?" There was no point in looking for the sound's origin in the dense fog, but Ravlen was sure there was a clock nearby.

"I hear it. But what I want to know is what that smell is."

Only then did Ravlen notice the stench, like raw chicken left too long in the sun.

Ravlen's heart started beating faster.

"Listen," Marriel stopped. "Do you hear a voice?"

The two girls held hands and let their consciousness shift, sweeping around them in search of the voice's owner.

"Here… find me here… I cannot move…"

Ravlen and Marriel looked at each other.

"I can't tell where it's coming from." Marriel squinted but shook her head. "It could be left or right."

"I'll displace." Ravlen squeezed Marriel's hand. "I'll go above the fog and check out the surroundings."

Marriel frowned. "I'm not sure that's a good idea."

Ravlen took Marriel's shoulders. "It's totally safe. My body will be down here with you the whole time. It's only my consciousness that goes."

"I don't know…"

"Let's try." Ravlen took a step back. "Maybe I won't be able to do it, or maybe I won't see anything once I'm up there, but it's worth a try."

"Okay," Marriel said, but her taut cheeks showed that she hadn't been persuaded.

Ravlen let herself relax, even though her mind was running a mile a minute. She anchored her feet so she wouldn't fall, then straightened her spine, feeling an invisible thread attach itself to the top of her head.

Just like I was taught. Now, I have to find that place, deep within. Follow Janna's instruction and tap into the energy... Come on, it must be something like this.

Her feet were solidly on the ground, and so was her awareness.

Up. I have to go up. UP.

She tried to relax. Marriel's heavy breath reminded her of the lesson.

As easy as breathing. I can't force it; just allow it. Go deeper into myself.

She felt the sensation of lifting, her consciousness light as she left her body and floated up, up, up. The cool fog disappeared as she looked beyond it, into the distance. The sky was gray, almost the same color as the cloud-like swirls below her.

"I can sense you up there," Marriel murmured. "It's so strange to watch you, knowing a part of you is somewhere else."

"I see a tree." Ravlen tried to focus on it, but the heavy air held her back. "The atmosphere is thick, but I think I see individual trees."

The distant voice spoke again. "Come, I am here. I will wait for you. I'm not going anywhere, as you'll soon see. I cannot hurt you. Please, let me lay eyes on another, if just for a few minutes."

"That way." Ravlen opened her eyes. She was back in her body and pointed in the direction of the tree.

"Keep hold of my hand and watch your step. Why does

this place seem so dreary? I thought echoes were supposed to be people's desires. Who would want stench and misery?"

Ravlen didn't have an answer. They marched forward.

Dina wouldn't let us come if we could get hurt. Besides, the echo wants us to want *to stay. But why would we ever want to stay in a grim place with no sign of life except for a crying man?*

Dina's voice circled in her head. *"You still think all people wish for things which are good..."*

Ravlen stopped. Marriel's question. Dina's instruction. She had heard her words but hadn't understood the meaning.

What if people wish for things that are horrible?

The thought was inconceivable and that was why she had discounted it so readily.

Until the hard truth slapped her in the head like a wet dish rag that smelled of rotting chicken.

"What's wrong?" Marriel glanced around, looking for any sign of something that might jump out at them from the fog, but they were still alone.

"What if..." Ravlen began. "What if people wish for an echo where people suffer?"

Marriel's hand trembled. "You think that wish could be powerful enough to create one?"

Ravlen squeezed her hand. "I'm afraid."

"Me, too." Marriel rolled her shoulders back. "And that's exactly why we have to go. I'll protect you."

Ravlen knew they had to go on, even though she was unconvinced Marriel could protect her. How could Marriel know what they were up against? It seemed bigger than Ravlen's imagination.

She didn't have long to think about it. The voice reached their ears, much closer than before.

"Please, come see me. I haven't seen anyone in so long."

The tree came into view, the fog lifting as they approached.

"Girls. How wonderful to see girls." A man old enough to be their father, with matted brown hair and torn clothes, smiled at them through broken teeth. "I told you, I cannot hurt you."

His arms were pulled around behind the tree. Ravlen let go of Marriel's hand and walked around, leaving a wide berth in case it was a trick.

Behind the tree were chains that wove between the man's arms and around his wrists. But there was no lock. The chains entered into the tree, the bark growing around them. Ravlen stepped closer and saw the chains weren't made of metal. They were a thick liquid that took the form of a chain. She picked up a branch and touched it, but the branch bounced off as though they were solid.

"This is my fate," the man said.

"How did you end up like this?" Marriel's voice was filled with awe.

"I don't like to talk about such things in kind company."

Ravlen returned to the front of the tree. "Does it hurt?"

"What hurts is all the pain I've caused in the past. Now I am left here alone with the knowledge that I did wrong, I hurt others, and I must pay for eternity for what I've done. I only hope those who had the misfortune to cross my path can forgive me. That is my singular wish. I deserve this eternal solitude, though I am grateful for these moments to set my guilty eyes on your lovely faces."

Ravlen inched closer to Marriel.

"You can't leave?" Marriel asked him.

"Never."

"And you don't try to fight it?" Ravlen jumped in. It was absurd that he could be content to stay in this condition.

"Watch." He lifted his foot, and immediately one of the tree roots lifted like a lasso and pinned it back down. "Oh, it's tight this time. It must know you are here."

Ravlen and Marriel backed away.

"Will it attack us?" Ravlen scanned the tree, but it made no attempt to capture them.

"Oh goodness, no. Don't you worry about that, child. This is *my* tree of knowledge, and mine alone. It knows the blackness that existed in my soul and those who wished me into this torture. I get no comfort from knowing there are others like me out there." He nodded into the distance. "We are all blackened by the choices we made."

He closed his eyes. Ravlen watched his chest rise and fall while they stood silent.

He lowered his chin and opened his eyes, but they had gone black. Black eyes laden with desperation, and Ravlen felt evil seething off of him.

"Best you go now, girls. Don't you worry, I'll still be here the next time you come."

They didn't wait for another invitation. Ravlen led them back through the haze, her and Marriel's hands clasped so tightly there were red marks when they finally let go on the other side.

They stepped out of the haze into a forest a short distance from Georgie's place.

Dina stood from where she'd been sitting on a log. Her face was serious.

"You don't have to tell me. I know what you saw. There isn't any easy way to explain it, and that's why it has been so hard to break." She marched up to the girls who trembled before her.

"One day, you'll break this one. But to do that, there is a lot you have to learn about life on the mainland."

She settled herself between the girls, putting her arms over their shoulders and leading them forward.

"You'll figure it out. I know you will."

ONE YEAR LATER

4

Ravlen ran, her heartbeat pounding between her ears.

She was growing desperate.

"PULSE!"

The tsunami behind her was gaining ground. Her feet touched down and she ran, leaping forward with another cry.

"PULSE!"

The echo didn't care if she lived or died. A massive energy wave sucked in the air. The world was nearing collapse and though Ravlen knew exactly where she was going, time was not on her side.

"PULSE!"

She touched down, careful to avoid landing on any of the thousands of hopping balls of fur that covered the land below her.

This echo was the most bizarre she had ever chased. She knew the rabbits were moments away from disappearing, having never been real to start with, but that didn't mean she wanted to crush them on her way out.

I need them to part like the Red Sea. I loved that story... Focus, Ravlen! PULSE!

The haze came into sight ahead, a shimmer of promise. Ravlen fought the pull behind her, pressing forward until she was in the haze, rushing through the swirling colors that meant she wasn't far from home.

Ravlen stumbled through and fell onto asphalt, the haze closing around a pinprick of a diamond before disappearing altogether. In its place, there was nothing but a brick wall.

A seagull cocked its head at her while she checked herself for signs of injury.

"Yeah, yeah," she told the seagull. "I shouldn't cut it so close. Timing is not my strong suit."

Ravlen patted down her legs and found everything intact. She sighed in relief. She was fine except for a dull ache in her ankle that had never healed properly from her first echo mission back on the island.

She touched the spot on her stomach. *Thank goodness it wasn't like the last time I ran out. That gash took six stitches and two weeks to close. I've really got to handle exits better. Too close for comfort every time.*

She brushed herself off and took in the sight of the back alleyway in the oceanfront city. After a few months at Georgie's, they'd traveled across the United States, closing echoes along their way as Dina taught them essential mainland lessons. Ravlen and Marriel had now been with Joan and Tom for four months in this coastal location, and it was to be their home base for the foreseeable future. They had to learn to fit in.

Ravlen loved the place. The vast ocean view from the small-but-sweet bungalow was the stuff Ravlen's dreams were made of. But unlike the echoes that Ravlen and Marriel chased, this dream was very real. Long beaches, the rising moon over the Atlantic Ocean, and finally attending school.

A real school with a real marching band and, best of all, orange trees.

If only all the echoes could pop up here, I'd be set!

She kicked herself for the thought as she strolled along the sidewalk, the seagull waddling at her side. The nice folks she'd met here were not deserving of that, in spite of her own selfish desire to stay.

Her watch beeped.

Georgie had given it to her just before they'd left her. The kindly carer had also noticed Ravlen's terrible sense of timing. The watch had proven itself to be very useful.

Ravlen looked at it now, her lips pursed in post-echo-closing confusion, trying to remember why she'd set the alarm in the first place. Then it hit her.

She silenced the alarm on the run, calling out to the startled seagull, "Band practice! And I'm late!"

Ravlen huffed as she entered the school's music hall. Between running for her life in the echo and running again to avoid the bandleader's stink eye – she was wiped out.

"You have to set the alarm for *before* you're supposed to arrive," Marriel chastised, passing Ravlen her trumpet with the mouthpiece attached and ready. "I even cleaned inside the valves for you."

"You're a lifesaver." Ravlen's sheet music was a mess in her bag, even though she already knew "Sweet Caroline".

"Alright, kids!" Mr. Johansson called to the crowd of brass-equipped adolescents. "It's time to show me what you've got! We start with 'Sweet Caroline', then go straight into 'Twist and Shout'. Got it?"

"'Twist and Shout'!" Ravlen hissed at Marriel. "I haven't rehearsed that one."

Marriel didn't take her eyes off Mr. Johansson. "Not even the trumpet solo?"

"Solo!"

Marriel was unimpressed. "You need a secretary."

"I was busy! This last one was covered in rabbits. I mean, *everywhere*. Do you know how hard it is to pulse and not land on one when the fields are covered in the things? They were so cute though. That made it hard to shut it down."

Marriel's shoulders relaxed. "Sorry, I should have reminded you about 'Twist and Shout'."

"It's okay. I should have taken better notes."

"We start in…" Mr. Johansson raised his hands and the students raised their instruments to the ready. "A-one, a-two, a-one-two-three-four!"

The forty-strong mix of trumpets, trombones, saxophones, and percussion kicked off. After six weeks of rehearsals, the cacophony of marching band madness was starting to sound like something that resembled "Sweet Caroline" and "Twist and Shout". They hit the closing note – except for one rogue French horn – and Mr. Johansson raised his fist in victory.

"Way to go, kids! Instruments away and then we'll debrief."

"Hi, Ravlen." A tall blonde, whose eyes doubled in size through thick glasses, flashed Ravlen a toothy smile.

"Hi, Greta." Ravlen made a point of looking into the horn of her trumpet, hoping Greta would get the hint that she didn't want to chat.

"I thought you did that trumpet part in 'Twist and Shout' real good. Like, *real* good." She laughed, then cleared her throat, seeing that Ravlen wasn't laughing with her.

"Yeah, thanks." Ravlen had faked her way through the whole song. Fortunately, she was gifted at following the other trumpets, almost in real time. But Emma, who played second trumpet, had given her a dirty look.

"Alright, kids." Mr. Johansson gathered up his sheet music

from the stand. "Take these notes. First Oboe, no extra breath on 'Sweet Caroline'. Don't think I didn't hear that."

A lanky boy shrunk behind the other oboes.

"And trombones, reduce the lag on the second phrase, please. No one wants to hear that in a marching band. As for the trumpets," Ravlen looked at her feet, "that'll do for now. It's not great, but it's good. Work on smoothing those rough edges. Feel the music."

Ravlen let out her breath, again catching Emma's scathing eyes.

"Ravlen, stay behind please."

Darn it.

Ravlen kicked at snags in the music room's old brown carpet as the others shuffled out. Once the room was almost empty, she dragged herself toward Mr. Johansson. Marriel leaned against the doorway, just out of earshot.

"I get the sense that your mind is elsewhere today." Mr. Johansson propped himself against his stool. It was the stance he took whenever he was trying to get to the heart of something.

Dina had taught Ravlen and Marriel all about 'tells'. Not only did they explain strange behaviors of the mainland people, but every single person had at least one. The way he was standing was one of Mr. Johansson's.

"You know, Mr. Johansson, you're right," Ravlen said. "My mind was absolutely elsewhere. Like *far, far* away." She wasn't about to tell him that a part of her was still wandering in the echo she'd just closed, transfixed by the thousands of rabbits that had hopped about the unreal land.

Mr. Johansson nodded knowingly. "I've seen it before. Some of the most gifted students struggle to apply themselves…"

Ravlen closed her eyes so that he couldn't see her rolling

them. If she heard one more adult on the mainland talk about "applying herself," she just might…

"…But I don't think that's your case." Mr. Johansson's eyebrows rose. "Am I right?"

Ravlen's eyes darted left and right. How was she supposed to answer such a direct question?

"Uh, I suppose you are." That seemed like the safest answer.

"New girl in school, new girl in band, loads of talent, and fleeting focus." He inclined toward her. "I'm going to give you a pass this time. But if you want to stay in first trumpet, then you're going to have to learn 'Twist and Shout' by next rehearsal. Got it?"

His lips were stern, but his eyes crinkled and Ravlen felt she'd found an ally.

"Yes, Mr. Johansson, you bet."

"Good. Now run along. I'll see you in class." He nodded toward the door. "Someone is waiting for you, and she doesn't look too happy about it."

Ravlen grabbed her backpack. "Coming, Marriel!"

***

THE GIRLS BOUNDED INTO THE BUNGALOW WITH NERVOUS energy. Binner jumped and licked at Ravlen's hand, knowing his after-school treat was coming. Ravlen tossed him a rawhide bone while she recounted the final details of the echo closure to Marriel.

Marriel's eyes narrowed with disbelief. "The closure was a *wave*? Come on."

"I'm telling you, it was a wave – a huge one – coming right toward me!"

"I've never seen that before. This was supposed to be an easy one."

They settled onto the stools in the kitchen, which were set for after-school snacks the way they always were. Carer Joan – though she only wanted to be called "Joan" – liked routine. Binner munched on his organic rawhide bone like it was the best day ever.

"It was easy, all things considered. The logic was pretty faulty, being surrounded by thousands of rabbits and all."

"Thousands of rabbits?" Joan entered.

Ravlen swallowed hard. She wasn't allowed to share the echo details with Joan and Tom. Though they were Ravlen and Marriel's new carers, and while they knew the basics of echoes and the girls' missions, they had never gone into an echo and weren't to know of the specifics that lay within them. It was one of the many rules for echo chasers Dina had taught them. These rules had been passed down from Madame and her unknown, unseen, and unidentifiable mainland counterpart, created to protect the complex network of mainland carers. And they weren't to be broken at any cost.

"Never mind, don't tell me." Joan threw up her hands. "I just serve the veggies around here." She pulled out a plate of carrots and celery with homemade ranch dressing that had quickly become one of Ravlen's favorites.

"I'll need a note for science class." Ravlen crunched into a carrot. "I had to miss it again."

"Science again? Can't you do your chasing over lunch?" Joan was already pulling out the notepaper she kept by the phone.

"I was doing my science homework over lunch." Ravlen gave a wide, cheeky smile. They had an agreement in place with the school, a note on Ravlen's file that she had "unique health considerations" that required her to sometimes leave school immediately and with little warning.

So far, that had worked. No one asked questions about a

new girl in school who had health issues and lived with a foster family.

"Can I have honey?" Marriel asked. Her sweet tooth was getting worse by the day, but Ravlen didn't comment on it. Last time she did, Marriel swiped her around the ear and it stung.

Joan strutted across the kitchen, waving a card like a fan.

"I don't suppose you know who this postcard might be for..."

Ravlen's heart skipped a beat. Marriel looked at her and flicked her eyebrows up with a knowing glance.

"Is it for me?" Ravlen leaned so far forward she almost fell off the stool.

"Hmmm." Joan looked at the card. "The originating location is hard to pin down. But the scrawl of an adolescent boy is unmistakable..."

Daniel!

"It's for me!" Ravlen jumped off the stool and rushed over to the teasing carer. Binner began turning circles in the kitchen, knowing something exciting was happening.

"Oh, I don't think you're interested in what he has to say." She winked at Marriel.

"Give it to me!"

"You've outgrown that childhood crush on him, haven't you?" Marriel chuckled.

"GIMME THE POSTCARD!" Binner jumped the same height as Ravlen who waved frantically after the postcard. Joan laughed at the bouncing duo and let Ravlen snatch it out of her hands.

Ravlen ran into the living room and threw herself onto the bouncy sofa that absorbed her into its upholstered grasp. Binner landed in her lap.

The front of the postcard had a dancing cow with a speech bubble that said, "Moo-ving on up!" She didn't care about that. She cared about what was on the back. No return address. She ran her hand along Binner's back to calm herself as she read.

Ravlen, how are you? It's silly to ask because you can't answer me. Still not allowed to share where we're located. I've finally made a couple of friends. Paul is a baseball fanatic and Dave plays guitar. I'm running out of room on this postcard, so I'll just say goodbye. Daniel

Scribbled at the very bottom, and with a different pen, were two words that made Ravlen lightheaded.

Miss you.

She looked toward the kitchen where Joan and Marriel were both standing in the doorway watching her.

"You can wipe those smirks off your faces," Ravlen said, knowing her own face was beaming. "It's just Daniel."

"*Just* Daniel." Marriel giggled.

"Come finish your veggies. You can ogle over the post-card from 'Just Daniel' while we wait for Tom to get home for dinner." Joan winked at Ravlen.

Miss you.

She read it again and again. She'd forgotten how much she missed Daniel until it was scribbled in front of her.

She slept with the postcard under her pillow, along with the five others he'd sent, and the good luck charm from Marriel.

Miss you.

She tried to imagine what he looked like now. Fourteen years old and a year of training at the boy's encampment had likely changed him. Ravlen was thirteen now, but when she looked in the mirror, she thought she looked exactly the same.

She fell asleep to the memories of being on the island, with good old Daniel and Binner by her side.

5

"How are my all-star echo chasers this morning?"

"Dina!"

Corn flakes flew out of Ravlen's mouth as she jumped off the stool to greet Dina.

Dina shook her head. "I see we still have manners to learn." She looked down her nose at the youngest member of the group.

Marriel smiled but stayed lost in her daydream, as she'd done for the last couple of weeks. Dina's visits were always unannounced and usually meant there was an echo somewhere in the vicinity that was pulling originals in.

Dina hip bumped Ravlen. "You're growing, R-girl."

"You think?" Ravlen looked down at herself. She still wasn't accustomed to the mainland clothes after years in the brown uniform dresses of the island. But her jeans were hovering above her ankle as though she was going to wade through a river. "I guess you're right."

Joan popped her head into the kitchen. "I told you, we need to go shopping!"

"I've been busy." Ravlen shrugged. "Dina, you should have seen the echo yesterday. It was filled with—"

"Rabbits?"

"How did you know?"

Dina winked. "That new kids movie, *My Bunny Paradise*, is causing rabbit-themed echoes all across the country. Who knew people would have such a fascination with bunnies?"

"I saw the movie, and I have to say…" Ravlen scratched her chin, "I wouldn't mind living in that bunny wonderland myself."

Dina leaned into Ravlen and whispered, "What's up with Marriel?"

"A boy at school has been talking to her," Ravlen said in a half-whisper out the side of her mouth and raised her eyebrows conspiratorially.

Marriel snapped her head toward them. "Are you talking about me?"

"Absolutely not." Dina smiled innocently. "We're talking about the boy who's paying attention to you."

Marriel's face went a new shade of pink. "He's not 'a boy,' he's Conrad."

"He's not a boy, he's Conrad." Ravlen and Dina repeated. Ravlen fell into giggles and even Dina had a wider smile than usual.

"Would you both grow up?" Marriel protested, but then she too got snagged into the gigglefest.

The three of them continued, each egging another one with "Oh, a boy!" and "Marriel's got an admirer!" until Joan stepped in with a fake stern face. "That's enough, girls. Get ready for school. Dina, you can brief them about the mission on the road. I'm not writing any excuse notes today."

The three girls made their peace with Binner, who was disappointed not to be going with them, but it was the same every day. He was the happiest to see them return home each afternoon.

Once they were out the door, Dina got straight to it. All signs of their morning mirth disappeared as she spoke.

"This weekend I'm taking you into the swamps. A haze opened up that's pulled in some people, mostly fishermen struggling to make a living since last season's drought."

Ravlen was rapt. It had been a couple months since she'd been in an echo with originals. Closing those – saving people from echo destruction and delivering them home – always felt the most satisfying.

It was only Wednesday. The weekend seemed like ages away.

"Can't we go now?" Ravlen stepped through the gate and onto the school grounds. "I can miss school."

"I can't," Marriel jumped in. "I have a school parliament meeting."

"You're not in school parliament." Dina did not look amused.

"Conrad invited me to volunteer."

"Regardless, we go on the weekend. The haze is tucked away far enough that it shouldn't pull anyone else in unless they're really unlucky. And it's important that you don't miss school." She looked at Ravlen. "Joan told me you have a math test on Friday."

"Oh. That."

Math was her worst subject. It wasn't because of the material, it was because the teacher hated her. Well, maybe the teacher didn't hate her, but she acted like Ravlen was a nuisance, and that was enough to make Ravlen hate math.

"Yes, that." Dina swung around, chains hanging from her belt loops jingling as she walked, and for the first time, Ravlen saw a tattoo on the bottom of her back. "Don't be so sensitive to what people think of you. What you think of yourself is more important. And learning fractions and ratios matters."

"I hate ratios," Ravlen muttered, low enough so the others couldn't hear. "And I'm not sensitive."

The first part was true. The second part was a lie, and she knew it.

Marriel headed to the high school while Ravlen trudged toward the middle school.

Mrs. Brand is going to tell me off for not finishing the home-work for chapter six. I know it. I just wish she wouldn't look at me like I'm some kind of weirdo.

Ravlen adjusted her collar to make sure it covered the mark of the unreal that ran down her neck and back. Something she'd never given a second thought on the island, had become an important part of her daily routine – making sure that line of sparkling air remained hidden from any curious eyes.

At first, she'd been obsessive about it – constantly adjusting her shirt, wearing scarves when the sun burned high in the sky, keeping her coat on indoors. But Joan had told her that first of all, wearing coats year-round in the southern United States was a recipe for dehydration, and secondly, that the sparkle was hardly noticeable against the fabric of a long t-shirt.

Still, Ravlen had become self-conscious. The kids at school were all right. It was the teachers who made her uneasy.

The teachers… and one boy in her class who stared at her longer than was normal. Not in a nice way.

She rushed up the stairs with a crowd of her classmates, the tinny bell ringing over their heads, signaling five minutes until detentions would be assigned to anyone left in the hall.

"Watch your step," a low voice stung her as she rounded the corner and nearly walked straight into the only person she would have preferred to run away from. The boy who stared too long. Christopher Duke.

"Sorry," she muttered and shuffled left to go around him, but he moved so that she couldn't slip by.

"I'm watching you." His dark eyes pierced her.

She turned sideways, her eyes steady on the floor as she pushed against him to get to the classroom door beyond.

She ran to her chair, flopping heavily into it. The chair protested with a dangerous crack. She glanced down the side where the evidence awaited her. The chair had a fracture up the middle of it, the wood dangerously close to snapping.

She sighed.

I guess it's going to be one of those days.

Christopher Duke, who was taller than all the other boys in the class, taller than anyone in eighth grade, stepped in just as the bell rang. Ravlen felt his eyes on her again, but she kept her own gaze on the blackboard.

A cheerful voice popped behind her. "Hiya, Ravlen!"

Ravlen didn't turn around. "Hi, Greta."

"I was wondering if maybe this weekend you might want to come hang out at my dad's place. He's got a pool and he makes great burgers – veggie ones, too, if you prefer. What do you say?"

"Sorry, I have to go to the swamp this weekend."

"Oh. Sure. Okay." The disappointment in her voice tugged at Ravlen's heart. Going to the swamp probably sounded like a lame excuse. But then again, so would saying she had to go save people from a parallel world.

Maybe I should have just said I have plans with Marriel.

She swung delicately around on the damaged chair to see Greta's downtrodden face.

"I'm visiting some people inland, that's what I mean. But maybe..." Ravlen didn't know how to end the sentence. Pools and barbeques sounded nice, but with Greta's boundless enthusiasm, Ravlen didn't know what to expect. It was like Greta was built out of a ball of happiness, and that got tiring when she had echoes to close.

"Eighth graders, books away. Quiz time." Mrs. Brand's dull face looked over the room. With flat brown-gray hair that hung like wet shoelaces and lips that were perpetually pressed into a line, Mrs. Brand was in a competition with day-old toast for the most uninteresting part of the day.

Groans filled the classroom, except for Greta.

"Oh, a quiz? That will be such good prep for Friday's test!"

Mrs. Brand distributed the quiz with royal disdain, dropping a single sheet of paper on each desk. Ravlen scratched her forehead waiting for the quiz's arrival, but froze when she caught Christopher watching her again. His head tipped awkwardly to the side, as if he were sizing her up. The intensity was so uncomfortable that Ravlen only managed to look away just as Mrs. Brand dropped the quiz on her desk.

"Eyes on your quiz now, Ravlen. Stop staring."

Me? Doesn't she see anything?

Ravlen huffed and set her attention on finding two-thirds of three-quarters.

"Time's up."

Ravlen could have sworn it hadn't been more than five minutes. She madly scribbled an answer to the last question she thought was close to correct, as Greta passed forward two quizzes from behind. Ravlen added hers, then handed the stack to a lanky boy named Tony who sat in front of her.

"Dang, question two was six-thirteenths? How did you figure that out?" Tony's eyes showed his surprise as he passed the stack forward.

"You don't want to ever copy off me when it comes to fractions, Tony," Ravlen told him with a sigh.

The lesson passed in a blur of pie charts and multiplication. They were in the middle of a strange analogy about submarines when the bell rang. Ravlen waited for Christopher to leave. Otherwise, she'd have to walk past his desk, and the thought alone made her nervous. She was the last to go.

"Move along now, Ravlen. You've got other classes to get to."

"Yes, Mrs. Brand."

"No need for you to be here any longer than necessary." Mrs. Brand's arms were crossed, but Ravlen saw more than typical teacher annoyance in her stance. Her toe anxiously tapped the floor and she kept looking up at the clock. Ravlen stuffed her notebook in her bag and rushed out of the room.

She's acting like she can't wait for me to get out of here, like I might bite her or something. Why would a teacher be afraid of me?

English literature was a breeze. Ravlen couldn't get enough of haikus, and Christopher Duke was pulled from class for a meeting with the counselor, which meant Ravlen could breathe easier.

Games day was the afternoon. Ravlen was getting good at baseball. She didn't let anyone know that her talent, smacking the ball dead-on, was the result of a tiny cheat. Just a little one, involving her ability to disturb.

The pitcher threw the ball. When it was only a few feet away, Ravlen disturbed just long enough to adjust her bat.

Smack!

She knocked it far into left field to the squeals of joy from her teammates as the score hit two-zero.

Ravlen jogged to second base with a mischievous grin.

Disturbing during games day is keeping my skills in practice, that's all. I need to be sharp for this weekend's echo chase. Nobody can hold that against me... even if it is a little cheat...

Her newfound baseball skills didn't hurt her social status either.

"Check out Ravlen's hit! I want her on my team next week!"

Ravlen was bounding with energy as she and Marriel walked home. "Listen to this haiku: Into the green swamp, into the deepness of echoland, there we will save them. Oh, wait, too many syllables on the second line. Maybe more like…" She pointed in the air, but Marriel's eyes had that glazed look she'd been wearing more and more lately. She dropped her hand and put on a teasing tone. "Marriel! I'm reciting poetry for you. A little respect, maybe?"

Marriel took several beats before replying. "Huh?"

Ravlen shook her head. "Is this what eleventh grade is all about? Getting googly-eyed over any boy who shows you some attention?"

That snapped Marriel out of her daydream.

"You wouldn't understand. You're only thirteen. This isn't being googly-eyed. I *see* something in him."

"See something in him? Like what?"

"You wouldn't understand," was all Marriel said before her eyes again took the far-off look.

Ravlen kicked at the ground as she thought up more haikus under her breath.

"A dog named Binner… waits for me to give him food… his love is edible. Nope, too long…"

A sense of cold air swept through the street and Ravlen's skin prickled. She frowned. The sun was still hot in the May sky.

Someone is here. Someone from the echo.

She stopped and twisted around, but life looked the same as it did at four in the afternoon every other day. Groups of kids running home, parents holding hands, some teenagers bouncing a basketball between them, perilously close to the edge of the road.

"Marriel…"

"What now?"

"I have a strange feeling."

As if yanked out from her boy-crazy musings, Marriel turned back and took Ravlen by the shoulders.

"Nearby?"

"I think so."

"Let me sense with you."

The two girls stood in the middle of the sidewalk, and for once, Ravlen didn't care if everyone was watching them. She was put here for a reason, and she had a job to do. The opinions of others faded into the background as Ravlen listened to her surroundings for any sign of something out of place.

"The ocean…" Ravlen murmured. "I think it's coming from that direction."

Marriel took Ravlen's arm. "I feel it, too. Let's go. Not too quick – we're going to have to pass through that private dune and we don't need anyone catching us on the way."

After nine months of sneaking their way through farms, hotels, and amusement parks to reach an echo entry, they were getting good at looking like they belonged somewhere they had no business being.

"Grandma told us to meet her right over here. I'm sure of it," Marriel said. She was using a fake voice she only used when they were echo chasing, the pitch higher than her natural tone, and her eyes big and innocent.

Ravlen wondered at her every time she used that voice, but right now she just nodded in return. She hadn't mastered the fake voice herself, but she could act like she was just following Marriel, mainly because she was.

"This way, sis," Marriel continued. "Or was it over there? Do you remember?" She looked at Ravlen in the way that meant she'd lost the direction and needed Ravlen to sense more closely.

"Hmm." Ravlen closed her eyes, her skin prickling as she let herself scan the area. "Left. Definitely left."

Their steps slowed, more hesitant now that they were closing in on whatever it was that had caught their attention.

"Pounding feet," Ravlen said as her own foot caught on a vine that laced the dune's edge. "And there's more than two feet running. Whoever is out there isn't alone. Slip-ins... running this way..." She looked up at Marriel with dread. "They're running right for us."

Marriel crouched. "Who are they? The sound is too far away for me, too faint."

"I don't know." Ravlen's breathing grew shallow. "But whoever it is, we definitely can't outrun them. The speed... the momentum ..." The pounding of feet on sand filled her consciousness and she closed her eyes. She thought she might faint.

"Hold me, Marriel!"

"I've got you. Don't worry, I've got you."

Marriel's arms wrapped around her like a mama bear as Ravlen waited for the echo people to appear before them. The pounding of feet matched the pounding of the blood in her brain.

Please, let them pass right by us. Let me disturb, or whatever it takes, let me... wait...

"Do you hear that?" Ravlen tried to unravel herself from Marriel's grasp, but Marriel's arms were boa constrictor tight. "I think it's... could it be..."

"You stay right here. I'm not letting anyone get you." Marriel cradled Ravlen's head in her chest, but Ravlen tapped her shoulder, then pushed herself free.

"You're strangling me, I think it's..."

The sound of panting filled the air.

"Binner!"

Ravlen launched herself at the galloping dog and they

landed in a pile of cheek-licking, fur-smooshing love. They rolled down the dune to the beach below as Marriel flopped into a seat at the edge.

"That's why we heard four feet." Ravlen managed to maneuver out from under the dog's undying affection. "How did you get out of the yard?"

"Binner." Marriel scratched him behind the ears. "I don't think I've ever been so happy to see this dog."

6

Thursday and Friday flew by as Ravlen and Marriel took every break between classes to brush up their skills and remind each other of the key aspects of rescuing originals. There would be no room for error once they were on the other side of the haze.

"We can't use the pulse until we've rounded up as many of them as possible."

"Do we know how many originals are in the echo?"

"Dina didn't say."

The bell rang and they rushed back to their regular classes. During lunch they were back at it, meeting under the tree between the middle and high schools.

"Remember to move slower than usual in the echo." Marriel pointed her finger. "You forget that the rest of us aren't as quick as you."

"I'll remember this time. And if I take off, it will be for a good reason."

Marriel nodded. "That works."

"Marriel?" A male voice invaded their conversation.

A boy with broad shoulders and a shiny smile approached them.

Ravlen watched, fascinated, as Marriel transformed before her eyes from echo chaser extraordinaire to mushy teenage admirer.

Ugh. I will never be boy-crazy. No way, not me.

The boy, with his collared polo shirt and neat khaki slacks, flashed another smile. "I thought I'd walk you to class."

"Oh yes, Conrad," Marriel chirped. "That's a great idea."

Ravlen looked at her watch. "But we still have fifteen minutes and a lot to talk about."

Marriel didn't even look at Ravlen. Her eyes were transfixed on the teenage heartthrob. "We can talk later."

And with that, Marriel was gone. Ravlen watched as she walked away, her hands swinging, brushing into Conrad's hand as if by accident.

Ravlen sighed and headed to gym class. It was the one class she didn't mind getting to early – and since Christopher Duke, with his incessant staring, was in the boy's gym group, she could at least have peace.

And maybe hit another home run.

Dina drove down a road that was as straight as an arrow into the center of the swamp. While they had closed out several echoes in desolate places, none had been quite like this. Water on all sides, jungle-like greenery, and insects Ravlen could swear were the size of her fist.

Even the air was different. On the coast, the air was often heavy with humidity, enough to cover cars with a film and leave Ravlen feeling like she was inhaling as much water as air. But as they approached the swamp, the air was charged with something more.

"Beasts. Human and otherwise," was all Dina said when Ravlen asked about it. But it didn't make sense to Ravlen. There were more people on the coasts than in the middle of the state.

"It's like the wind stops here," Dina said after driving a long way in silence. Marriel was asleep across the back seat. These days Marriel would be in her room by nine and wouldn't come out again until it was almost time for school. Joan explained that it was normal for a girl Marriel's age to sleep like a rock, but Ravlen had long ago given up on what normal could or should look like for an echo chaser.

Dina's eyes narrowed as she looked into the distance. The landscape spread out around them was nothing but swamp now, the road manufactured for humans to pass. But Ravlen couldn't help thinking they didn't belong there. This was a place only for wild creatures to live, thrive, own.

The idea sent a chill down her spine.

Why would anyone want to come here? And why would an echo end up here, of all the isolated places in the world?

Someone had been the tipping point. One person alone didn't do it, but the wishes of someone in the swamp had acted as the final push, bringing the echo into being.

And now Ravlen had to shut it down.

"Not far now."

Ravlen watched Dina's hands on the steering wheel, small tattoos of flowers and birds on her fingers.

"Are we here?" Marriel spoke from the back.

"Good morning, sleeping beauty." Irony dripped from Dina's lips. "How nice of you to join us."

Marriel rubbed her eyes. "This place looks terrible."

Ravlen didn't quite agree. If she let her eyes unfocus, the colors of the swamp were pretty. Blues and greens with occasional swatches of brown. It was as natural as nature got, though it still seemed foreign and strange to her.

"It's fine," Dina said, "if you stay out of the 'gator's jaws. You don't want to be their next meal." Dina winked in Ravlen's direction.

"Alligators!" Marriel shuddered and lay back down. "Just wake me up when we're there. I can't stand alligators."

"There it is! The haze!" Ravlen pointed ahead, where purples, pinks, and yellows shimmered over the water. "In the middle of a swamp. How are we supposed to get to it without—"

Dina cut her off. "Don't worry. I've got a boat in the back."

"You do?"

The car's trunk was barely big enough to fit two suitcases. Ravlen didn't know how a boat could possibly fit.

"It's inflatable."

"Inflatable?" Marriel perked up again. "That's all well and good until an alligator jumps out of the swamp and digs its fangs into it."

"Alligators can't jump," Ravlen laughed.

"Actually…" Dina inhaled between her teeth. "They *can* jump – up to six feet in the air."

"What!" Ravlen and Marriel cried together.

Ravlen clapped her hands over her eyes. "Their legs are so short, how on earth do they jump?"

"They're not pushing with their legs," Dina said, but with their heavily-muscled body and that giant tail pushing them out of the water…"

"Why don't they teach us *this* stuff in school?" Ravlen said.

"Ohhhhh." Marriel groaned. "I wish we were back in that desert echo with the scorpions. At least most of those were harmless. Hungry, *jumping* alligators? We're doomed!"

"Relax." Dina laughed. "I wouldn't do that to you. There's *mostly* no alligators in this area, which is how the haze was able to establish itself near the wisher, who is likely someone who knows the area well and was curious about the shining portal that appeared before him."

"*Mostly* no alligators?" Marriel repeated.

Dina pulled over, but there wasn't much of a shoulder.

"Look over there." Ravlen pointed deep into the swamp where a small collection of boats were neatly bumped into one another.

"The fishermen." Dina nodded. "They were expected to be away for days. No one has reported them missing except one who didn't call his wife as planned. But even she said he regularly lost network out here."

Ravlen had to get out of the car carefully to avoid falling into the swamp, as there was a drop of two feet from the edge of the road straight into the muck.

She edged around to the front of the car, leaning over it for balance and cleaning the car's hood with her t-shirt on the way. "You said there's more than one original in this echo, right?"

"We're pretty confident that there are at least three. But judging by the boats out there, it might be more. It'll be up to you to determine once you're in." Dina opened the trunk and pulled out a red pack the size of a suitcase. "Marriel, get the boat filled up. You'll see where to plug it in. Ravlen, let me show you some of the specifics of the entry point."

Marriel huffed, trying to unfold the cumbersome boat, as Dina led Ravlen around the side of the haze.

"It's *over* the water. First time I've ever seen this, but I'm guessing that's because of how thick the swamp is here. You might have to try a few times before getting in, especially if you and Marriel are going to go through at the same time. Worst case scenario, if you lose hold of each other, you'll arrive at separate points in the echo."

"We won't. It's never happened before." Ravlen put her hands on her hips with youthful assurance.

Dina smiled with one side of her mouth. "Mmhmmm. Well, if for some crazy reason you arrive through separate entries, your first goal is to find each other." She called out, "Did you hear that over there, Marriel?"

"If we're separated… we find each other," Marriel panted trying to hold the boat in place while the whir of the pump continued. "How big is this thing? It's making my arms tired."

"Keep going. The effort is good for your heart, sleeping beauty." Dina turned back to Ravlen. "If my assumptions are correct, the echo won't be a hard one to break. But the challenge will be to locate the originals, since we're not sure how long this one has been around. The echo could be large in scope."

"Large in scope?" Just when Ravlen thought she was getting the hang of this echo-breaking stuff, Dina would come up with something new.

"It could be quite an advanced world, fantasy though it may be. And geographically spread out if the originals have explored their way through it."

"Got it."

Marriel joined them in inspecting the haze. "It's literally floating in midair."

Dina pulled the boat over. "You two up for this?"

Marriel and Ravlen looked at each other.

"Something different." Ravlen shrugged.

"We've seen worse," Marriel agreed.

"Good answer!" Dina smacked her hands against the side of the boat and pushed it in. "Everybody, in the boat. I'll try to keep it steady as you make your way into the haze. Step in over the right edge there. Careful now, Marriel! You're rocking the whole thing!"

"I've only ever been in big wooden boats before!" Marriel

wobbled left and right, looking as though she was about to belly flop into the water before finding her balance.

"The key is to sit down as quickly as you can. Ravlen, your turn."

Ravlen got in and sat down. "Easy-peasy."

Dina stepped into the boat and sat at the back. She produced a collapsible paddle and maneuvered them close to the entry point.

"Alright, both of you, stand up… careful… That's right."

Ravlen took Marriel's hand as tightly as she could. She stepped into the haze, finding a kind of floor on which to stabilize her foot.

But the boat wobbled and Ravlen's other leg slid under the unseen landing, knocking her backward and into Marriel with a slippery, "Oof!"

Marriel pulled her back to her feet as the boat rocked beneath them. "Let me go in first. I can get my foot on there and then lift you in."

Marriel's approach went more smoothly. Dina gently guided them forward, Marriel put her first foot up, hopping up off the boat, to get her second foot into the haze. It sort of worked, except that the hopping motion sent the boat bouncing around as Ravlen struggled to stay upright.

"Marriel, careful, I'm going to… I'm almost…"

"Come on, Rav! I've got you! Jump in!"

"I'm trying but the boat keeps moving…"

"Stop jumping, Ravlen!" Dina shouted. "Let Marriel pull you in, or else… oh no."

"Whoa!"

Ravlen's motion pushed the boat away from the haze. Marriel tried to hold onto Ravlen's wrist, but within seconds the boat was too far, Marriel too high, and Ravlen's grip slipped.

She dropped straight into the water.

"Take my hand!" Dina called, leaning over the front of the boat. "Gotcha." She pulled Ravlen back in, covered in wet, muddy grasses and looking like a drowned rat.

"I tried! I didn't know I could push the boat away. Let's try again, Marriel. Marriel?"

"She fell backward into the haze when she lost hold of your hand." Dina paddled back to the entry point.

"Then she'll come back through in a minute, right?"

"In theory."

They waited. Five minutes passed, then ten.

No Marriel.

"You're going in, Ravlen," Dina said.

"Without Marriel?"

"She's in there, and from the looks of it, she needs you."

This was not going to plan. "But you said this could be a big echo."

"It could be massive," Dina agreed. "A fisherman went missing four weeks ago, and we suspect that he was the wisher. Four weeks is a long time to explore inside. And he's probably experienced the numbing touch of echo people."

Ravlen groaned. "So much for this being an easy job."

"I never said it was going to be easy. I just said that the logic flaw will be obvious." Dina stabilized the boat beneath the entrance. "Off you go. I'll give you a boost."

Dina launched Ravlen into the haze.

7

Ravlen stumbled forward, the floor of the haze roiling like a dock floating on troubled water. She didn't have a chance to say goodbye to Dina before toppling through the swirling colors, the light of the echo world just ahead. Water dripped from her but disappeared into the haze entry's invisible ground.

I hope Marriel isn't far. I hope I can find her position with an easy disturb or two. If only I knew what happened to her. What's inside this echo anyway?

She didn't have to wait long to find out. She took one more step and then the ground disappeared beneath her. She had just enough time to pinch her nose before tumbling into crystal blue water.

She kicked frantically to drive herself back to the surface. Her head emerged into sunrays glistening off gentle waves.

"Dunked twice in a day!" she shouted to no one.

She swam to the water's edge, grateful for the swimming lessons they'd been given on the island. Madame had always talked of how the skill of swimming could decide between life and death. Ravlen had thought she was being dramatic, but not anymore.

She pulled herself out of the small lake onto a patch of perfect lawn, luscious and soft. She squeezed out her t-shirt and took in the sights.

A collection of lakes and ponds of all sizes, separated by swatches of green grass with pleasant benches, stretched on for as far as she could see. The lakes were nothing like the lakes she'd seen during their travels. The water here shone like gemstones, clear enough to see to the bottom. Some of the ponds were no bigger than a child's swimming pool, while others extended to the horizon. Ravlen squinted. Silhouetted forms moved in the distance.

Echo people or originals? Is one of them Marriel?

On a bench three lakes away, an old woman sat with a playful grin on her face. Ravlen's referent. She tipped her head to Ravlen and then made a wringing motion with her hands, mimicking Ravlen twisting her t-shirt. She broke into a hearty laugh that Ravlen could hear even though the old woman wasn't that close.

Nothing like being teased by a referent.

Ravlen focused herself.

Must find Marriel. That's job number one. The rest can come after.

She closed her eyes and silently called upon the energy to disturb. Like a wave of electricity, the echo paused in place. Only the originals continued to move, unaffected by Ravlen's skill.

Whoa. There are more originals here than Dina thought.

Ravlen counted at least eight, more likely nine. One of them, she hoped, was Marriel.

She looked around, lakes left and right, but where was she supposed to start? Where could Marriel have arrived that she didn't immediately turn around and come back to the swamp?

Did she hit her head? Was she taken away by echo people?

The list of possible disasters grew longer as Ravlen twisted around, not yet ready to move forward.

Her referent giggled again, the sound jarring Ravlen from her thoughts.

"Well?" the old lady spoke. Ravlen intensified her hearing to make out the words. "You have to start somewhere, don't you?"

Ravlen squinted at her referent.

She's right. Marriel isn't going to find herself. I have to start somewhere. Wait, what's wrong with my referent's legs?

Even with her farthest degree of focus, Ravlen couldn't make out what was odd with her referent. A long skirt covered them almost to her ankles. Almost, but not quite. Something green shimmered in the sunlight.

Are those fish scales on her legs?

Ravlen shook it off.

Marriel. Finding her is my number one priority. I've got to remember Dina's instructions.

She ran.

She darted between the lakes, paused to disturb, listened for anything she thought might guide her to Marriel, then continued on.

The lakes became larger and the green between them smaller, the horizon turning into shades of blue.

"Where are you, Marriel?"

Ravlen scanned but knew disturbing wasn't going to be enough. She had to displace. Ravlen took in a deep breath. The last time she'd displaced, she'd grown dizzy and her stomach turned.

But she had no choice. She had to find Marriel, and the sooner, the better.

They had originals to save.

Ravlen calmed herself. She connected with her breath, following the movement of her lungs – expanding and then relaxing. With a delicate shift of her shoulders, she opened her chest, feeling the pull upwards. She let it happen.

That's better. More like an elevator than a roller coaster.

She sensed across the distance. Figures came clearer for her, though none seemed to be Marriel. They all had something strange happening with their legs.

Is it related to the logic flaw of this echo? I've got to see who these people are.

She tried to make out more of their details, but stopped herself.

Marriel. This is all about Marriel.

A sound, far but familiar, reached her.

"Ravlen?"

It's her!

Marriel continued, "If you can hear me, I'm by a lake."

That's not very helpful.

"I'm going to need more to go on than that," Ravlen called out, but Marriel's hearing had never been as powerful as Ravlen's. She likely wouldn't hear anything until Ravlen was closer to Marriel's spot.

"Can you hear me? Ravlen? A big lake."

"More, Marriel." Ravlen scanned, but there was still no sign of her. "Tell me more."

As if she heard, Marriel went on. "There's a bench, and many – uh – people. Sort-of people. Are they people? Am I dreaming this?"

"Focus, Marriel! More detail!" she shouted into the sky.

"The sun is behind me. My shadow is long. I will walk in this direction, as it passes between two lakes ahead."

Now that is useful. Ravlen followed the shadows, still displaced and seeking from above and below.

I think I see a spot with a trail between two lakes...

"Is that you, Marriel? Can you hear me?"

"Ravlen! Yes, I hear you now! Can you see me?"

"I can! Stay right there, I'm coming! I'm – ouch!"

"Ravlen?"

Ravlen was sucked back into her body, her stomach flip-flopping on the way.

Someone had touched her shoulder.

"Child! What in heavens are you doing?"

"Oh, I'm dizzy." She turned away from whoever had yanked her out of the displacement and threw up on the grass behind.

"Child, oh, child. You are not well." A syrupy southern accent drawled as Ravlen rested on her knees, waiting for the nausea to pass.

"I knew somethin' wasn't quite right. I knew you was strugglin'. You'd been talkin' to yourself for minutes!"

Ravlen's stomach settled, but a new kind of knot took place there. She had to get going quickly to find Marriel. Echoes had a habit of trying to keep her from her goal, thinking they knew better what she needed. She had to get away from this woman as soon as possible without drawing any unnecessary attention to herself.

"I really appreciate your concern." Ravlen managed to get herself upright while controlling the wave of queasiness. "But I'm okay. I was just lost in a daydream is all." She turned. "But I appreciate your... your... whoa."

All words were stolen out of Ravlen's mouth. She forgot how to make her lips work.

Standing in front of her was a mermaid.

"I..." she started again. "I... Aren't you supposed to be in the water?"

The mermaid laughed, deep and hearty. The scales that

ran along her entire body trembled with her laughter, glistening iridescent in the sun.

"Where *did* you come from, child? It's as if you never saw a morpher before!"

Ravlen couldn't stop herself from staring, but she did remember that gawking with an open mouth was rude. She snapped her jaw shut and took in the sight before her.

The woman's face looked like any other woman's. Full cheeks and deep-set wide eyes that had a diamond-like shine when the sunlight hit them. Her skin waved green and blue and brown, like the vapor that rose from asphalt in hot weather. But her lips were red as roses and she was one of the most beautiful women-creatures Ravlen had ever seen.

"Cat got your tongue, child?"

"It's just… I…" Ravlen stumbled over her words. She let out a quick breath and composed herself. "It's very nice to meet you, Miss…"

"Esmerelda." Her eyelashes sparked like a princess as she batted them. Ravlen felt lost in the undulating blues of her eyes. They were like waves that pulled Ravlen into their current.

Ravlen shook her head. *She's charming me. I've got to stay laser focused or she's going to suck me in…*

"Miss Esmerelda. There's someone waiting for me, so I've got to go, but I hope our paths will cross again sometime."

"Sure, sugar. You come around this evening for the Big Splash. It's a competition we've got going and everyone will be there."

"Oh yeah? Where does that happen?" It might be the perfect opportunity for her and Marriel to bring the originals together.

"The Bay of Wee Waters."

"Wee Waters?"

"'Wee' as in 'little.' It's right over there, where you yourself was just swimmin' about."

"Ooooh."

This information would be useful indeed.

"I'll be there, Esmerelda."

"Then I'll see your beautiful face later." Her voice soothed like a lullaby. "You just stay as sweet as honey, now." Esmerelda flashed that brighter-than-life smile and Ravlen tripped over her feet as she walked away, spellbound.

Esmerelda waved at her.

Ravlen waved back.

And then walked straight into a big, soft someone. A man.

Ravlen's head snapped upward.

He's an original.

The smack had zapped Ravlen out of her trance. He had to be an original because she hadn't felt a single thing when she'd knocked into him. No tingling or electric current, just a regular thump. He was one of the originals she and Marriel would soon have to round up.

"Sorry about that, sir. I wasn't looking where I was going."

He didn't reply. His eyes were on Esmerelda. He wore rubber overalls and knee-high boots. His face was red, as though he'd been in the sun for way too long. His bald head was peeling.

"Never you mind, it's no problem," he said, but he didn't look at her. He only had eyes for Esmerelda.

Ravlen followed his gaze and caught her breath.

Esmerelda had changed.

She wasn't a mermaid anymore. Now her body glittered in gray from head to toe, her hips still wide and round but her waist had grown to the same size. Her face was unchanged, but from the neck down, her arms were now welded into gills at her sides. There was no question.

"She's a fish," Ravlen exclaimed, but the man only smiled.

"Most beautiful fish a fisherman ever laid eyes on. I'm in love with her."

"In *love* with her?" Ravlen clapped her hand over her mouth.

"Never in the world has anyone been kinder, truer, or more loving." His eyes widened and his head tipped to the side in the same way as those who'd been touched and numbed by echo people.

The false logic of the echo is easy to see... but if he's in love with her... and of course he would be...

By the time she'd finished the thought, the man was at Esmerelda's side. She caressed his cheek and bald head with her gills.

"There you are. I knew my fisherman would be back for me."

"Of course, Esmerelda. You're my favorite."

"But can you catch me?"

"I'll do my best."

Esmerelda waddled in fish form to the water's edge. "Come on, fisherman. Catch me if you can!" She jumped into the lake, a small splash the only evidence she'd been there.

"Weeeehoooo!" The man yodeled to the sky, his knees bent and leaning backward like a wolf-turned-southern angler.

Esmerelda's head emerged from the water, long hair and princess face superimposed on a shape-shifting mermaid-trout.

Ravlen gawked, the sight at once terrifying and mesmerizing. *She turns herself into whatever we want her to be. The shimmer of her scales, the blues of her eyes, the curve of her cheek...*

She shook herself out of the spell. She wanted to stay. But she couldn't. Not yet.

She turned her back on the scene and ran.

Marriel. I've got to get to Marriel.

8

She found Marriel sitting in the same spot as when Ravlen had displaced, legs crossed and head resting in her hands. "Thank goodness! Did you lose sight of me or something?"

"I got detained. By a mermaid. Or a fish. I'm not sure which – what – she was."

"I see."

The good thing about having explored so many echoes with Marriel was that they both knew how the unexpected – and sometimes downright ridiculous – could happen.

"What happened to you?" Ravlen helped Marriel up. "Why didn't you come back through the haze?"

"See that lake over there?" Marriel pointed to a large lake, so big Ravlen couldn't see the other side of it. "I arrived right in the middle of it. There wasn't any boat for me to climb on and launch myself back through. The haze was too high. It took me ages to swim to land. Thank goodness for swimming lessons."

"I thought the exact same thing when I plopped into one of the ponds over there."

"The haze is in the middle of a pond?"

"Sure is."

Marriel sighed. "This doesn't get any easier."

"Hey," Ravlen gently punched her on the shoulder, "cheer up. It's better than the middle of a lake."

"I guess. " Marriel brushed herself off and pulled her still-wet hair into a bun on the top of her head. "The good news is that we're back together." Marriel put her arm around Ravlen. "What did you see when you displaced? How hard is it going to be to find the originals here?"

Ravlen described the eight originals plus the two of them.

"That's more than we've ever done at once." Marriel's doubt spread across her face. "How will we round them all up?"

"Have you heard of the Big Splash?" Ravlen rubbed her hands together.

"No…"

"That's our answer."

Even though every echo was a little different, after a year of saving people, they'd found tried and true methods to get the originals out.

The originals who were quickly convinced to go back to the normal world they called 'easy-leavers'. Some of them had family or jobs or had seen enough of a fantasy world and had grown tired of it.

And then there was everyone else.

Those who loved the echo. Those who were still eager to explore. And those who'd been touched by the echo people enough that they'd succumbed to the belief that the echo was real.

With all the originals together at the Big Splash, they could get the easy-leavers out through the haze first, and then pulse for those who refused.

So far, no one had ever refused after witnessing a pulse.

While Ravlen thought this watery world had a simple enough logic to break – mermaids who turned into fish and such – the man's reaction made her pause. He had been captivated, in total awe and charmed by Esmerelda's presence. Just like she'd been.

It might not be a straightforward closure after all.

Ravlen kept track of the originals by disturbing briefly. As the day passed, they'd all made their way toward the Bay of Wee Waters. Ravlen and Marriel headed that way, too.

"Do you see this?" Ravlen whispered as they advanced.

"How could I miss it?" Marriel swallowed hard.

The grass paths between the ponds were now full of water creatures.

"What kind of echo is this?" Marriel gasped. "Fish and octopus and mermaids and…"

"What is *that*?" Ravlen pointed with her head.

Marriel raised up on her toes to check. "A manatee."

"It's huge!"

They all had human faces, though their skin matched their chosen animal. And as Ravlen had seen with Esmerelda, each was capable of changing, evolving into another type of creature as different originals joined the conversation.

"Fascinating." Ravlen watched as an eel turned into a clam with a giant pearl in her chest.

"It creeps me out."

"But the originals love it. What would make these people wish for human fish?"

Ravlen counted eight of them, seven men and one woman. They were all there. The woman held hands with a man as they laughed with a dolphin.

"Welcome to the Big Splash!" a woman called out over the waiting crowd. "I am Mama Mermaid. I know many of you have been waiting for this moment, the Celebration of the Catch!"

Cheers erupted. Ravlen and Marriel clapped hesitantly.

"Tonight, we feast on the spoils of our travels. Snapper and bluegills and trout and catfish. More than enough for everyone!"

The girls' mouths dropped open.

"Are they going to *eat* each other?" Ravlen hissed.

"For our newcomers," Mama Mermaid gestured toward Ravlen and Marriel, "we shall enjoy the nutritious and delicious results of our own creation. Every fish being grilled tonight was brought into being for this very purpose."

"That's how the fishermen have rationalized it for themselves," Marriel whispered. "Or else the echo would have collapsed on itself at the very beginning. They can't have a relationship with the life-size creatures and eat them, too. Instead, they say the fish being grilled were *intended* to be eaten."

"Seems kind of fishy to me," Ravlen sniggered.

Marriel looked at her sideways. "Bad joke."

"The games will begin shortly, races and chases and catches galore!" Mama Mermaid called out, the crowd enraptured by the sight of her diamond smile–a smile just like Esmerelda had used to captivate both the man and Ravlen earlier.

"This is our chance!" Ravlen rushed ahead, checking out the various equipment for the games. Marriel reached her side. "Look, rafts over there. And there's the pond with the haze." It was only a couple ponds away, easy enough to move the rafts to it.

"All right, let's move those rafts."

"Wait. I have an idea." Marriel tapped her head. "I've got the sense that we'll catch more flies with honey in this echo." She traipsed over to Mama Mermaid who was leaning over a grill, wafting the fumes her way.

"Mmmm, yes. A great catch, wouldn't you say, Artie?"

An original stood beside her, his head cocked. "Yuh-huh."

"I know the look on his face," Ravlen whispered to Marriel.

"Me, too. He will not be an easy-leaver."

"Look at how Mama is caressing his arm."

"And look at how his eyes droop every time she does it…" Marriel cleared her throat. "Excuse me, Mama?"

"Why, hello! One of our new visitors. Such a delight to see you." Mama grew taller, sleeker, slimmer before Ravlen's eyes. She turned into the mermaid from one of the movies she and Marriel had seen during their early days on the mainland.

"Whoa," Ravlen hushed under her breath. "She just turned into Serenna the Mermaid. Weird…"

Marriel smiled. Ravlen could tell her mind was racing, looking for the right thing to say. But Marriel was always gifted with words. Where Ravlen excelled in the skills of the echo, Marriel could convince a monkey it was an elephant. But could she convince a mermaid that they were there for fun and games?

"Mama," Marriel began with a playful grin. "I have a great idea for a game. Would you let us move the rafts into that pond over there?"

"The one with the shimmery cloud? Why certainly! What's the game?"

Marriel smiled wide, and Ravlen knew it would all come clear soon enough. "It's a surprise."

"Oh!" Mama clapped her hands together, just the way Serenna the Mermaid had done in the film. "I do *love* surprises. Don't you, Artie-boy?" She turned to the man, her body changing back into the wide-hipped, large-busted mermaid she'd been before.

"Yuh-huh," Artie replied.

Marriel leaned in. "I'll take care of the easy-leavers, but

you're going to have to do some work on that one." Marriel tipped her head toward Artie.

"I got this." Ravlen wore a crafty smile, a plan already forming in her mind.

An octopus and a merman moved the rafts to the haze pond as Marriel supervised, her arms crossed and chin lifted. She'd easily taken on the role of matriarch.

"So what's the plan?" Ravlen murmured behind Marriel.

"It's a game. A game where the originals disappear."

"Wow. It will be so believable, it's brilliant! But wait... what if the creatures want to play, too? What if they want to disappear into the haze?"

"I'll get the originals out. Your job is to keep the echo creatures in while you shut it down."

"Figures. You always get to do the easy stuff."

Marriel chuckled.

Ravlen poked Marriel in the ribs. "You're laughing because it's true. But that's fine. I can take care of that part."

"I know you can, Rav. And here we go..." Marriel rubbed her hands together. "Everyone, everyone!" she shouted over the crowd. Most creatures hushed and Mama shushed those who didn't. "I need all the folks with skin – no scales or blowholes – to head over this way. That's right. You and you, too. Artie, come this way."

Artie dragged his feet, his back hunched over, but he came. That already made Ravlen's job easier.

"My friend Ravlen here is going to stay on this raft with," Marriel pointed, "one, two, three, four. You four kind folks. The others come on the raft with me. We've got to be careful now, no tipping the raft. That sure isn't the game!" Marriel broke into a wild laugh, which the sea creatures on land repeated. "You all see this foggy spot just here. I promise you that what you'll find on the other side will amaze, and for those of us left behind, we will stare in wonderment!"

"What's through that colorful fog?" the lone original woman asked. She seemed to have her head about her better than the others.

"Home," Marriel replied with a kind smile.

"Oh, good. I was just wondering if I'd be able to make my weekly bridge competition. Harold? Harold? You get over here."

"What's that, Rhonda?"

"No more mermaids. You were getting a little too googly-eyed for my liking. Out you go!"

Harold stepped into the haze with Rhonda behind, pushing him through.

"Ta-da!" Marriel lifted her arms in victory. "Two people, disappeared! We will search for them in a bit. See, this is grown-up hide and seek!"

"Look at that," Mama Mermaid cried out. "They disappeared! What delightful magic!"

The creatures erupted in cheers and applause and cries of "Do it again!"

"Yes, it's time," another man on Marriel's raft nodded. "Come on, Stan."

Stan shook his head. He was a man of about sixty with a big, round belly. "Haven't you seen what's around us? This is incredible."

"I think someone put something in our beers. I hope the boat is still waiting for us. Come on."

The two men fell through, disappearing to the crowd's delight. Ravlen rowed closer to the haze as Marriel remained alone on her raft. She maneuvered out of the way for Ravlen to get closer.

A younger man from Ravlen's raft was up and out without another word.

"Look at that one go!" an octopus shouted.

The only originals left on the raft were the bald man

Ravlen had encountered earlier, the man called Artie, and a third man who kept looking between the haze and the creatures on land.

"It's best you go now," Ravlen whispered to the third man. "It's about to get real bleak in here."

The man nodded and was off.

The crowd cheered with more vigor. Only two remained – Artie and the bald, sunburned man.

"All right," Ravlen began. "It's the two of you now. Who's first?"

They both stood silently, the bald man staring at her, his mouth agape while Artie sat in a stupor, a far-off, glazed look in his eyes.

"Not going," the bald man said, and began trembling. "This is the place I've dreamed of my whole life. I can't leave."

Ravlen maneuvered her way across the raft to him. "But it's not real."

"That doesn't matter."

"It does. Because it's all going to come crashing down around us, in minutes."

He crossed his arms. "Then I'm going with it. I'm going with Esmerelda. She loves me." He looked back at the mermaid-turned-trout. She blinked vacantly into the distance.

Ravlen softened her voice. "She can't love you. She's built from imagination."

"She does love me, she does…"

But even Ravlen could see the doubt spreading across his face. Esmerelda, for her part, just stood there, staring blankly ahead. When she saw that he was watching her, she shook her head, making herself look alluring, a wave of change coming over her body.

"I see you there," she called out to him. "I see you

watching me." She curtsied and did a twist like a runway model.

But there was no love in her eyes.

The man saw it and the logic was broken.

He looked at Ravlen. "She was perfect. So perfect. But she becomes perfect to whoever is looking at her, doesn't she?"

"Yes." Ravlen nodded solemnly and sympathetically.

"I'll come with you." Marriel slid over from her raft to Ravlen's. "We'll go together." She took his hand and led his first step up, into the haze. He stopped and looked back at the land.

Esmerelda waved expansively, from side to side as if drawing a rainbow over her head. "You go on now, get disappearing! Show us all that you can hide!"

"Let's go," Marriel gently persisted.

He lifted himself heavily upright, balancing on the raft. Ravlen adjusted her footing so they didn't tip, and by the time she looked up again, he was gone.

The crowd went crazy.

It was him, she thought. *His wishes were the tipping point, and he was the first one in. That explains the sunburn and the emotional ties to the echo. Poor man.*

Ravlen examined her final charge, Artie. His mouth hung open. He was unaffected by the events around him.

"Artie." She tapped his arm. "It's your turn."

"Nuh-uh." He shook his head.

"I'll come with you. We're going back home. Back to real life."

He blinked, turning his head to her. "*This* is real life."

"It's not. You've been made to feel that way through the touch of these unreal people."

"They are *real*."

"You'll see. When you step through that haze, it'll become clear to you."

For the first time, he looked straight at Ravlen. "You want me to go in *there*? Have you seen it? It's a portal to who-knows-where! Looks mighty strange to me."

"You came through it to get here."

Artie's eyes narrowed. "You're trying to trick me."

This is not going well. I'm going to have to pulse to show him.

Ravlen started gathering her internal resources. If she was going to pulse strong enough to illuminate the echo's falsehood, she had to get centered.

Artie's lip curled. "I get it. You're trying to trick me into leaving this real world behind so that I end up in some scary place, a half-world or something."

"You've got it backward." Ravlen tried to focus, but it was hard with his bloodshot, accusing eyes on her.

"You're a witch!"

Ravlen shot her arms out from her body with as much energy as she could muster, crying out to make it work.

"Look around you, Artie!" Ravlen had to keep her eyes tight shut or she was going to lose her power. But she knew what Artie was seeing, the ghost-like figures, the vacant space where moments ago had been a magical world. "What do you see?"

"What – have – you – done?" Artie's voice stuck as he spoke.

"None of this is real. It's all based on dreams and false hopes. And it will eat you up with it. Because real creatures don't change form to suit the person looking upon them."

"They do. It happens in nature all the time!" Artie cried out.

He's right, I learned about that in science class. I've got to declare the false logic. If that's not it, then what is it... I've got it!

"No creature would stand by and let you eat their young, roasting the very creature they are – if they were real fish, they'd be saving the fish! They'd be saving themselves and fearing all of us."

"Well, yes, but…"

"But it's not real!" Ravlen heard the telltale bells ringing in the background, the ringing growing louder, bells she hadn't heard since she closed out the echo on the island. But she couldn't think about that now. "We've got to go, Artie. You and me both, before the waters rise up and dry up and suck us away with them."

"But it used to be so nice here… what did you do to them? Why are they flashing like that? How has it all turned so horrible?"

"Go, Artie!" Ravlen released the pulse and pushed Artie into the haze. His shins knocked into the haze's entry, making the raft rock. He climbed in and Ravlen looked around at the water creatures. Their faces were blank, waiting.

It's as if they know.

She scrambled up and through the haze as a pull with suction like a vacuum cleaner approached in the distance.

She landed in the brackish water of the swamp, arriving into a battle. The originals they had just freed from the echo were pushing and grabbing, shouting and screaming.

"The police are coming!" Dina called to her. "We've got to go!"

"What's going on?" Ravlen rushed to the little boat and climbed in.

"Let me back in! Let me back in!" The bald man was fighting with the other three men. "I never wanted to leave! I should have stayed!"

"Why is he like this?" Ravlen asked as they rowed away.

Ravlen couldn't imagine why someone who knew it wasn't real would ever want to stay in an echo. But the bald man was in total denial about the end of the echo.

Dina looked sadly back at the scene. "There are those who have been convinced by the echo that the fake world is real. And then there are those who convince *themselves* that it's real. They have a much harder time returning to the real world."

9

Joan wrote Ravlen a note to get out of class on Monday. It said "Specialized treatments."

It meant "Recovery."

Ravlen hadn't slept well since she'd returned from the swamp. She rolled around in bed, trying to figure out how she could ease the transition from echo back to the real world so that people like the bald man wouldn't suffer on their return.

Or at least suffer less.

It was something no one had ever talked about since this adventure began. Not Madame, not Janna, not Marriel, nor Dina. No one talked about what happened after the echo closed. Ravlen's mind rolled over the thought all night long.

Marriel, however, was eager to get to school. She was up earlier than she'd ever been, her hair pulled into a neat braid.

Ravlen stumbled out of her bedroom with Binner trotting close behind.

"You're up early." Ravlen dropped to the floor to tousle with Binner. She looked up and scrunched her nose at Marriel. "Are you wearing lipstick?"

"Never mind that." Marriel waved her off. "Conrad is going to be here any minute, and I can't find my black bracelet!"

Ravlen rubbed her eyes. "So go without it." She yawned. "You don't need a bracelet to walk to school."

"It makes my wrists look more dainty."

"It makes your wrists *what?*"

Marriel groaned. "Never mind. Joan! Joan! Have you seen my—"

Joan appeared in the hallway, holding a black bangle high in the air. "Exactly where you left it."

"I looked beside my bed, and it wasn't there."

"No, it was in the fridge. The chocolate milk, however, I found beside your bed." Joan passed Marriel the bracelet but didn't let go. "You need some rest, Marriel. This was not an easy mission. Reconsider going to school…"

The doorbell rang.

"It's Conrad!" Marriel snatched the bangle and slipped it on as she ran to the door. "See you later! I'll miss snack, but I'll be back for dinner."

"Just a minute—" Joan began.

"Bye!"

The door slammed.

Joan sighed and then joined Ravlen on the floor, giving Binner's belly a scratch. "She's the first teenager in this house so eager to go to school."

RAVLEN LOOKED OUT THE CAR WINDOW AT THE STATUE OF A dragon that stretched toward the bridge they were driving across. It was dressed up in gold and red sashes.

"Check that out," Tom said, pointing.

"So pretty!" Joan's voice was filled with child-like glee.

"Who dresses up a statue?" Ravlen thought it was weird, but there were plenty of mainland customs that struck her as strange. Plastic pink flamingos on lawns, iced tea with sugar added, and a Greek festival attended by non-Greek people.

Even though Ravlen loved the Greek festival, she still wasn't used to these things after having spent years on the island with the carers and Madame, where celebrations were few and always emotionally charged.

The dragon, however, was weirder than the flamingos and the iced tea combined. She couldn't figure out why people were so keen on it. They drove across the bridge to a surprise location Joan and Tom promised she would love. After the weekend she'd had, Ravlen was perfectly happy to be driven around with Binner snoozing in her lap.

The driver's side door slamming jolted her awake. She hadn't realized she'd drifted off.

"Tom!" Joan hissed. "She was sleeping!"

"She was sleeping? Finally?" Tom pressed his face against the car window, staring in at her.

"She was until you tried to tip the car over."

"It's okay, it's okay," Ravlen said, sitting up groggily in the back seat. "I'm up." She climbed out of the car and took a few steps around the parking lot to get her bearings. Binner trotted alongside her, firmly attached on his leash. The sparkles down his back were less visible here than in other parts of the country. Ravlen chalked it up to the humidity.

Tom shrugged in reply to Joan's dirty look and then turned to Ravlen. "You can rest if you like. Where we're going will still be here when you wake up."

"No, that's okay." She stretched. "I'm curious. And I'm awake now. What is this place?"

Tom opened a glass door that jingled and creaked. "After you, mademoiselle."

Ravlen stretched her head up to read the sign. "Chez

Marie. Is it *French?*" The question came out as a squeal and a cry. "Do they have croissants?"

Joan whispered in Ravlen's ear. "Almond croissants."

Ravlen ordered two, much to Joan and Tom's satisfaction.

She ate them slowly, letting the almond paste melt on her tongue before she dared take the next bite. While they weren't as good as the ones on the island – or at least her memory of the ones on the island – the taste brought back vivid images of years past.

The time she found a wounded sparrow and nursed it back to health.

The time Marriel gave her the handmade shell good luck charm.

The time Daniel said he had feelings for her.

"Ravlen?"

"Mmmm?" She looked up to the adults' waiting eyes. "I was just thinking about the island."

"I bet you miss it, huh?" Tom asked.

It was hard for Ravlen to swallow. She felt the absence of her mentors and friends, Janna and Madame, Yuna and Donelle, more with the taste of the croissant on her tongue.

"Yeah. I do." She glanced at her croissant, then smiled, pushing aside the wistful feelings. "Not that I'm not happy here. I love the sea and band practice, and I love living with you guys. Marriel and Binner do, too."

Binner lifted his head in mid-lick from the crumb-laden floor.

"I'm glad to hear it," Tom said with a jovial smile. Everything about Tom was fun-loving and good-humored, from his brightly colored Bermuda shorts to his big belly laugh. He was known to break into song from time to time, bouncy tunes from his youth. Where Joan was clever and loving, Tom was the work-hard, play-hard guy. Living with the two of them was the best arrangement Ravlen could have asked for.

"And now," Joan said with a voice that meant they had to talk serious, "we need to talk about school."

Ravlen groaned. Her grades were adequate. She wasn't drawing any extra attention to herself, not any more than was absolutely necessary for the purpose of leaving class to close an echo. It wasn't her fault that the teachers treated her like she had the plague.

"I know," Joan continued. "It's not a joyful subject for you, but we got a call from Mr. Johansson this morning and it's time to set the record straight."

"What's wrong with my record?"

Joan and Tom looked at each other in the adult way that meant Ravlen was missing something.

Ravlen straightened her spine. "What did Mr. Johansson say? I'm doing well in music class, and in marching band. I know I forgot to rehearse 'Twist and Shout', but I've already figured out the fingering for the chorus…"

"It's not that." Tom folded his hands. "Mr. Johansson thinks there's something unusual going on between you and the other teachers. What can you tell us about that?"

It felt like a trick question. How could she know what was going through the other teachers' minds?

"Mrs. Brand has it out for me because I don't *apply myself*," Ravlen said in a mocking tone while making air quotes with her fingers. "As for Miss Markham, she clearly thinks my French accent is terrible. She makes faces at me every time I talk. My science teacher, Mr. Costello, is fine. He just doesn't look at me. Or call on me. Or say hello. No big deal."

Ravlen shrugged as if none of it mattered, except that it did. It mattered to her even if she pretended it didn't. She worked hard to fit in, and despite all her efforts, these teachers still eyed her with suspicion.

Joan and Tom exchanged a look.

"What?" Ravlen asked. "Why are you guys doing that *thing?*"

"What thing?" Tom asked with innocent eyes.

"That thing where you know something and you won't tell me what's going on."

Joan scratched her head and they sat quietly for a minute.

"Mr. Johansson," Joan spoke slowly, drawing the words out, "believes that… that the teachers have a mistaken idea about you."

"What kind of mistaken idea?"

Tom shrugged. "He wasn't forthcoming about that, though we tried. You're not the first echo chaser to attend this school. We've had others stay with us, but none of them had this… issue."

Ravlen felt heat rising up the back of her neck. "What's the issue then? Why am I being singled out?"

"We don't know. But Mr. Johansson seems to want to help. He's asked for a meeting with all of us."

Ravlen groaned.

Joan tapped her hand. "Don't worry, we'll handle this. It's our job to protect you. We'll go all together, but Tom and I will do the talking."

Tom put his hand on Ravlen's shoulder. "Your mission is hard enough as it is."

Ravlen felt a wash of relief. She smiled meekly at the comforting faces of her mainland carers and wondered if this was what it felt like to have parents.

THE NEXT MORNING, MARRIEL AND RAVLEN WALKED BEHIND Tom and Joan on the way to the school. Marriel's arms served the dual purpose of calming Ravlen while also pulling her close so they could discuss this ominous meeting with Mr. Johansson.

"I know you'll be careful about what you say," Marriel whispered as a couple of kids ran past, "but you don't know what he's looking for. Don't try to outsmart him. You have to just be you – while not giving anything away."

Ravlen nodded and let out a tight breath. "I'm going to look so nervous. I'm not like you, Marriel. You always put on such a good show. I can't pretend, and I can't lie." Ravlen kicked at the dirt, wishing she were just a little better at faking it.

"You don't have to," Marriel comforted. "You're going for a meeting with the teacher. That makes everybody nervous. See?" Marriel offered a reassuring tap. "Just be yourself. And don't say anything. That'll be best. Tom and Joan will do the talking."

"Marriel," Joan turned from the top of the stairs into the middle school, "I believe someone is waiting for you."

Conrad stood off to the side, just past the stairs, his hands in his pockets. He made eye contact with Marriel and flashed the million-dollar smile that gave Ravlen the heebie-jeebies.

"Just a second," Marriel called out with her girlie voice.

Ravlen fought not to roll her eyes.

"You can do this." Marriel patted Ravlen on the shoulder. "This is a walk in the park compared to everything else you do."

She hurried off to join Conrad, who placed a hand on Marriel's lower back, leading her toward the high school.

Ravlen climbed the stairs to the middle school, for the first time seeing it as a place full of dangers and pitfalls, risk and menace. Before she only had Christopher Duke to worry about. Now there was a whole bunch of teachers to add to the list.

Starting with Mr. Johansson.

Mr. Johansson was just sitting down at his desk when Tom, Joan, and Ravlen walked through the door. He stood.

"Mr. and Mrs. Cravner, welcome. Ravlen, hello."

Ravlen peeked shyly from behind Joan. "Hi, Mr. Johansson."

"Please," Tom shook hands with him, "call us Tom and Joan."

"Tom, Joan, lovely to meet you. Ron Johansson. Music teacher, marching band leader, native of our fine state, and – I like to think – a good judge of character."

Joan raised an eyebrow at Ravlen, but Ravlen did her best to remain stoic. She didn't want to give anything away. Following Marriel's guidance made sense.

"Please sit down." He gestured to the middle school-sized chairs in front of his desk, which were barely sufficient for Tom and Joan's adult bottoms. "I've asked you here today because I have seen a pattern that worries me." He paused, bringing his pen to his lips, then set it back down on the desk. "It comes both from my observations of Ravlen's behavior and that of her other teachers. It seems that their relationships are… strained."

He stopped there, assessing the impact of his words on Tom and Joan. Ravlen also looked at the two of them.

They didn't react at all.

He tapped his pen on the desk. "Do you have any response to that?"

"I assume you are going to tell us more about this so-called 'strain,'" Joan replied.

Mr. Johansson tapped his pen again and looked at Ravlen. "Ravlen, do you feel any strain, awkwardness, perhaps even tension with your other teachers?"

Ravlen looked at Tom and Joan, who both gently nodded their heads, encouraging her to speak.

"Maybe," was the only word that came to mind. "But maybe it's just normal teacher-student stuff."

"I see." Mr. Johansson leaned back in his chair. "So you don't feel as though they look upon you with contempt?"

Tom interjected. "What are you trying to say, *Ron?*" Tom put emphasis on the name, notes of threat underscoring his statement.

She looked back at Mr. Johansson.

The music teacher furrowed his brow. "I'm trying to ask Ravlen if it feels as though she's being – *chased* – away." He leaned toward Ravlen, looking her deeply in the eyes. "Could that be it?" he whispered.

Joan and Tom stood up.

"It seems you have misread the situation." Joan's smile was tense.

"Ravlen is still adapting to her new home here," Tom continued. "And while we appreciate your concern, Ravlen is doing perfectly well."

Mr. Johansson hadn't taken his eyes off Ravlen. She shifted in her seat.

"You can tell me," Mr. Johansson said. His voice was barely above a whisper, but Ravlen heard him clearly. "Do you feel *chased*? Or maybe you are the one *chasing* them away…"

"Thank you for your time, Ron." Joan nudged Ravlen to stand beside her. "Ravlen does enjoy marching band so very much. I've been helping her with 'Twist and Shout'. But now she'd best get to her other classes."

Mr. Johansson continued to watch Ravlen. He tapped his pen on the desk and leaned back in the chair. "Yes, her classes with the other teachers. But Ravlen, it's important that you let me know if ever they give you trouble, all right?"

Ravlen nodded.

"Good," he replied and looked over to Tom and Joan. "You're doing a wonderful job supporting her. We need more people like you."

Joan put her arm around Ravlen's shoulders and guided her toward the door.

Ravlen glanced back to find Mr. Johansson nodding at her, his eyes transfixed.

What does he know? Ravlen wondered as the classroom door closed behind them.

———

"You think he knows about echo chasers?" Marriel dropped her sandwich in the box. "Why would he talk so much about 'chasing' unless he knew?"

"It was like he picked the word on purpose." Ravlen tried to take a bite of her own sandwich, but she wasn't hungry. "He's always been the nicest to me. Maybe he does know something about our work. Maybe he knows previous echo chasers. Maybe he's on our side."

Marriel scooted closer to Ravlen and looked around to see if anyone was listening. "Or maybe it's the opposite. Maybe he's an echo master."

"No way, he couldn't teach full time and be an echo master."

"Maybe he fits it in on weekends."

Ravlen shook her head. "No, not an echo master. But you're right that there's something about him. He knows something. I just don't know what."

"Hi, Marriel." The adolescent male voice was becoming awfully familiar.

Conrad leaned against a tree. Ravlen couldn't help thinking that he was trying too hard. Trying to look cool, trying to look smart, trying to look charming. She couldn't put her finger on exactly what it was.

But she didn't like it.

"Let's go for a walk before class. What do you say, Marriel?" He winked.

Marriel looked at him and then back at Ravlen.

Ravlen jumped in before Marriel could reply. "We need to discuss this – uh – problem." Ravlen leaned forward on her knees. "I really need your help, Marriel."

"We can talk about it later." Marriel smiled and nodded quickly. "I promise."

"But I have to get through the whole afternoon, and I have Mrs. Brand *and* Miss Markham."

Marriel rested her hand on Ravlen's shoulder as she stood. "You'll do fine."

"You know, kid," Conrad piped up. "It's important for you to learn to fight your own battles."

"Pffft." Ravlen couldn't stop herself.

If only he knew the slightest thing...

"I'll catch you after school. Okay, Rav?" Marriel smiled meekly. "We'll meet right here. Promise. Bye!"

Conrad was already walking away by the time Marriel turned around. She caught up to him and he placed his hand on Marriel's back.

As if Marriel needed to be led anywhere. He's got some nerve.

Ravlen angrily ate the rest of her sandwich.

If Marriel is going to leave me on my own, then I'd better prepare myself for Mrs. Brand. Was Mr. Johansson right? Is she trying to chase me away? Is that what all those teachers are trying to do?

The bell rang.

"Already?" she said to her half-eaten sandwich. "But I don't even have my books yet!" Ravlen's locker was on the other side of the school, and the final bell rang as she jogged through the halls toward class. Ravlen grasped the doorknob and took a deep breath before opening it.

"So you decided to join the rest of us, Ravlen?"

"Sorry, Mrs. Brand."

She stepped in, kicking Christopher Duke's desk leg on the way.

"Hey, watch it," he hissed. "And I thought we were lucky enough to go on without you."

She ignored him, but only on the surface.

Christopher Duke. The teachers. Conrad the slimeball. I can't catch a break.

"Hi, Ravlen," Greta's enthusiastic smile awaited her. "How was your weekend?"

"Full of fish."

Greta did a double take. "Full of fish?"

Mrs. Brand clapped her hands. "That's enough. Ravlen, the least you can do is slip in quietly next time you rudely interrupt my lesson." She turned back to the blackboard with her hand on her head. "*Slip in...* Where was I... Can't seem to remember anything... She's late, she's constantly watching, Ravlen, one of *them...*"

She's off her rocker. Ravlen gawked. *How can my presence be so distressing for her?*

"Compound ratios, that's it." She turned back to the class. "Open to page three hundred and thirty-eight, students." Her voice resumed its normal tone. Composed and cold.

But Ravlen saw the line of sweat on her brow.

10

Ravlen woke with prickles running down her arms. She peeked out the curtains, but the sun had yet to rise. The moon cast slivers of white over the waves of the Atlantic outside her window.

An echo opened. Somewhere close.

It had to be recent, either an emerging echo or a new entry to an established one, as Ravlen hadn't felt it before.

She grabbed her watch and pinched the light-up button.

4:37 am. Ugh.

She let her head drop back on the pillow as she considered her options.

Option one, go back to sleep and pretend the sensation over her skin was not an echo threatening to invite originals into it. As much as she wanted her sleep, there was no way Ravlen's conscience would ever let that happen.

Option two, wake Marriel and drag her to the echo with her. But the last time she tried this, Marriel was barely able to help, her bloodshot eyes still half-asleep.

Option three, Ravlen would do it herself, popping in and out, closing it down before first period.

As far as Ravlen was concerned, option three was the only option. She scribbled a quick note and left it on the table, even though she intended to be back for breakfast.

"Closing a nearby echo. Back soon. Or else meet you at school. R"

She signed it off with a flourish of her initial, something she'd been practicing. It felt artistic and fancy.

She stepped outside the front door, closed her eyes, and sensed. She let her awareness roll over the ocean, though it was most unlikely an echo would open there. The ocean waters were simply too restless. Scanning south, all was peaceful but for the early risers who were expected at that time. Truck drivers, bakers, morning shift workers at the big factory just inland from Tom and Joan's home.

There. She looked inland. *It's that way.*

She crossed the near-deserted road, the sensation on her skin growing with each step closer to the factory. Though only a few blocks from Tom and Joan's apartment, this part of town was rougher around the edges. Manufacturing and commercial blocks took the place of residences, and trash was piled on the curbs, behind the buildings, and around the designated garbage containers. A paper cup blew in the wind, bouncing off Ravlen's shin as she looked up at a street sign.

"Hope Drive," she read aloud. *Not a very hopeful feeling place. I bet there are a lot of people wishing for things around here.*

A seagull squawked overhead as someone dropped a garbage can on the corner across from her.

"Hey," a man in coveralls called out. "What'cha doing? You shouldn't be around these parts alone."

Ravlen looked behind her. "Me?"

The man scratched the back of his head and set his hands on his hips. "Yeah, you. You lost or something? Running away? I caught a runaway back here once. Turned out she was getting a regular beating back home. Is that what's happening to you?"

"Oh no. Not me." Ravlen shook her head. "Absolutely not."

"Then what'cha doing here?"

I've got to lie. I can't tell him I'm chasing parallel worlds, he'll call the cops on me. He seems harmless enough, but I can't take any chances...

"I..." she looked back down the road for some kind of inspiration. "My dog! My dog ran away. Yes, that's what happened, really. I'm looking for my dog."

She gave a firm nod and hoped she'd sounded convincing.

I've got to get better at lying!

"Your dog. I get it. I've got a Pittie at home. Best darn animal in the world." He snapped his fingers. "I'll help you! My name's Mac. I'm a welder over at Blue Piece Manufacturing. I'm sure we'll find your dog in no time."

Ravlen gulped. The last thing she needed was someone witnessing her disappear into the haze. It was one of the most sacred rules of echo chasing.

No one could ever know she did it.

He might follow her in, or alert authorities before she could shut it down – worse, he might tell tons of people about it and blow her cover.

"That's really nice of you." She racked her brain for a possible solution. She could tell the haze wasn't far, if she could find it and get in while he thought she was heading home... "Why don't you look for him that way, while I look this way."

Mac's eyes narrowed. "I don't know how separating is going to keep you safe."

"The minute I find him, I'm going home, you can be sure about that." She cringed at the insincerity in her voice, like it was a line from a play. "I think it's best we cover separate ground, in case... in case he's hiding somewhere, afraid."

She knew Binner wasn't afraid of anything, but she didn't have to say it to this guy.

"I see..." He didn't sound sure. "You shout out if anything weird happens, y'understand?"

"I sure will."

"I'll go this way." He pointed in the exact direction of where she sensed the haze. "That way you stay on the main road."

Find an excuse, find an excuse...

"The main road is scary. Someone might see me and stop me from finding my doggie."

Doggie? Now I sound like I'm five years old. Though he doesn't seem to notice.

"I hadn't thought of that. Okay, you go that way then. What's the dog's name?"

"Binner."

Ravlen kicked herself.

I should have made up a name!

He wiped his greased-up hands on his coveralls. "Binner. Okay then, let's find Binner. Binner!" he shouted at the top of his lungs.

Ravlen looked at her watch. 5:12 am. She hoped Binner was fast asleep and couldn't hear someone calling his name from four blocks away.

But she had her doubts.

"Binner..." she called, but not too loudly, just in case he was more tuned into Ravlen's voice.

"He won't hear you if you whisper like that," Mac called from a street over.

"He might be scared. I don't want him to feel like he's in trouble."

"Ah, good point." Mac lowered his voice. "Binner..."

There's the haze.

Behind a forklift, Ravlen caught sight of the shifting air. The echo entry was tucked neatly into a backend access of a wood-chipping plant.

Mac was shuffling half a block away. In the stillness of early morning, Ravlen could hear him turning over wood pallets and garbage cans. "You in here, Binner-boy?"

Please don't hear us, Binner. Please just stay snuggled under my bed at home.

She approached the haze, slipping behind the forklift. She was out of sight of the main road and tucked away from the entrance to the plant. There was a single light on inside the building, on the second floor facing the back access door.

I bet the wisher is in there. If only he knew...

"Binner!" Mac's voice grew closer. "You in here?"

Ravlen cleared her throat. She had to throw him off the scent. "Oh look!" she called from her hiding place behind the forklift. "I've found him! Hooray, Binner! We're going to head home now. Thanks for your help, Mac!"

"You found him! That's great, where was he?"

Ravlen held her breath, hoping he'd think she was already gone.

"Hello? You found Binner?" He paused. "Guess she went home already."

Ravlen made a silent fist of success, just as the hairs on her arm prickled.

Oh no.

The click-clack of dog claws on pavement was unmistakable. Binner rounded the forklift and jumped on Ravlen's legs, panting with the exuberance of a dog that just found its long-lost master.

"Shhhh, Binner. Quiet."

Binner closed his mouth and looked left and right, waiting for Ravlen's next command.

"You wait here, Binner. Stay hidden, and I'll be back."

Binner set his paw on Ravlen's foot.

"You have to stay. I don't have long." Ravlen stood, but the loyal dog stood, too, leaning against her leg.

She sighed. "Well, boy. Looks like you're coming with me."

He jumped, front paws pressing against her legs and his ears perked, ready for whatever adventure Ravlen would throw at him. She lifted him up and held him close, then stepped through the haze.

They arrived on an island.

Not an island like the one where Ravlen grew up. Nothing like it. She and Binner stood on smooth white sands with the shade of a palm tree overhead. Looking left, she saw the shore, curving out of sight. Looking right, she saw its limits there, too. It was the smallest island she could have imagined, the whole thing taking up no more than the size of the middle school.

Directly in front of her was a suitcase. When she opened it, she found bars of gold, a pillow, and a stack of comic books.

"If you were stranded on an island, what would you want with you?" Ravlen recalled the writing prompt from her English class the previous month.

Someone had taken that idea to heart.

Binner ran to a nearby palm tree and began barking.

"What's up there, buddy?" Ravlen joined him and could hear a clicking, some kind of animal sound. Through the branches she could make out a monkey.

"A golden monkey?"

The monkey replied with a sassy smile and hopped to another branch.

"It's brass."

Ravlen swung around to find her referent sitting in a

lawn chair under a parasol.

"A brass monkey?"

The referent shrugged. "People imagine all kinds of things on a desert island in the middle of the sea."

"Who would *want* to be on a desert island with a brass monkey and a suitcase full of gold?" Ravlen grumbled.

"Someone who is surrounded by noise and chaos, by commotion, disorder, and poverty." Her referent lifted a big glass of a foamy white drink complete with a straw, slice of orange, and a tiny umbrella stuck in it. She took a loud slurp.

Ravlen strolled away from the old woman. "This is the problem around here. New worlds popping up every day based on wishes and desires, like nobody is happy with the life they have." She looked down at the dog. "How do you explain that, Binner-boy?"

If dogs could shrug, that was what Binner did.

"Yeah, I get it. Everybody imagines some version of what they think could be better."

A drink stand built out of a giant coconut popped up in front of her. Ravlen jumped back and Binner growled.

Her referent stood behind the counter, filling a glass with the white drink.

"Thirsty? Here you go." She passed it to Ravlen and whispered, "Don't drink it."

Ravlen swirled the drink but took the advice and didn't dare a sip. They stood, each observing the other.

"Are you helping me?" Ravlen shot out quickly before she regretted asking.

"I can't help you. I can only cast a little light into dark places."

"That's a riddle."

"Life is a riddle. You are surrounded by it in this very moment."

Ravlen couldn't argue with that. Without thinking, she brought the drink to her lips.

"What did I say?" the old woman said.

Ravlen quickly lowered the drink and then put it back on the counter. "Thank you. I didn't even want to drink it."

"And yet you would have." The woman's eyes twinkled with experience.

Ravlen leaned forward on the counter, the closest she'd ever been to her referent. She could see the deep lines that crinkled by her eyes and the faintly cracked skin of her lips.

Ravlen's heartbeat grew louder as she dared to ask the question that had been on her mind since her first trip into the echo.

"Who are you?"

"Ah." The woman crossed her arms. "I was wondering when you might ask."

"Can you tell me?" Binner scratched at Ravlen's foot. "What, Binner? I'm having a conversation here."

"He's right," her referent nodded. "Listen to the dog. There are some questions you don't want answered. Instead, think about what you have seen of me. What have you observed since your first foray into these lands?"

Ravlen thought back to the first time she'd seen the woman, sitting on a bench in the park when Marriel and Ravlen had come with the animals, back when she was first learning to disturb.

"What have I revealed to you over this time, young Ravlen?"

"You know my name?"

"I wouldn't be a good referent if I didn't."

Ravlen wondered if this might be a trick, if there was something more to the question than she saw, but so far, she had no reason not to trust her referent. She had only ever been there for Ravlen with a word of guidance, a riddle, and the occasional mocking gesture.

"You're always there."

"I am." The woman nodded solemnly, her lips forming a straight line and her eyes looking deep into Ravlen's soul. "Always. There is much you cannot know, not now and perhaps not ever, but of this you can be sure. I will always be there."

A cloud blew into the otherwise perfect sky, a dark cloud turning black.

They both looked up. Binner whined at the sight.

"Not long now," her referent sighed. "Our meeting this time is brief."

"But we're finally talking about things that matter! I have so many questions, so much I don't understand…"

"And if I were to reveal it all to you, the very sky would crumble upon us. And yet, another sky will be born in eternity, just as you close the lights down on this one."

"That's the whole problem!"

Binner jumped and tugged on Ravlen's shirt. The single cloud was growing, spinning, danger breathing out from it like a squall from the heavens.

"That is the greatest riddle of all." Her referent smiled, generous and gentle. "Where one ends another will open, but you can only end it with the very beginning."

I can only end it with the very beginning?

"Best you be going now." Her voice was soft but firm with warning.

The cloud covered the sun and nighttime descended in an instant. Binner yanked on Ravlen's pant leg.

"Coming, Binner!"

Ravlen cast a glance back. Her referent's eyes reflected the black of the sky, speaking volumes to Ravlen in their silence.

Ravlen didn't say goodbye. Binner jumped into her arms and together they stumbled onto asphalt at sunrise, the fork-lift unmoved.

Ravlen sat down, trying to gather her rushing disorder of thoughts. Binner licked her cheek as the near-silent suction signaled the end of the echo behind her.

I can only end it with the very beginning... What does that mean?

11

"We were worried about you."

Joan and Tom sat with her at the table. Tom's hands were clasped so tight his knuckles had gone white, and Ravlen could swear that the line of Joan's brow was deeper than it had been before.

"I'm sorry. I thought I'd be back sooner."

Joan and Tom lectured Ravlen about the dangers of going out in the early morning hours by herself. She wasn't to do it again. Joan and Tom would always get up to at least accompany her as far as they could.

Ravlen wasn't sure how practical that would be, or even if it was allowed.

"But what if…"

"No but's, not now." Joan clenched her fist on the table.

They're both angry, even if they're trying to control themselves. I guess this isn't the moment to work out the details…

By the time Marriel and Ravlen left for school, first period was already well underway.

"You could have woken me up," Marriel chastised as they headed out for school. "I could have helped."

"No need." Ravlen kicked at the asphalt and avoided Marriel's eyes. "I could tell it was going to be an easy one to close."

Marriel gently poked Ravlen's head. "And *I* can tell you're lying. You didn't know what it was going to be. And taking Binner with you? What if he'd run off just as the echo was closing? What if he felt more at home there and you had to make a terrible choice?"

The thought hadn't occurred to Ravlen at the time, but now she knew where Binner's loyalties were. And they weren't to the echo worlds.

He was loyal to her.

"You should have seen him, Marriel. He grabbed hold of my pant leg and wouldn't let go. He was taking me to the haze. He saw the danger I faced and wouldn't let me fall for it."

Marriel stopped and put her hands on Ravlen's shoulders. "Don't do it again."

"I won't."

"Promise?"

"Promise."

"Good," Marriel carried on, "because I've got things to do these days. You're going to be on your own more."

"*Things* to do?"

"My boyfriend, Conrad," Marriel grinned, "asked me to be the secretary of student parliament."

"Your *boyfriend?*" Ravlen's mouth fell open. "You can't just drop that into a conversation like it's peanut butter and jelly."

"What does that even mean? Don't be immature, Ravlen."

"I'm not. You getting a boyfriend could have serious consequences for our mission."

"Now you're being both immature *and* dramatic. Maybe once you're sixteen you'll understand."

Ravlen threw her head back. "Don't start on that again."

"Remember what Dina said. We can't be like other kids. We have to grow up. And that's what I'm doing."

"This is not what she meant."

Or was it? What exactly did Dina mean? It made sense at the time, but now...

Marriel was already several paces ahead of her as they reached the edge of the school grounds.

"I'll meet you after school. Conrad and I will walk you home. We agreed on that."

"Gee, don't do me any favors."

"Don't be late, Ravlen." Marriel pointed at her. "Set your alarm and don't keep us waiting." Marriel turned and waved to Conrad who was waiting for her at the top of the high school stairs.

"Late again," Mrs. Brand announced as the math class door creaked open and Ravlen poked her head in.

"I have a note, Mrs. Brand."

"Always a note," the irritable teacher muttered under her breath.

The only good news was that Christopher Duke's seat was empty.

"Hiya, Ravlen!"

"Hi, Greta."

"You all set with *Twist and Shout*? I thought we could rehearse together before band practice tomorrow."

Marriel has a new boyfriend. She won't be hanging out much with me now, not unless she and Conrad are chaperoning me home like I'm a baby. I can make my own plans.

"Let's do it," Ravlen grinned.

"Quiet, Ravlen!" Mrs. Brand's voice rang out.

Greta leaned forward.

"Why does she always pick on you?"

"I wish I knew."

That was a good enough answer for Greta, who raised

her eyebrows and stuck out her tongue when Mrs. Brand turned her back. Ravlen giggled.

"Ravlen, quiet!"

"Pick up your feet, kid." Conrad put his foot underneath Ravlen's from behind, making her stumble forward.

"What the heck, Conrad?" Ravlen righted herself.

Conrad laughed and looked at Marriel. "I love kids."

Marriel giggled.

"You've *got* to be kidding me," Ravlen mumbled under her breath as she quickened her pace.

Conrad was impossible. She'd barely spent ten minutes with him, and he'd already managed to boast about his polo victory, his A+ in chemistry, and even mention the fortune his family had made from a luxury hotel chain. All that, and he'd even found time to pester Ravlen along the way.

"I told you, Marry. She's got to learn to be more independent. You can't have her depending on you for everything."

"I'm working on it."

Ravlen spun around. "You're *what?*"

"The adults are talking." Conrad made a hand motion for Ravlen to spin back around, the same motion Ravlen used with Binner to get him to do a trick.

Heat from the insult burned up Ravlen's neck. She quickened her pace and reached the bungalow before Marriel and Conrad turned the last corner. She slammed the door shut and turned the deadbolt.

"She has a key, you know," Tom said from the living room, his face hidden inside a wide newspaper.

Ravlen collapsed onto the sofa beside him. "Why does he have to be such a jerk?"

"The boyfriend?"

Ravlen nodded and rested her head on Tom's shoulder.

"He's sixteen. It's pretty much obligatory at that age. A rite of passage."

"Daniel was never like that."

Tom turned to look at her. "So I gathered. And speaking of Daniel, there just might be a postcard with your name on it waiting by the microwave."

Ravlen jumped up, all thoughts of stupid Conrad flying away. "Why didn't you tell me?" She ran into the kitchen.

"I just did."

"Ravlen, hi. How's school? How's Binner? I'm learning finally how to disturb. It's so cool! I tried it with a frog..."

"A frog? Why would he try it with a frog? That won't work."

"What's that?" Tom called from the living room.

"Nothing."

"...but it didn't work. It didn't occur to me that animals are like humans. Go figure! Let's compare skills next time we're together. Daniel"

Ravlen came back into the living room, postcard in hand. "Do you think I'll ever see him again?"

Tom looked over his reading glasses and seemed to see her anxiety. She couldn't stand the idea of never hanging out with Daniel again. He closed the newspaper and tapped the sofa beside him. Ravlen sat down and hugged her knees in.

"I can't make you any promises, but I do know that if anyone can make something happen, it's you."

A high-pitched giggle interrupted them. They looked out the big bay window to see Conrad leaning in as Marriel turned her head and he planted a long kiss on her cheek.

"Yuck."

"I'm with you on that, kid."

GRETA AND RAVLEN MET BEHIND THE MIDDLE SCHOOL AFTER the final bell rang. Although they were in the same class, Greta always left during the last hour. Once Ravlen overheard a classmate say that she had to go because she was 'too special to stay', but Ravlen didn't understand what that meant.

They pulled out their instruments and began the tedious act of cleaning. Greta played the flute and stood at the back, not far from where Ravlen marched with the trumpets.

"What happens when you go – you know – where you go?"

"You mean my tutoring?"

"That's where you go?"

"Yep. Miss Markham helps me with homework. Sometimes my brain gets stuck."

Ravlen wasn't sure if it was okay to ask what that meant. She took a minute to figure out the right words, but Greta saw her expression and answered the question without being asked.

"Brains are like machines. If too much gunk builds up, then nothing else can get through. I understand the lessons, but after a while, I just can't make sense of them. Miss Markham breaks it all down into smaller pieces."

"It's too bad you have to do it with mean Miss Markham."

Miss Markham cast Ravlen the stink eye on a near-daily basis in French class. Sometimes Ravlen thought she deserved it since she knew her accent sounded more like a choking cat than French. But sometimes she hadn't even had a chance to do something wrong and Miss Markham would be staring over her bent wireframe glasses.

"Miss Markham, mean? What are you talking about?" Greta squinted into the end of her flute. "Miss Markham is one of the nicest teachers around this place. So calm, so friendly."

"To you, maybe," Ravlen grumbled. "She's never liked me. You'll see, I'll point it out in next class."

"How can you be sure she'll do it?"

"She does it every single day."

"Hmmm." Greta rested the flute in her lap. "Did you say something insensitive about the French Revolution maybe? That's the only time I saw her get a bit uppity."

"Of course I didn't! Why would I ever say anything about the French Revolution?"

"I don't know, but if you want to give *Twist and Shout* a try before marching band begins, then we'd better get going. Ten minutes to rehearsal."

When their ten minutes were up, they rushed into the music room. Ravlen scanned for Marriel, but she wasn't with the trombones. She wasn't anywhere in the room.

Marriel late? That's a first.

"Good afternoon, band players! When you walk through that door for rehearsal, you are no longer the students of our fine middle and high schools. No!" Mr. Johansson glided between the students, his arms open wide. "You transform. You become one. One marching band, one unit, one orchestra of enthusiasm and tenacity."

Someone groaned.

"I mean it!" Mr. Johansson crossed back to the front of the room. "In here, you are not a twelve-year-old, not an adolescent, not a student, and not a boy or girl. You are an artist! Now let me hear that emotion, that energy in your playing. 'Twist and Shout', we'll run it all the way through and then spot-check the verses and chorus. Ready?"

The students all set their instruments to mouths, and the drummers had their sticks in the air. Ravlen looked around, but Marriel was still nowhere to be seen.

Blowing off band practice? That's not like Marriel at all.

"A one, a-two, a-one-two-three!"

Ravlen got through the ninety-minute practice and rushed home to find Marriel sitting on the front step of Joan and Tom's place, with none other than Conrad stuck to her cheek.

"Double yuck," Ravlen muttered as she walked up the path. She gathered herself. If she was going to have to deal with Conrad, she couldn't stoop to his level. "Marriel, did you forget that today is Thursday?"

"No, why?"

"Marching band?"

"Oh, yes, that." She looked over at Conrad, who had a crooked smile on his face. "Conrad wanted to talk about some stuff, so I had to miss it."

"You know that Mr. J. only lets you skip twice and then you're out."

"I know. I won't."

Conrad jumped in. "It was important." He put his arm around Marriel. "A couple has to have certain things in place. Marriel and I had to talk about those things. *Grown-up* things." He winked at Ravlen, which made her gag.

"Coming through, let me in." She made a point of stepping between Marriel and Conrad, tapping Conrad's shoulder with her foot on the way.

"Watch it!" Conrad brushed himself off. "Kids," Ravlen heard him say before she slammed the front door shut.

Binner rushed at her, the branch of a palm tree in his mouth.

"What have you got there, Binner?"

"It seems Binner enjoys when I garden," Joan said. "No sooner do I get a pile of stuff together to take to the garbage than he's in it, rolling about, and tossing it everywhere. It's not even a big garden, but he's having the time of his life." Joan shook her head. "He's cute, but terribly untidy."

Binner jumped to play with her, so Ravlen yanked back in

a merry competition of tug of war. The game ignited Binner's dog instincts to pull with all his might, even if the prize was just a palm leaf.

Ravlen cast a glance through the living room window to the front step, where Conrad was talking in low tones to Marriel. Marriel's face was smiling, her eyes wide with adoration. They hardly knew each other, and already Marriel was falling head over heels.

Conrad then stood, touched her cheek, and walked away. Marriel waved widely, then climbed the steps to the door. She smiled weakly at Ravlen before turning to watch Conrad walk away.

She's got it bad for him. But I don't see how they can live happily ever after with all the echo chasing we have to do.

Ravlen sighed.

As long as she doesn't get too attached...

Ravlen kept turning to the car's empty backseat while Dina set her eyes on the highway ahead.

"You going to be all right on your own?" Dina was taking her one state over, where, as Dina called it, "...a plethora of echoes had emerged at once..." Another echo chaser had managed to close out several already, but she needed a break.

And Marriel had 'plans.'

So she said. Ravlen knew that meant Marriel was going to be 'doing nothing' with Conrad. Apparently, if you were doing nothing but it was alongside someone else, it was good enough to be called 'plans.'

It wasn't that Ravlen felt she couldn't do it on her own. She'd already closed lots of echoes without Marriel.

But this was different.

Marriel *could* have come. Ravlen thought she *should* have come. But she didn't.

"I'll be fine." Ravlen bounced as Dina turned off the highway onto a dirt road. "It just feels weird."

Dina slapped the steering wheel. "It happens all the

time. Girls become teenagers, and they have to do things their own way. It's part of growing up. For Marriel, it's exploring other possibilities. For you, it's doing what you know, but without Marriel. It's a perfectly normal progression."

They hit a pothole and Ravlen's head smacked into the window.

"Maybe it's normal," Ravlen rubbed her head, "but it's still weird."

The car lurched left and right on the bumpy country road.

"Out here?" Ravlen opened the window that had become covered in dust. "There's nothing here." At that moment her skin began to prick. "Then again…"

"Close the window!" Dina coughed in the dust.

"Over there." Ravlen pointed where a line of trees jetted out perfectly straight from the road. "How can trees grow in a row like that?"

"It's a way of marking fields – maybe a different crop or different owner on either side of the line – or it could be a windbreak for a farmer's house."

"There's something stable about using a tree as a marker. Even if it's strange to see them all in a straight line."

Dina grinned. "Still a lot of this mainland stuff left for you to learn, huh?"

"Honestly, every day there's something I don't expect," Ravlen said, "starting with Marriel and Conrad being a couple. Then there's this girl in our band who's super nice to me. But then there's this guy at school whose eyes have hurricanes in them every time he sees me. And the beach – I saw the most amazing crab! It almost crawled into Joan's garden!"

"Wait, wait. Hold up a second," Dina said. "Did you say a boy with hurricanes in his eyes?"

Ravlen's stomach knotted. Christopher Duke was the last person she wanted to think about.

"Not literally hurricanes, but his eyes definitely do something funny when they reflect the light. They're dark gray, and they get even darker when he looks at me, even though I've never done anything to him, I swear!"

Dina kept her eyes on the road, but her knuckles turned white as she gripped the wheel tighter. Her lips opened as if she was going to say something, and then she stopped herself.

"Watch out for that guy," she finally said. "We don't know what he knows."

"But how could he know anything?" It was maddening to think that all along Christopher Duke might be harboring secrets about her when she'd never exposed her mission to anyone, not once. She pounded her fist on her leg.

"Earth to Ravlen!" Dina poked her in the arm. "Don't get sidetracked by that, we have a mission to fulfill."

Ravlen pointed to the left. "There's something happening over there."

Dina pulled into a laneway that barely looked passable for her small car.

"Stop here." Ravlen felt the pull of the haze. It was close. "Save your car, I can walk the rest of the way." She stepped out and left the car door open, something strange in the air calling her forward. "This one's different…"

"What does that mean?"

"I don't know."

"Describe it to me," Dina asked as she caught up to her. "If it's something different, we need to document whatever you're feeling. It might be something important for the future."

Ravlen wasn't sure if it was important, but it sure was *different*. Little pops of energy danced across her senses like the sparklers kids wrote their name with on the fourth of July. It was a haze, no doubt, but the consistency of it was different.

"It's popping," Ravlen said. "The waves are growing."

Dina gasped. "It's a brand new entry! Quick, Ravlen, let's find it. I've never seen a new entry being created!"

Ravlen led Dina to the place, not far from their makeshift parking spot.

"There it is."

Dina shook her head, her mouth open in wonder. "It's stunning."

A nearly transparent prism floated in mid-air. Sunlight shone through it, casting gentle rainbows – but the light wasn't coming from above. It was coming from *within*.

"Wow." Even Ravlen was transfixed by the sight, like watching an egg hatch or a flower bloom.

It was the beginning of a new world.

"How can something that's not real be so beautiful?" Ravlen watched the colors shift and grow, the prism spreading, splitting, and finally transforming into the haze she'd come to know so well.

"There is great beauty in the human imagination." Dina held herself, her arms crossing over her chest. "If only it weren't so dangerous."

They stood, not speaking, not moving until the haze had finished its expansion into a wave of a shimmering entry.

Ravlen tried to imagine what was on the other side. "Can I go in?"

"Think about it for a second." Dina kept her arms tight around herself. "It's like being at the birth of a powerful weapon. I don't know how I feel about it. And more so, I don't know what you'll find in there."

Ravlen had to know. The words of her referent reverberated in her ears:

You can only end it with the very beginning.

This was her chance to see what that meant. Was it possible she could use an emerging echo to shut down all echoes forever?

Her heart raced at the thought.

"I've got to go in, Dina. There are secrets on the other side. I have to know them. This could change everything!" Ravlen's muscles tensed; she had an overwhelming desire to run through the haze, but she knew the dangers all too well of rushing into an echo. She might find herself on the edge of a cliff, or in the middle of traffic, or who-knew-what.

Dina unwrapped her arms and without warning, embraced Ravlen, holding her close and tight.

Dina had never hugged her before. Ravlen was too surprised to react, but when the embrace lasted longer than she expected, she raised her arms and gently pushed Dina back. She felt Dina's shoulders relax, her whole body release, like she'd just let out a breath she'd been holding for years.

"You be careful in there," Dina whispered in Ravlen's ear. "I'll be right here when you come back."

By the time they separated, Dina was back to herself. Strong, hard, clever Dina, with her tattoos and piercings and sharp eyes. But Ravlen had caught a glimpse of what was inside her, and it was soft, fragile, and vulnerable.

"I'll be back soon," Ravlen reassured, but Dina just pursed her lips and nodded, like she always did.

Ravlen stepped into the haze.

The air was warm and wet, like having her face in a blanket that just came out of the washing machine. Each breath was an effort, but she could get enough air. Everything around her was a fleshy color of pink, like looking at the sun with her eyes closed.

Is this echo ready for humans?

The idea had never struck her that the echo might not be

able to sustain life. She looked behind her. The haze was still there. She could leave if she wanted to.

I need to calm down. If I stop breathing so quickly it'll be easier.

She took in a deep, slow breath. There was less resistance. The pulsating pressure in her head slowed, too. Her body took on a new state, tranquil and settled.

That's better.

She smiled at herself. She could do this. *But now what? There's nothing here...*

Even as she thought it, the world began forming around her, molded out of nothing, shapes created in the thick air.

"Whoa."

Creatures took form, like a coloring book sketching itself with living, breathing animals. Elephants and tigers, eagles and camels. She was watching the page of a coloring book come to life.

Her eyes struggled to make sense of the creatures who walked across the sky like it was a piece of paper, while her feet remained firmly on pink ground.

What is its logic? And what if I get it wrong? What if it's going to become something much more complex?

As she debated with herself, life sprang into action. She watched the jungle images moving in two-dimensional space on a screen while the animals themselves were larger than life.

This seems pretty easy to close down... Oh, a leopard!

Far above her head, the leopard slinked across the pink expanse. It seemed to hear Ravlen's thought, and paused, meeting her eyes.

The leopard smiled. Ravlen froze.

I didn't know leopards could smile... but then again... they can't. Yes, I can shut this echo down easily but what if...

The "what-ifs" swam through Ravlen's brain until a voice in her head interrupted her thoughts.

You can only end it with the very beginning.

"This is it!" she called out and all the animals looked at her. In perfect unison, they cocked their heads. "If I can get to the echoes as they emerge, then at some point there won't be any left to bring in originals!"

She was sad to shut down a place with some of the most beautiful animals she had ever seen.

It's okay, she consoled herself. *They couldn't be happy living a three-dimensional life in a two-dimensional world.*

When she went back through the haze, her head was high and her chest puffed with her newfound knowledge of how echoes emerged, and more importantly, how she could stop them before any original ever found their way in.

Dina was leaning against the car but rushed over on hearing the suction of the haze closing. "So? What was it like?"

Ravlen smiled. "I'll tell you. But first, I have an idea."

13

———

Ravlen described her big idea. Shut down the echoes before they finished forming, and maybe uncover the secret to preventing them from opening in the first place.

"No kidding," Dina snarked.

Wasn't that the best thing that could happen? Dina was skeptical as the plan was short on detail. Very short.

"You don't understand what luck it was that you came across the birth of that echo today. It was a pure accident."

"Was it?" Ravlen wasn't ready to give up that quickly. "Or was it that there was something in the nature of it that I was able to sense, something… unique. Maybe we can identify exactly what that thing is, and train the other echo chasers to seek it out."

"Echoes are more like earthquakes than hurricanes. Hurricanes you can predict. Earthquakes, you only find out about when the ground starts to shake under your feet."

"Still… maybe…"

"I don't mean to burst your bubble, kid," Dina led Ravlen to the car, "but we've got another echo to close down. This one isn't emerging, and it isn't going to be as easy as some of your recent assignments."

Ravlen was still bounding with excitement at her big idea. Confidence oozed through her. "Don't worry, I got this."

Dina looked sideways at Ravlen. "That's why I worry."

They hadn't driven more than fifteen miles before Ravlen felt gentle waves sparking over her skin.

"Already? What's happening to make all these echoes?" She looked to Dina for insight about what was happening in this desolate and deserted part of the country. The nearest town was a few miles away. Houses were few and far between.

"Now you understand why we needed you. It's out of control. There's an echo master operating in this area. Seems he has his sights set squarely on this region. He seeks out the more depressed parts of the state and feeds on their poverty and destitution." Dina shook her head. "It's pretty depraved."

"Wait, wait, wait!" Ravlen needed to understand what Dina was saying. It might have an impact on what she was trying to do, and she'd never heard anything like this about the echo masters before. "Pull over."

Dina did so and looked at Ravlen with a big question mark in her eyes. "You know we're in a rush, right?"

Ravlen ignored the question. "What do you mean, echo masters feeding off the wishes of the poor? That's not what we were taught. That has never been the explanation for why echoes appear."

Dina looked out the driver's side window to see if anyone was coming, despite the fact that they hadn't passed another person in ages.

"It's not the most popular theory, but all we have are theories."

Ravlen crossed her arms. "Tell me more. If I'm supposed

to be ending these echoes, then I have to know how they start."

Dina scratched her leg and looked away. "I don't see why that matters."

Why won't she tell me? Why would Dina hold anything back?

"I see how you're looking at me." Dina sighed. "Okay. Here's what I *can* say: As mentors, we try not to speculate. We're supposed to help you build the skills to shut down the echoes, skills the rest of us have learned the hard way. Certainly, you'll learn new ones too, abilities I can't even imagine. That's the natural order. But we've seen the dangers of speculating about the 'why' of things in the past."

"What kind of dangers?" Ravlen saw possibilities opening in front of her, but she had to keep Dina talking.

"Dangers… like losing you inside an echo. As it is, there are so few of us able to chase echoes, fewer still able to close them," Dina said. "Most girls on the island never will be able to. They may have been found in an echo, but not born in one. If we get sidetracked, pulled into missions that aren't part of our primary goal of saving originals from certain death, then we end up putting more people in danger."

"But Dina, I'm talking about *ending* the echoes altogether."

Dina shook her head. "Are you going to end human desires? Are you going to end the suffering that leads to those desperate wishes? Never."

"But maybe there's another way…"

"Stop, Ravlen."

"Imagine if we could end all this…"

"I said STOP!"

Ravlen blinked. Dina's face had gone beet red, the vein in her neck throbbed.

"It's not just that it's foolish, it's *dangerous* to talk like that. You can't pretend you're bigger than you are. We are all expendable in this world, and even more so in the echo.

Every minute you're not focusing on shutting down the existing echoes, you risk killing someone in there. Do you understand that?"

Ravlen could only nod, but her thoughts were clear.

She's wrong.

If there was a way to make sure humanity could have their desires without being sucked into another world that wouldn't hesitate to risk their demise... that was a worthy mission.

But now wasn't the time to say it.

"Over there." Ravlen pointed toward the middle of an overgrown field with no tracks. "The haze is that way."

"You're really good at this, you know that?" Dina pulled the car as close to the edge of the field as possible without driving into brambles. "I've never met another chaser who can sense the specific direction of a haze like you can. It usually takes a lot more reconnaissance work, mentors trying to identify missing people, or piece together stories and folklore that might help us find a haze. But you... you just feel them from miles away. That's one of the reasons it's so important that you stay focused on this work."

"I understand why you say that."

She tapped Ravlen's leg. "I'm sorry I yelled at you. It's personal for me."

"I know, Dina."

She's waiting for the day when someone finds her sister and brings her back. I don't blame her for wanting all of us to be focused on the goal of bringing originals home... it's just that I know we can do better... I feel it...

She'd explore the idea later with Marriel, if Marriel weren't fully consumed in her new boyfriend-girlfriend status.

Ravlen rolled her eyes as she walked to the haze even though there was no one to see it.

Marriel and Conrad. Ugh. How long is this going to last? Forever? She's only sixteen. Nobody gets married when they're sixteen. But eighteen? Two years and Marriel could be married?

The haze came into sight.

I can't think about Marriel now. I'll totally blow this echo closure.

She paused in front of the haze.

Then again, I know what I'm doing. Like Dina said, I'm almost the best there is. Maybe I am the best...

She stepped into the haze.

Maybe I can shut down echoes with a single thought....

She moved smoothly through the haze, no more than a moment passing.

After all I've seen this past year, there's nothing that can surprise me.

She arrived in a field of wildflowers, a daisy tickling her nose and a butterfly floating around her cheek.

She should have enjoyed the easy arrival. They weren't always this welcoming, that was for sure. And yet, she was anything but relieved. She clutched at her stomach, immediately feeling like she might be sick.

I know this garden. I know it too well.

It was the garden of her first echo.

Her head began to pound as flowers swayed in the gentle breeze, and shimmers of sunlight peaked through the brambling bushes.

The garden where her echo master father had brought her. The garden of her own infancy. A garden of memories she'd buried since she'd uncovered them a year earlier.

"Hello, Ravlen."

She turned slowly, hoping she'd heard wrong. Wishing he wouldn't be there. But there he was.

"Hello, *father*."

1 4

"I wondered when I might see you again." Oaken's deep, dark eyes were full of nostalgic longing that Ravlen remembered from their first encounter by the pond. "Were you? I wasn't."

She put on her imaginary armor. Anything he said would slide right off her. She had spent many nights imagining what to say and do when this day came. Witty words to sting him, and powers to overwhelm him. But now that the moment was here and he was standing in front of her, she forgot it all. So many great conversations that had played out in her mind, all gone like a wisp of fog under a bright sun.

He laid a hand on her shoulder, casting waves of electricity through her skin. "Perhaps I can convince you to leave. This world is well-managed, and the people here are safe, leading the most extraordinary lives. This isn't like the last time. You won't find a fault with this world."

He said it as if it was true, but Ravlen didn't fall for it.

Every echo is built on false logic. There is no reality in a world where everything goes perfectly to plan.

"Even if you were to find originals here, they wouldn't

want to leave." There was no malice in his tone, only self-confidence.

My father, arrogant and self-righteous as always. He thinks he's right, even though we both know it isn't true.

"Then you have nothing to fear if I walk around and see for myself." Her voice came out with a whine, more like a snarky adolescent than a poised echo chaser. She kicked herself for not being more mature.

"You are always welcome wherever I am, Ravlen."

Ravlen searched for a clever reply, something that would show just how much she'd grown in the last year, how far she'd come, and how advanced she was.

But nothing came to mind.

She kept her expression neutral, responding through a cool silence. Maybe that would get to him more than dueling words, especially since he didn't listen anyway. Why waste the breath?

Oaken nodded and walked away.

Next time, I'll do better. Put him on his heels, next time.

She huffed as she explored the echo, annoyed with herself.

I could have said, "I never want to be wherever you are." No, that's too childish.

She kicked at the asphalt of a smooth pathway that ran from the garden to a city block. She was not in the mood to revisit the memories of the wildflowers. As it was, she was losing focus on her mission.

Forget about Oaken, if that's even his real name. I've got my mission.

She scanned the surroundings but, as Oaken had said, nothing looked out of place. She caught a hint of sound in the distance and closed her eyes.

Hone in on the sound. Ignore everything else. Just like the carers taught. Listen by deepening one sense at a time... let every-thing else fall into the distance... Is that a marching band?

Ravlen opened her eyes and ran to the center of town where she found a parade in progress. She joined the edges of a crowd. Children waved flags that said, "Me!" and "My turn!" and "I'm waiting for you!"

"Excuse me," Ravlen found a woman who had a small child at her side. "What's the parade for?"

"What's the parade for? Why, it's the parade of every day!"

"Oh." Ravlen went on her tiptoes but couldn't yet see any floats coming down the street. "So, we're just celebrating that it's, uh, another day?"

That's a reasonable enough reason for an echo to throw a parade. No flaw in the logic there.

The woman laughed. "Of course not! Did you come from up north? I heard rumors that they were only just beginning to consider the parade."

"Yes," Ravlen lied badly. "Yes, of course. I come from up north."

"Ah, well that explains it. This is the matching parade. Just past the band are floats with the united families of the week, and beyond that are the parents who will pick their child from the crowd."

"*Excuse me?*" Ravlen couldn't stop herself from making a face.

"It's so much more natural than the *other* ways. I picked out Junior here just a couple of weeks ago. Isn't he adorable? Isn't he the sweetest?" The boy gave a toothy smile and grasped his mother around the leg. "We were meant to be. My husband is in the band. You'll see him coming in a moment."

The marching band's song was familiar, though Ravlen couldn't remember the name of it.

"Wait a second," Ravlen raised her voice as the band approached. "All these kids holding up signs…"

"The children without parents? They're waiting to be picked."

Ravlen's stomach sank.

"All of them? Poor kids."

"Oh, don't feel sorry for them. They will get to live in wonderful conditions once they are selected. The family is gifted with an in-ground swimming pool and their choice of either a pony or a sailboat. We took the sailboat. My husband is allergic to horses."

The logic of this echo is super, duper warped. All these kids waiting for families? All of them suffering until they are picked, and then they get a pool and a pony?

"Look over there." The woman pointed. "See that float way at the back? There is at least one, maybe two adults on it. They'll pick their child today. Isn't it grand? Every day at four in the afternoon, after lunch is tidied and the children have had their nap, it's parade time! The atmosphere is just electric, don't you think?"

"Something like that."

Ravlen raised to her tippy toes and could just about make out a woman on a float, waving. She wore a sparkly blue dress with a wide skirt, feathers floating along the bottom of it. White gloves came up to her elbows like a fairytale princess.

Everyone here dreams of a princess mother? I suppose that makes sense given the swimming pools and ponies and all.

The float approached and Ravlen focused on the future mother's face. Her cheeks were flushed with emotion and her hand trembled as it waved.

She's an original!

Ravlen walked to keep up with the float, following alongside it. She observed the woman who at once was laughing and smiling while the hand at her side was clenched in a fist.

She is terrified. And happy. At the same time. Adults are so weird.

The cacophony of voices mounted as the parade slowed. Children rushed at the barricades with their signs, eager to be seen and selected, to become the son or daughter of the original woman dressed like a princess on the float.

Ravlen got an idea.

She ran toward the barricades. She didn't have a sign, so she'd have to make herself seen, heard, and wanted all at once.

The echo children obeyed the rules, jumping or waving their signs from the designated spaces on either side of the parade.

Ravlen scaled the barricades.

"What's she doing?" someone behind her asked.

"Is that allowed?"

A guard approached the barricades but was blocked by mobs of children. "Come back with the other children, young one!"

Ravlen ignored them all.

She reached the bottom of the float. "Excuse me, ma'am?"

The princess-original looked down at her. "Your enthusiasm is very sweet, but..."

"Hang on, lady. I've got to tell you something. I'm coming up."

"You're doing what?" Surprise danced across the woman's face. "They never told me this could happen."

"You!" the guard cried, climbing over the fence. "You have to come back. This is outside acceptable practice. You must wait with the others."

An older woman's shrill voice rang out over the others. "Carry on! Do as you must!"

Ravlen sought the source of the familiar voice. Her referent waved, indicating she should continue. Ravlen nodded back to her.

"Look, ma'am. I'm not from here. I'm not trying to be your child. But you have to pick me."

"I don't understand." The woman's chest lifted and fell with quick, heavy breaths.

"Don't be afraid, but I have to take you home now. This has gone too far."

The woman gave several short nods. "Yes, I think you're right. I got completely carried away. It just seemed like such a wonderful idea after so many years of wishing. We tried, you see, and a child is all I ever wanted. But I'm living in a dream. I know it. Nothing ever happens like this, though it seemed like maybe, just maybe…" Her voice trailed off.

"I know." Ravlen took her arm. "I'm sorry it can't be any other way."

"Yes. Yes. I see that now."

The guard was nearly upon the float. "You come back down, young one. Join the others."

"She can't," the woman replied. "She is definitely the one I pick. I saw her from afar and knew she was the one. I… I called her over."

"Are you sure?" The guard tilted his head. "This is highly unusual."

The woman looked at Ravlen. "It was as if she knew all along that I was going to pick her."

"I see!" The guard threw his arms up as he turned back to the crowd. "The woman has a child! And the child has a family! We can celebrate at last the unification of these hearts into one household!"

Cheers erupted. Even the children who weren't selected applauded as though it was the greatest moment of their lives. Ravlen thought of her father. Her mother. Her own lost childhood spent without family.

A profound sadness settled on Ravlen's heart.

"Let's go," she whispered to the woman. "This dream will end soon, and we need to be out of here when that happens."

"Lead me on, child. What's your name?"

"Ravlen."

"Ravlen. What a perfect name for a hero."

"We've got to go quickly." Ravlen didn't want to run into her father again. Every second they stayed, she risked seeing him.

"This world is false," Ravlen declared, both for the woman and to begin the process of closing the echo. "Children and parents cannot be matched according to a whim and a wish. They need love and support from the very beginning of their lives and the world has to care for them. They can't be left to suffer, waiting for their lives with a family to begin."

Ravlen was relieved that she didn't need to pulse, sparing the original woman from the horrible sight of the echo's truth, the screeching and ghostly figures that lay beneath the facade.

They were nearly at the haze.

"This is the way back?" The woman looked at Ravlen, then at the haze, and back to Ravlen. "I have to go in there?"

"When you go through, you'll be back in the same field where you first came in. My friend Dina is waiting for you there."

The woman took one hesitant step. Ravlen would go through behind her, to make sure she didn't change her mind. She'd learned that trick early on when an original had taken off in the other direction moments before the echo was too close. Fortunately, Marriel had grabbed his ankle and together they got him through.

But Marriel wasn't there now. Ravlen had to do this on her own.

The woman took another step deeper into the haze. "I see, then let's go." She paused. "But I wasn't in any field. There was this strange shimmer just around back of the post office in the center of town. But we'll figure it out on the other side, I suppose." She took a deep breath. "Home, here I come."

The woman walked through.

But Ravlen was stuck on the spot.

The haze wasn't in the field, that's what she said. There was a second place of entry.

The sky was already darkening, bells tolling in the distance, which marked the end coming closer and closer.

But the situation was urgent. She disturbed, reaching out with her senses and confirming her fears. The echo was closing but she couldn't leave.

...There are two more originals in here.

15

A twister was coming her way. Already the gusts of wind pulled Ravlen's hair forward and around her face. She brushed it away, but the flurries were growing in strength. She looked left and right, her senses blurred by the building storm.

How could I miss other originals in the echo? I can't believe there were more here all along and I didn't sense them. How could I let that happen? How am I going to find them now?

She ran back to the town center where the parade floats shook in the force of the twister's pull. Ravlen didn't have time to figure out how everything went wrong. She had to find the others and find them now.

"PULSE!" she cried, thrusting out her hands.

A mile away, through the crowd of echo phantoms, two children held onto each other, trembling. Ravlen released the pulse and ran for them.

"PULSE!" she declared as she leaped, desperate to cross the ground faster than her feet would let her. She flew forward, shoes barely getting a grip before she launched herself again.

"PULSE!"

She walked the last stretch toward them. Their fear was palpable, and all Ravlen's doing for not finding them before breaking the echo's logic. She moved quickly but put on the most reassuring face she could.

"Hello. I'm Ravlen. I can't explain everything to you now, but you have to come with me, okay?"

The younger child buried her face in the chest of the bigger one, who couldn't have been older than eight or nine. The older one shook her head vigorously and held the younger one tightly.

"You've got to come with me. It's not safe here – this place is about to come crashing down. Look. Ravlen pointed at the rush of air swirling into a tower of madness toward the sky. "That twister is coming for us. I know you're scared. I'm here to protect you. But now, my job is to help you. I'm going to take you home."

"No!" the older girl cried. "You can't take us back there!"

"I'll take you wherever you want to go, but we can't stay here!" Ravlen felt the pull stronger now. They had seconds, not minutes, to escape. "Give me your hands, now!"

Ravlen dragged them forward through repeated pulses, their cries buried in the growing rush of winds. Tears streamed down their faces, and they struggled against the harshness of coming reality.

"Faster!" The haze was flickering like a light bulb about to extinguish. She launched the two girls into the haze and followed them through, landing with a hard drop in the field on the other side.

Dina left the woman by the car and ran to them.

"What happened in there?" Dina's voice was shrill with strain as she scooped up the sobbing girls.

"There were more originals than I thought." Ravlen was breathless with effort and emotion. The weight of what she'd almost allowed to happen weighed heavily within her chest. "I almost missed them, Dina."

Dina enveloped the girls, who couldn't be consoled. "That's okay, you cry it out. That was scary, it sure was. Go ahead and cry. We'll figure this out."

The princess-woman had changed into one of the real world outfits Dina kept in the car, and insisted on walking home. She was dazed and disoriented, as most adults were when first yanked out of the echo. Like the other adults, her memories would be fuzzy, dream-like more than reality.

Ravlen sat in the middle of the field, trying to understand what had happened as Dina coaxed the girls into the backseat for a nap. Dina gently closed the car door and then stomped to Ravlen's spot in the field.

"What's the matter with you? Missing originals? And *children?*"

"I rushed."

"Rushed? The whole purpose of our mission is to save people, *especially* children from the end of these horrible, awful, terrifying places. And you rushed?"

Ravlen couldn't find her voice. Dina was right. But Ravlen had been desperate to get out of there, anything not to see her father. And yet, because of her own fear, she was almost responsible for the loss of the two innocent lives now resting in the car.

Ravlen mumbled.

"What's that?"

"I'm sorry," Ravlen choked up. "I didn't realize."

Dina pointed in Ravlen's face, trembling with fury. "This can never happen again. Never."

She turned and marched away, but then stopped. She looked back at Ravlen.

"What if one of them had been my sister?" Dina's face creased as she held back her tears. "What if?"

DINA DROVE TOWARD TOWN, THE TWO GIRLS SLEEPING IN THE back.

Ravlen leaned her head against the window, letting it smack as they hit potholes on the country road. The sting felt like fair punishment.

Dina watched the girls through the rearview mirror. "They are out for the count."

Ravlen turned around. Their faces were tear streaked and stained, the younger one's dress was ripped and the older one had smudges of dirt all over her. But the pink of their cheeks and breath heavy with sleep captivated Ravlen.

"They look like angels."

"What was in that echo, Ravlen? How could this happen?" Dina's tone was gentler now, her anger subsided. Ravlen didn't hold it against Dina, she was angry with herself, too. She had been too weak, too easily pulled back into Oaken's mind games.

I'll never forgive him.

She punched her leg with her fist. A part of her knew it wasn't his fault. She had to better manage herself. She was responsible for her feelings and reactions. He may have been her father, but she was an echo chaser, and she had to be stronger than that.

"Tell me, Ravlen. Don't keep it in. Remember what you were taught on the island. Debriefing is as important as breaking the echo itself. Otherwise, you risk running yourself into the ground." She tilted her head toward Ravlen. "And I won't let you do that."

"The echo was warped. The logic of it wasn't like anything I've seen before." If she could keep Dina's focus on that, then maybe she could avoid talking about her father.

"Children waited to be picked by parents who rolled by in a parade each and every day."

"Do you think it was the woman who was the tipping point, or the girls?"

"I don't know." Ravlen instinctively looked at them in the backseat. "But they didn't want to go home. The older one screamed it." She looked over their clothes again. "How did they get so dirty? There wasn't anything in the echo to explain that."

"You might have just figured out why they don't want to go home."

Ravlen watched the road go by, wondering what they would do with children who wouldn't go home.

"You can't take us back."

Ravlen swiveled in the seat to face the older girl. She hadn't moved, but looked up at Ravlen, her eyes full of terror.

"Back where? Where do you come from?" Dina asked.

The girl's eyes opened wider, the whites of them glowing in the orange light of dusk. "I'm not telling. You can't take us there. They are horrible. We had to run away."

"Do you mean your parents?"

"No. They're gone. When we were little, I found the spot where people came and went. I saved Claire and me."

Claire's eyes blinked open at the sound of her name.

"You've gone through the haze before?" Ravlen faced Dina. "They were in another echo."

"You can't take us to the place for children. You can't take us back, no matter what."

Dina pulled the car over and turned around. "You don't have to worry, I'm going to make sure you're safe. What's your name?"

"Alison."

"Alison," Dina spoke gently. "Can I see your back, please?"

Alison twisted and lifted the bottom half of her shirt, revealing dirt smudges but nothing more.

Dina shrugged at Ravlen. "Not what I thought," she murmured. "I thought maybe…"

"Are you looking for the sparkles?" Alison interrupted.

Both Ravlen and Dina spun to look at her.

Alison put her hand on her sister's shoulder. "Show them, Claire."

Claire turned and lifted part of her shirt.

Just like Ravlen, a line of disrupted air glimmered just above her skin. It was the unmistakable mark of the unreal.

Dina nodded slowly and for a long time they sat in silence at the side of an abandoned country road.

"Alison, Claire, you don't have to run anymore. You are going to be safe from now on." Dina put the car back into drive. "Madame will take care of this."

ONCE ALISON BEGAN RECOUNTING THEIR STORY, SHE couldn't stop. The drive back to Joan and Tom's flew by as she narrated her tale. Claire occasionally jumped in with details that her five-year-old eyes had seen.

"After we got out of the first one of *those places*," which was how she referred to the echoes, "I found a grown-up who said he would take care of us. But he was a bad man and took us where there were other bad men who sold us to a family who seemed pretty nice and we got to eat and everything, but they wouldn't let us go to school and even in *that place*, we got to go to school." She paused to take a breath and glanced over at Claire who was nodding in agreement with her story.

"But then there was this other man who wasn't bad at all found us," Alison continued, "and he took us and this woman where we lived and another woman and four other children who he'd found in other families but who couldn't stay there. And then nobody believed us when we said that we *hadn't* been with other families but that we'd been in *that place*."

Ravlen did her best to keep up, but Alison's story came out in long breaths. She got the gist of it:

Alison was born outside the echo. Then her parents took her into an echo, and a well-established one from the sound of it. Claire was born there.

The echo was closing when Alison saved Claire, but their parents wouldn't come.

Ever since, Alison and Claire had been moved from home to home until they were supposed to have a permanent arrangement…

"They didn't feed us." Claire's little face clouded over. "They locked us up when we did something they didn't like. We weren't bad on purpose."

"Of course you weren't," Dina reassured. "And I'm going to talk to someone who understands very well what you've been through. Until she is able to figure something out, the two of you will stay with Ravlen and her friend, Marriel."

The two girls looked at Ravlen.

"We live in a nice place. And I've got a great dog named Binner." Ravlen winked. "You're going to love him. He has sparkles, too."

Claire's face lit up. "I love dogs."

J oan took Alison on a tour of the small bungalow while Tom showed off the snails in the garden to Claire. She was fascinated by the creepy crawlers, which gave Ravlen, Dina, and Marriel time to talk alone.

"I'm going to need a few days to arrange things," Dina began as soon as Alison was out of earshot. "Alison is in a state of hypervigilance. That won't pass any time soon so it's important that I take care of this outside the house."

"Hypervigilance?" Ravlen didn't know what that meant, but it didn't sound good.

"She's been watching over Claire for years now. She's on the lookout twenty-four-seven for any kind of threat or danger. She can't relax, because she expects that something horrible might happen at any moment or someone will try to take them away."

"Oh." Ravlen thought back again to her own childhood. Even though she'd had bouts of loneliness, she'd never had to be hypervigilant.

"What can we do to help them?" Marriel peeked out the

window where Claire was giggling at a snail in the palm of her hand.

"Maybe start by not taking off to see Conrad tonight." Ravlen heard the accusation in her tone, but this time Marriel deserved it.

Marriel rubbed her head. "It's the elections student parliament meeting. He needs me there. I already explained this to you."

"And I already explained that *we* need you here. And you know what?" Ravlen felt heat rising and words she hadn't intended to say boiled up. "I needed you today."

"You did not. You don't need me for echo closures, you do them all the time. Don't exaggerate."

"I'm not exaggerating." A wave of emotion tinged Ravlen's voice. "You know why I almost left these kids behind?"

Marriel crossed her arms and snapped, "You probably saw something cute and cuddly, and you just had to go check it out."

Ravlen shook her head. "I saw my father."

"What?" Marriel dropped her hands to her sides, her mouth falling open.

"You did?" Dina rushed over to Ravlen and reassuringly put a hand on her shoulder. "Why didn't you say anything?"

"Because just when I should have been able to stand up to him, I couldn't. He walked away from me, just like when I was a baby, and left me there tripping over my words. I had to get out of there at all costs. When I found the original woman, I just assumed she was the only one. If you'd been there, Marriel, maybe I wouldn't have gotten so out of control. Maybe he wouldn't have made me feel like I was two inches tall..." Her voice cut out as a sob caught in her throat.

"Ravlen?" Alison walked in from the kitchen.

"I'm here." Ravlen swallowed her tears. This had to be about Alison and Claire now. She could work through her own issues later. She put her arm around Alison's shoulder. "Say, Alison, did you know that Marriel can draw better than anyone I know?"

"No…"

Marriel picked up on Ravlen's lead. "It's true." She smiled, big and warm. "Do you want me to teach you how to draw an elephant?"

Alison looked at Ravlen.

"You can if you want." Ravlen gently tapped the girl's shoulder.

"I'd like that."

"Good." Marriel put on a cheerful face. "I just have to make a phone call to change my plans for tonight, and then we'll get right down to it. I even have some crayons so we can color the jungle around him."

Ravlen mouthed, "Thank you" to Marriel.

"I'm sorry," Marriel mouthed in reply.

"THERE YOU ARE!" CONRAD CALLED OUT TO MARRIEL AS THEY arrived on the school grounds the next morning. "I was wondering what happened to you. You missed all of first period."

"We had some things to do at home." Marriel raised her eyebrows in a way that told Ravlen to keep quiet.

"You cut out on student parliament, and on top of that were late for school. I'm not sure I like that." As if noticing that his true colors were shining through, he stopped himself and smiled widely. "At least you're here now, and we have a few minutes before class." He rubbed the sides of her arms.

Ravlen shuddered.

"I wouldn't have been late if it weren't important," Marriel gushed, goose bumps rising on her arms where he touched her. "I wouldn't miss our morning snuggle time." She nestled her head into his neck and Ravlen rolled her eyes, bigger than she'd ever rolled them in her life. It was all she could do not to gag.

"You should be getting to class, kid," Conrad chided as he rubbed Marriel's back. "You're going to get in trouble for skipping."

Ravlen trudged off, leaving the sickening scene of adolescent affection behind.

"Skipping first period, Ravlen. Not good." Mrs. Brand clicked her tongue in disapproval. In the five minutes between classes, the posse of middle grade teachers trolled the hallways in search of students who'd cut class or slept in or were dragging their feet. Bumping into them was certain to result in a reprimand of one sort or another.

"I have a note." Ravlen pulled the folded paper from her pocket. It said that she'd had an appointment. In reality, she'd helped Alison and Claire settle after a chaotic night of tossing and turning.

"She always has a note," Mrs. Brand muttered to Miss Markham under her breath.

"Just another sign," Mr. Costello piped up.

Ravlen walked through the group of teachers, who parted down the middle to let her pass as though she had something contagious.

Mr. J. was right. They've got it in for me.

"Ravlen!" Mr. Johansson appeared from the music room. "Lovely to see you early for class."

Ravlen dared a look back at the trio of teachers who were shaking their heads at Mr. Johansson.

Mr. Johansson raised his voice and looked straight at the teachers, not her. "Great to have my *star trumpeter* in music theory." He held the classroom door open and whispered, "Quick, let's talk before the other students get here."

Ravlen dropped into her chair, her teeth clenched.

Mr. J. sat on the desk in front of hers. "I'm working on them."

"Why have they got it in for me? I haven't done anything to deserve it!"

He bit his lip, visibly weighing his words. "They have a misguided belief about you. It'll take time – they aren't as experienced as I am – but they will come around."

"As experienced as you? Experienced in what?" Ravlen leaned in, at once anxious and eager. Finally, she might get to know what Mr. J. had been talking about all along.

"Ravlen!" Greta bounded through the door. "I saw you come into class early. What plans have you got for this weekend?" Her smile was innocent to the daggers Ravlen was launching with her eyes.

Mr. Johannsen walked back to his desk, the opportunity for her to learn more about his knowledge was lost.

I was so close!

Ravlen grumbled, "Hi, Greta. Your timing is impeccable."

Christopher Duke walked through the door.

This goes from bad to worse! Just sit down, don't say anything. Pretend I'm not here.

No such luck.

"Ravlen again. You've always got to stir things up, don't you? Can't leave well enough alone."

"I don't know what you're talking about." Ravlen turned on her chair to face Greta, but even she was drawn into Christopher Duke's dark demeanor.

"The teachers here see right through you." He bent forward. His breath smelled strange and blew cold on her cheek. "They know the same thing about you that I know. That you're not from here, that you shouldn't be here, that all you do is create trouble for everyone around you. Why don't you just go back where you came from?"

"Where I came from?"

He stood up straight. "You heard me. Keep up what you're doing here and you're going to ruin it for everyone. Joan, Tom, Marriel… And did I see a couple of new kids hanging around you? Girls who just showed up… out of nowhere?"

Ravlen gasped.

"Trouble will follow you, Ravlen. Everywhere you go. No one is safe around you."

He spun and muttered something else that Ravlen couldn't make out before walking to his seat at the far back corner of the music room. Other students filed in, entirely unaware of the exchange that had just taken place and shaken Ravlen's world.

Greta leaned into Ravlen's ear. "I think he uttered a curse."

Ravlen couldn't reply. Her mind was reeling.

Alison and Claire. They aren't safe. I've got to get out of here, but how?

Music class went on as normal for everyone but Ravlen, though over the course of the hour, Christopher Duke didn't look at her once. Ravlen felt some of the pressure pass. Maybe it wasn't as bad as she thought. Maybe it was regular bullying, like Donelle used to do back in the old days on the island, before Ravlen had saved her life.

The bell rang and Christopher was the first one out of the room, giving Ravlen space to breathe and to try to figure out what was going on.

"What is *up* with him?" Ravlen shot him a quick glance down the hall where he'd stopped at his locker. "Is he like this with everybody?"

Greta shrugged.

"You've been here longer than me." Ravlen turned to Greta. "You've lived in this neighborhood your whole life. You must know something about him."

If I can get to know his background, maybe I can figure out why he's picked me to torment.

Greta shook her head. "He got here just before you. Nobody knows anything about him."

"Nobody?"

"Even before you came, he was weird. He keeps to himself. He doesn't have any friends."

"With that cheery personality? I never would have guessed."

Greta gestured for Ravlen to lean in closer. "I think he was in jail."

"In jail? He's a kid."

"Kid jail. Look how white he is, like he hasn't been in sunlight. And the way he acts… rude and standoffish. That's how jail people are."

"You mean prisoners."

"Yeah, prisoners."

Ravlen stole another look at the pasty-skinned boy. His eyes were set on the inside of his locker, his cheeks taut with tension and his hands in fists at his sides. The collar of his leather jacket was pulled high even though it was shorts weather.

"Maybe he's just an angry person."

"I don't think that's it," Greta whispered. "There's something not right about him."

Ravlen couldn't argue with that. She didn't think it was prison, but she couldn't come up with a better answer. The fact that he'd been watching her home, seen Alison and Claire, was enough to make her believe there was more to him than a regular school bully.

He turned, catching Ravlen watching him. Even from a distance, his gray eyes were cold. Dead cold.

Ravlen shivered.

"Shhh, Ravlen. Don't tell Binner where I am!" Claire giggled from her hiding spot under the chair where everyone sat to put on their shoes.

The weekend had been so relaxed with the girls, Ravlen had dreaded Monday. But it hadn't been so bad since Christopher Duke was off sick. Ravlen had come home to find Alison and Claire playing hide and seek with Binner.

With Binner's nose, it didn't seem like a fair game.

Binner waltzed into the hallway and dramatically lifted his nose in the air. He twisted his head, immediately sighting the little girl. His tail wagged but he didn't approach her.

He's pretending he doesn't know where she is...

Ravlen admired the dog's ability to play along. She'd never met another dog like that.

Claire lifted her finger to her lips, which Ravlen did in return. Claire covered her mouth to prevent the giggles from escaping.

Binner took one step, then another, and then ran to her hiding place with a playful bark.

"You found me! You found me!" Claire threw her arms

around his neck. "But it took you longer than last time. I'm getting better at hiding."

The dog looked up at Ravlen, and if she didn't know better, she would have been sure he gave her a knowing wink.

"Alrighty-oh!" Joan emerged from the kitchen. "Enough fun and games. It's time for serious stuff. Your snack!"

"Snack!" Claire jumped up. "I love snacks!"

Alison joined them from the living room and whispered to Claire, "Don't eat too much. We don't want them to get angry with us."

Joan put her arm around Alison. "And the good news is that we have as many snacks as you would like. Today is the day when you can eat snacks all the way until dinnertime, if you want."

"Really?" Claire's blue eyes widened with delight.

"Both of you can. It would make me so happy to see you eat. After all, it's veggies and dip and fruit. You can't go wrong."

Claire whispered to Alison in that childlike way that everyone could hear.

"I told you they were different from the others."

Joan ushered the two into the kitchen. "It's already set on the table. Help yourselves. I'll be there in a minute to get your drinks."

"Yay!" The two girls shouted in unison, then ran off to the kitchen hand in hand.

Joan looked at Ravlen, her eyes shiny. "Poor girls."

Ravlen followed Joan into the kitchen. The girls contained their enthusiasm, moving slowly as they picked out broccoli, celery, and carrots, cherishing each bite with loud "Mmmmms".

Joan poured a glass of orange juice. "And Marriel?"

Ravlen shrugged. "I waited for her after school, but she didn't show up. I guess she went off with gross Conrad."

Joan frowned. "She didn't tell you she wasn't coming back for snack time."

"Nope."

"That's unlike her. She's always at least told us her plans. I don't like this."

"I don't like Conrad." Ravlen walked to Joan where the girls couldn't overhear. "They hardly know each other and suddenly he acts like he's the most important thing in Marriel's life. And she lets him!" Ravlen threw up her arms but then hushed her voice. "It's like she forgets who she is."

Joan delivered fresh orange juice to the elation of the girls. "She's discovering new things about herself, about the world. You'll do it too, Ravlen. In some ways you already have, just differently."

"Doesn't mean I like it," Ravlen grumbled.

"You don't have to." Joan mussed Ravlen's hair. "You just have to let her do it. And then you have to be there for her when she comes home."

Marriel didn't come home.

Ravlen's eyes were glued to her watch and the window that faced the front door. Dinnertime came with everyone watching the door, but she didn't walk through. Dina came over and watched the girls while Tom, Joan, and Ravlen discussed what to do.

"She's got to be with Conrad," Ravlen insisted. "If we find him, then we find her."

"It might not be so straightforward." Tom scratched his head. "When was the last time you saw her?"

"When we got to school." Ravlen's stomach was twisting.

While a part of her was certain she was with Conrad, another part of her knew Marriel wouldn't put them through this. She'd come home or call or *something.*

Dina came into the kitchen. "I've got the girls settled in front of the T.V. with cartoons. What can I do to help?"

Ravlen looked at her watch and jumped from her seat. "Of course! It's Monday, the student parliament debate. She must be there with Conrad and forgot to tell us!" Ravlen and Dina took off for the school while Tom and Joan stayed with the girls, who were beginning to pick up on the fact that something wasn't right.

Breathless, Ravlen and Dina burst into the auditorium of the high school. The debate had finished. Several kids were still hanging around, others were getting ready to head home, packing bags and laughing in small groups.

"Look, over there!" Ravlen pointed to where Conrad was in a full-on embrace at the other side of the room, only Marriel's hair visible beyond him. Ravlen ran. "Don't you both know what time it is?" she yelled at them.

The couple split, caught in the act. Ravlen slid in mid-step, her mouth hanging open as Conrad turned to face her.

The girl in Conrad's arms wasn't Marriel.

"Where is Marriel?"

"How should I know?" Conrad shrugged like it was the strangest question he'd ever heard. "I dumped her at lunch. Haven't seen her since." He looked at the girl hanging on his arm. "It wasn't serious. We were mostly just friends, but she wanted more." He turned back to Ravlen. "Julie here said she'd take me back, so how could I refuse?"

Julie waved meekly and turned to Conrad. "Who's she?"

"Nobody."

Dina was now at Ravlen's side. "She's not here. And jerk-face isn't going to help. Let's go."

Ravlen marched out of the room, feeling her neck on fire with rage and her skin prickling with frustration.

"Ravlen!" Dina called out. "Slow down!"

Ravlen stopped, rubbing her head as she waited for Dina to join her.

"Where *is* she?" Ravlen pounded her sides with her fists. "How could she just take off like that?"

"Maybe she didn't." Dina's face clouded over. "Maybe we've got this wrong. Something else might have happened – we have to consider the possibilities."

"Like what?" Ravlen rubbed her arms, the sensation of needles not subsiding. "You think someone might have taken her?"

Dina opened her mouth to speak and then stopped. She tilted her head to the side as she inspected Ravlen's arms. "What are you doing?"

Ravlen looked at herself. The waves of prickling continued. It was the same feeling she got every time she was in the vicinity of an echo.

It took a moment for the thought to sink in.

"Dina…"

"Yes?"

"I think it's…" She couldn't bring herself to say it.

Dina nodded solemnly. "I think so, too. Let's find the haze. I'll bet you anything Marriel is in the echo."

THEY DIDN'T HAVE TO GO FAR. THE PIPELINE BEHIND THE school was mostly a vacant stretch where people walked their dogs. The lines overhead hummed with electricity, underscoring the tension Dina and Ravlen shared as they looked for the haze.

Ravlen found the shimmer under one of the pylons and

had to climb a wire fence to get to it. Dina waited for her on the other side, her knuckles turning white from how hard she was gripping the fence.

"I'll be here. However long it takes, I'll be here."

Ravlen had never felt so unsure about going into an echo. "You can't come with me?"

"You know I can't."

Ravlen nodded. She wished for company, for backup, for support. It was supposed to be Marriel who was there helping her, but now everything was turned upside down and Ravlen had to save her partner.

"You can do this," Dina called out as Ravlen stepped closer to the haze. "It's just like every other time. This is a young echo. Don't look too deeply for the logic and it will come to you."

"Okay, Dina."

"Don't let her convince you of anything other than what you know is right."

"Okay, Dina."

"Ravlen?"

She turned away from the haze to see Dina's worried face.

"Come back soon."

"I will."

Ravlen took a deep breath and focused herself. Saving Donelle had been one thing. Saving Marriel, her overseer, her best friend... that was another.

She rolled her good luck charm in her pocket. She needed it now more than ever.

She stepped through the haze and found herself in the middle of a dark non-space. Ravlen couldn't think of any other way to describe where she was. It was like being in the middle of a big black room with only a single bit of light at the far end. She couldn't tell how big the space was.

If this is a brand new echo, then very few originals have been here. Or maybe none at all. Could we have been wrong? Maybe Marriel isn't here after all...

Thick velvet curtains appeared and were pulled back, revealing a throne room.

"Whoa."

A spotlight shone on a massive gold and purple velvet throne. Ravlen blinked to adjust her eyes to the brightness of the light. She couldn't yet be certain, but she thought she saw...

"Marriel?" Ravlen's voice came out as a whisper.

Marriel lounged on the throne, one hand dangling over the side while the other perched lazily on the armrest.

Ravlen blinked again.

By her side... who is that? Is it a... a prince?

"Your beauty surpasses every princess in every other kingdom I have ever so much as laid a foot in." The prince kissed the dangling hand.

He touched her!

Ravlen watched in horror as Marriel's body responded to his touch with a shudder. Her eyes fluttered closed. Ravlen waited. She had to assess the situation before confronting Marriel, especially if she was emotionally fragile following the breakup with Conrad.

The first prince was dressed in reds and golds, a large, red velvet heart sewn on the back of his doublet.

Another prince strode to Marriel's other side. "My princess. I have been looking for you everywhere."

"Me?" Marriel's head turned slowly and Ravlen watched as she tilted it in the same way as those who'd succumbed to the echo's effects.

This is not good.

Ravlen stood still, observing the scene, racking her brain for ways to convince Marriel to leave the mini fairytale behind.

"Yes, you, my princess," the second prince was saying. "You are my inspiration. I have fought mercenaries and pushed back armies, destroyed enemies – all because I knew you would be the spoils of my victory." He ran his fingers along her perched arm.

Marriel's eyes widened to the whites, then lulled into a half-open daze. "You fought for me?"

"You and only you."

The prince was covered in black leather and silver, with a black symbol on his back.

Clubs. I'm sure he's the prince of clubs. Hearts, clubs... But there's no prince in a deck of cards...

"My treasure! There you are."

A third! Ravlen felt her face scrunch in surprise. *How many princes does she need?*

He strode, bowing near where Marriel's left foot dangled over the edge of the throne.

Don't tell me he's...

He took her foot in his hand and removed her shoe. "Your foot is as precious as the world's most valuable diamond."

I had a feeling that was coming.

"So delicate, the arch. So strong, the heel. My caves may be filled with gold and silver and gemstones from the world round, but nothing compares to you. You are my greatest treasure, my prize, worthy of all my fortune and I shall indeed lay it all at your feet." His tunic was made of shiny red fabric with gold threads woven through it. The telltale diamond was woven in gold on the back.

A prince on each hand and a third at her feet. All of them touching her. All of them dragging Marriel deeper into the echo.

And Ravlen knew it couldn't be over yet.

Come on, Spades. Where are you?

"My princess!"

Right on cue.

Ravlen ventured closer, knowing it would soon be her turn to speak.

"How I have slaved over these lands, amassed my people to set the land to work, that we may live in plenty all the rest of our days. While others starve, we shall feast. When others cry for want, we will be surrounded by our fellow workers, all together, a team, a family, united in our quest to strive hard and reap the glorious fruits of our labor."

As Ravlen suspected, he knelt at Marriel's right foot and leaned his head against her knee.

"I have worked all my life for this one moment, to lay eyes on my worthy princess, to give you the greatest this land has to offer." The spade on his back was made of forged iron.

Ravlen cleared her throat dramatically. The four princes snapped their heads to see Ravlen standing there.

Marriel, however, moved as though through molasses. Her head turned in slow-motion, then tilted, and she inhaled leisurely. "Rav…" she swallowed, "…len?"

Oh. She's far gone. But she's only been here an afternoon!

Ravlen remembered the fisherman. The one who'd fought to try to go back in the echo as it was closing. Dina's words came back to her.

Those who convinced themselves that the echo was real struggled hardest to come out of it.

It wasn't hard to see why this world ticked all Marriel's boxes. Perhaps one adolescent false prince had let her down, but here were four dream princes, surrounding her with compliments, promises, and declarations of love.

"You know why I'm here, Marriel."

"I'm going to stay a while. You don't have to worry," Marriel's eyes drooped. "I'm fine. I'll come back when I'm ready."

"And when will that be?"

Marriel smiled. "When I get my happily ever after."

The four princes resumed their fawning and flattery. Words escaped their lips like "greatest beauty", "worthy of everything", "you are above us all", and "riches will fall at your feet."

Ravlen crossed her arms. She wouldn't have to close this echo. It was going to break itself. It was wholly unsustainable. She just had to show that to Marriel.

"You know as well as I do that there's no happily ever after here."

"And why not? Look at them, my princes are all content with making me the center of their world. We can live like this forever." She looked from one to the next, as each offered a caress to her cheek, her lips, her hair.

"You see what they represent, right?" Ravlen was going to have to walk her through this, slowly.

"Sure, I do. But isn't it woooonderful?" She drew it out in a sleepy state. "Adoration in hearts, riches in diamonds, commitment in clubs, and perseverance in spades."

"You've played cards, Marriel."

"And?"

"They don't work together. They are in competition with each other."

"They complement each other. Each fills a need the others don't."

"One of them will have to win."

Marriel looked benevolently over her adorers. "No… no… I don't think so…"

"Come, my princess, we have much to discuss." The Prince of Spades stood before Marriel. "The people look to you for guidance, for wisdom, for inspiration and motivation. Your words will move an entire population."

"Oh," pleasure lit across Marriel's face, "I cannot keep the people waiting."

"First," the Prince of Diamonds stepped in front of Spades, "my princess, let me bring you to the richest of riches in my kingdom. Allow me to show you the treasures that are to be laid at your feet."

The Prince of Diamonds took Marriel's hand and helped her to stand.

"My princess." The Prince of Hearts took her hand from Diamonds. "Before you are caught up in the trivial matters of the material world, let me fill your ears with words of love, to enchant you from beginning to end, to convince you of all the love you are worth."

"Come off it, loverboy." The Prince of Clubs pushed Hearts away. "Love is a battle. We must fight for what we love. And I will fight for you until the end!"

"This is not good," Ravlen muttered while maneuvering herself closer to Marriel.

"You're nothing but a brute!" Spades pushed Clubs back. "Too long the people have been under your authoritarian thumb! It's time the people rise up!"

"People-shmeeple." Diamonds leaned in to take Marriel's hand. "Where I'm taking you, you will need for nothing, you will be able to have all the world can offer and in abundance."

"But it will all be meaningless without love!"

Thunder sounded in the distance.

That woke Marriel up.

"Ravlen? What's going on?"

"You know as well as I do. The logic is breaking itself. This happily ever after was impossible from the start."

"But… But…" She watched as the princes argued, insults hurled, and someone, probably Clubs, threw a punch. Hearts fell to the ground. Marriel shook her head as she slipped away from the throne and the combatants. "This is not good."

"You took the words right out of my mouth." Ravlen inched closer to Marriel, hoping the princes wouldn't catch sight of them. She didn't want to know what they might do to keep them from leaving. But she didn't have anything to worry about; they were consumed by their own quarreling.

"You call yourself Diamonds? More like a Joker!"

"What would you know, you commoner! Go back to tilling the fields."

"What labor have you ever done in your life, Hearts?"

"At least I don't use my muscles to hide my emotions!"

"Let's go." Marriel took Ravlen's hand. "You were right. The shine has worn off."

"Not a moment too soon." Ravlen shuddered as the thunder deepened. "We don't have long."

As she promised, Dina was waiting where Ravlen had left her, on the other side of the fence. The night had almost fully descended, only a few orange streaks remaining in the sky when Ravlen and Marriel stepped out of the closing haze.

"Thank goodness." Dina helped Marriel over the wires. "I was worried you might not want to come back."

"I didn't want to. Conrad humiliated me." Marriel paused to help Ravlen over the fence. "How can I show my face again after the way he dumped me in front of half the class? He was so sweet, so funny, so everything until *she* showed up. And then with the flip of a switch, he was exactly the same… *with her.*"

"Jerk," Ravlen muttered.

"The echo was sensitive to my emotions. I'd run out of the school, desperate to get away, and there it was. When I saw the haze, I knew it was beckoning me. Me, someone who knows all the dangers, yet I let myself be drawn in by it." She put her hand on Ravlen's shoulder. "I was embarrassed by how I let you down. Too embarrassed to face you. Our work is more important than ever. Or maybe I'm just realizing how important it always was."

The three walked together, arms around each other.

Ravlen heard their heartbeats, felt them pounding faster than normal. They'd come too close to losing each other.

Marriel, in the middle, looked over at Ravlen. Ravlen looked at Marriel and then past her to Dina. Dina looked back at them both. The three stopped walking and pulled each other into a group hug.

"I'm so sorry."

"I'll always be there for you," Ravlen replied.

"We'll always be there for each other," Dina added.

The full moon rose high in the sky, casting white light over the path and illuminating their way home.

1 8

R avlen kept her ear glued to Marriel's door with Binner at her feet. Marriel had stopped crying but Ravlen didn't like the silence that followed.

Alison tiptoed over to her. "Ravlen, will you come play cards with me? Joan showed me a game called Memory. It's really fun."

She shivered at the thought of playing cards. "I will, Alison," she said, keeping her voice low in case Marriel could hear her, "but I'm busy right now."

"What are you doing?" Alison whispered in return, but in the way kids do where the whisper was as loud as her regular voice. "Is Marriel in there?"

"Yes, I'm in here and I wish you would leave me alone," said Marriel's muffled voice.

"I'm not doing anything!" Ravlen called back, through the door. "I'm just... uh... waiting."

"Wait somewhere else!" There was a long pause and Ravlen's stomach twisted at the emotion in Marriel's voice. More softly she added, "I'm okay, Rav. I just want to be alone."

"Come along, girls." Joan marched down the hallway and corralled Ravlen and Alison into a bundle. "Let Marriel take the time she needs."

Ravlen looked back to see Binner reposition himself outside Marriel's door. He lay down and rested his head on his paws, his tail thumping gently as he made eye contact with Ravlen. Always watching out for his humans. Ravlen smiled. Binner would be there if Marriel needed comfort. Ravlen knew well that sometimes dogs could do that better than humans anyway.

Ravlen settled in at the table in the backyard with Alison for a game of Memory, while Claire dug up corners of the garden in search of worms.

"Jack of hearts." Alison slapped down the card. "Why isn't there a prince of hearts? There's a king and a queen, but no prince. Where did he go?" Alison scrunched up her nose with thought.

Ravlen thought of the princes who had each been willing to have Marriel as their own at any cost. She shuddered. "Maybe the game is better without the princes." She flipped over another card. "Two of spades. No match."

"I saw princes once," Alison said, concentrating on the cards, her finger hovering over many different spots before making her selection. "Eight of diamonds. They rode horses into the castle where the powerful man lived. Oh! Six of diamonds, that was close!"

I've got to keep her talking.

"Eight of spades!" Ravlen took the pair. "That was a lucky find." Keeping the game going would make conversation easier, more natural. Alison didn't respond well to any kind of stress, so she had to keep it light. "Ace of clubs. Your turn to flip. What were these princes like? Were they really fancy?"

Alison shook her head while scanning the spread of cards.

"No. They were dressed really simple actually. All in the same way – shades of brown and black. They were nice enough, but they mostly kept to themselves. The powerful man didn't let them do very much."

"How did you know they were princes?"

Alison lifted her head and opened her arms. "It was obvious. Don't you know a prince when you see one?"

"I'm not sure I do. You must have some strong senses."

Alison blinked and looked back at the cards. "I had to learn to listen real good." She started to flip a card and stopped. "Otherwise, we might have been found. So I learned to listen and to see really far, farther than anyone I know. Except maybe you."

She looked at Ravlen with such intensity that Ravlen squirmed. Ravlen had learned her skills to fulfill her mission. Alison had learned them to survive.

The moment passed, and Alison looked back at her cards, choosing one almost at random.

"Ace of hearts! I got lucky that time!" Alison squealed.

"Well done!" Ravlen gave her a pat on the shoulder. When Alison recoiled at the touch, she quickly added, "I'm sorry, I didn't mean to surprise you."

Alison let out a long sigh. "I have to get used to normal things again." She glanced at Claire who was singing to herself while drilling her finger into a pile of mud. "I don't want her to react the same way I do." She stared at the cards. "I know I'm not normal."

This was a feeling Ravlen knew well. And this was her chance to be there for Alison the way Janna had been there for her. "I've learned that no one is normal. Other people see only the surface and make judgments, filling in the gaps of what they can't with their own guesses. But what they think of us isn't who we are and shouldn't change us." She smiled at Alison. "You know yourself better than anyone else knows you. What makes them think you're *not* normal is what makes you who you are."

"But I want to be like everyone else." Alison's eyes shone in the midday sun, tears brimming at their edge.

"That's just it." Ravlen nodded. "You *are* like everyone else. You don't see it because they're better at hiding who they really are. I always thought that I was strange, that there was no one else like me in the world. Like I was a big weirdo."

Alison's mouth dropped. "You? You're not weird. You're great!"

Ravlen smiled. "I'm glad you think so. But it took me a long time to realize that I am both weird *and* great! And that's what makes me who I am. We all have our own weirdness, Alison. We are unique, one of a kind. And without that, we would miss out on the beauty that makes us real."

"Weird is beautiful?" Alison scrunched up her nose.

"That's what I'm saying."

Claire rushed over. "Weird is beautiful? You're so funny! Look at this worm. It's weird and it's not beautiful at all." She thrust out her hand with a fat wriggling worm which made both Ravlen and Alison shriek. "See!" Claire couldn't stop laughing. "I told you it wasn't beautiful! But it's very weird!"

"Take it away!" Alison curled into a ball. "That's so gross!"

Ravlen saw a great opportunity to get the conversation back on track about the echo the girls had lived in.

"How can you love creepy crawlers so much, Claire? Did you play with them a lot in the place where you used to live?"

"All the time!" Claire smiled broadly as she set the worm on the grass in front of her. "You dig back into the ground, Willy the Worm. They don't like you here." She looked up at Ravlen. "I used to name all the creatures, even the bees and the caterpillars."

"It's true, she did."

"I did, until the servants arrived."

"Servants?" Ravlen hadn't heard of servants in an echo before, but that didn't mean it wasn't possible.

"What servants?" Alison asked. "There weren't any servants in *that place*."

"Sure there were. You were just talking about them. The ones who came on horses."

"They were princes."

"They weren't princes. They were servants."

"Servants don't ride horses."

"I heard them say they were going to be servants." Claire crossed her arms. "You can't tell me I didn't hear it because I did."

"Hang on," Ravlen interjected. "Alison thought they were princes on horses, and you heard them say they'd be servants one day. They could have been princes that would become servants."

"That makes no sense." Alison wagged her finger. "You can't be a prince one day and then a servant."

Ravlen knew well that there wasn't use in trying to find logic in the echo. Echoes defied logic. They ran on their own rules. But how to explain that to two young girls?

"It doesn't have to make sense," Claire declared with a nod of her head. "That's just how it was."

She was born in an echo and spent her first years there. She knows it even better than me.

"Anyway," Alison picked up, "The princes – or servants – were strange-looking boys…"

"They weren't boys." Claire lifted a finger. "They were teenagers."

"Fine, they were a strange group of teenage boys because some of them looked like they were really happy to be princes, while others looked miserable."

It doesn't have to make sense. Ravlen reminded herself. *This was in an echo. One that no longer exists. These prince-servants have disappeared.*

Alison's face clouded over. Her eyes darted left and right. Ravlen saw what Dina had described, hypervigilance, showing through Alison's body.

"Hey there." Ravlen reached over to reassure Alison through the power of a kind touch, but stopped herself, remembering how Alison had reacted. "You're okay. You got yourselves out of *that place* before it disappeared. You're safe."

Alison narrowed her eyes and shook her head. "No. It's still out there."

"I thought you said that the place you'd grown up in had disappeared."

"It did. You call them echoes, right?"

"Yes."

"We've lived in five different echoes."

"You have?" Ravlen felt like she'd just been hit by a truck.

Claire vigorously nodded while Alison stared straight ahead.

This changes things. Five echoes? How long had they been there? I've never been in an echo for more than a couple of days, but they might have lived there for weeks, or months.

The most important thing struck her.

Are they all closed? Or do these echoes live on?

Ravlen opened her mouth to speak, but Alison had shut down. Her eyes were wide and darting. Her whole body trembled. Claire caressed her sister's hair.

"It's okay, Ali. Look where we are now. This is a great home. People here are nice. We don't have to go back into any of those other places anymore, I promise. I'll never ask again. If it hadn't been for the servant on a horse, I wouldn't even have asked. He was the one who kept telling me it was better there. I'll never ask again, I promise."

Alison's shoulders relaxed a little.

"You need a nap, Ali," Claire coaxed. "Let's go have a rest."

Alison half-turned her head, the weight of the world almost visible on her shoulders, the shadows under her eyes stark against her pale face. "You stay here. I'll rest alone. You play with Ravlen."

"Okay, Ali. Whatever you want." Claire's blue eyes followed her sister as she went inside before turning back to Ravlen. "You have to stop the servants. Or princes. Whoever they are, Ravlen. You can't let them keep doing this."

"What do they do?" Ravlen felt like she couldn't breathe. Something inside her knew this might be one of the most important insights into the echo worlds that she'd learned since she first went in, because she was learning it from someone who had only known the echoes as home. To Ravlen, they had only ever been a dangerous trap.

Claire looked around but there was no one in earshot. "They are the ones who tell us to come," she said, her voice so low Ravlen had to lean in close to hear. "They tempt us with promises of wonderful things. And it's true, everything is wonderful in *that place*. But sometimes things go wrong. We've seen it. We lost friends in there, and if it wasn't for Alison... we might not..." Claire started panting, holding back sobs that threatened to burst.

Ravlen shifted and put her arm around the child.

"You don't have to tell me anything more if it's too hard to say."

"I want to tell you."

Claire took two deep breaths and swallowed hard. She leaned into Ravlen's shoulder seeking comfort. Ravlen held her close.

"You have to stop them. The princes."

"Tell me why."

"The princes Alison saw were learning how to become servants, servants to *that place*. I heard the powerful one say so. Their job is to bring people like us into their world and to keep us there."

Echo masters.

"But there are other prince-servants out there. They replace older ones who left their jobs behind. If you see one, you'll know who he is." Claire looked up at Ravlen in firm determination. "You know because he has storms in his eyes."

Ravlen gulped. Her throat was stuck. She knew someone just like that – someone with storms in his eyes. That had been exactly what Ravlen had seen. The thought drove an icicle into her gut.

Christopher Duke.

"It's your turn." Claire gestured to the cards, but Ravlen's mind was now far off, back in Mrs. Brand's math class, staring into Christopher Duke's eyes.

Christopher Duke... could he have come from the echo?

She shook her head and turned over a card. "Four of hearts."

"That's my favorite card!" Claire flipped over another one quickly. "Four of diamonds! That's my second favorite! I get that pair." Her smile beamed. She didn't realize the importance of what she'd told Ravlen. "Five of spades. Your turn."

It's just as well. She's too young to carry any more burden than she has already.

Ravlen's awareness suddenly pulled her away from the game, her senses operating faster than her consciousness. She lifted her nose in the air.

Hints of greenery, of fresh flowers and musk floated on a breeze. It was familiar and distant at once, like a song where she knew the tune but not the lyrics.

I know this scent, but not from here. Is it from our trip across the country? Or from one of the echoes?

She closed her eyes.

"Ravlen, you'll never pick the right card with your eyes closed!" Claire giggled.

"I smell something…"

Claire leaned against Ravlen. "What is it? Something good?"

"I think so… I'm not sure yet."

"I'll try with you."

They sat silent and focused, together with their eyes closed.

Ravlen felt a wave of warmth envelop her as the scent approached. Binner ran out of the bungalow and began circling the garden in mad dashes, barking and crying and wagging his tail hard enough to snap Joan's marigolds in half. He launched himself at Ravlen, nuzzling under her arm and pushing against her leg, persuading her to stand.

"I'm trying to focus, Binner!"

He barked again, and then Ravlen heard a familiar woman's voice cut through the air from a couple of blocks away.

"Hello, Ravlen."

Ravlen didn't wait a second longer. She was at the gate, flinging it open and practically stumbling down the driveway with Binner barking at her heels.

"Madame!"

The older woman turned onto her street, her long black dress tied with a bright blue sash flapping in the ocean breeze. To Ravlen, she was an apparition from another time, another life. And yet there she was, in the flesh, standing before her with the same benevolent grin and glint in her eyes.

Ravlen threw her arms around her waist. Laughing, Madame had to catch her balance before embracing Ravlen in return.

The lace of Madame's dress smelled like lilacs mingled

with blackberry tea, memories flooding Ravlen of the times she'd spent in Madame's hut learning about her mission, about her history, and about herself. She remembered the times before when she'd thought Madame frightening, in her black dresses with her long, spindly legs and ability to hear Ravlen coming from a great distance.

So much had changed since then.

"You're here," Ravlen spoke into Madame's shoulder, suddenly feeling young and vulnerable again. "I missed you so much. I didn't even know how much until right now."

Madame patted Ravlen's wild hair down. "It's good to see you too, child. In some ways, it has been very long, and in others, I never expected to see you so soon."

Binner ran around Madame's feet, jumping and playfully nipping at her sleeves. "And you too, Binner." She scratched him behind the ears, just the way he liked. He dropped dramatically in the middle of the sidewalk and rolled over for belly rubs.

Claire waited by the garden gate, suddenly timid. She twisted her hands together and rolled her feet into the grass.

"Madame, let me introduce you to Claire, who along with her sister, Alison, is one of the most amazing girls I have ever met."

Claire beamed.

"Why hello, Claire," Madame said in her well-practiced tone as head carer of the island. Claire didn't know that tone yet, but she would. Madame's voice would become an important part of Claire's childhood, just as it had been for Ravlen.

"Hello, Madame," Claire said shyly.

Madame gazed upon the house. "And Marriel?"

"She's inside. But I'd better explain our last echo to you first…"

Ravlen took Madame through the story of Conrad and the princes as Claire rushed inside to find Alison.

"I'm not surprised that Marriel had this experience," Madame said with a sigh. "It is part of growing up, but it is never a pleasant time."

Ravlen was shocked. "This is serious, Madame! That jerk dumped her and she was in tears over it, to the point of going into an echo!"

Madame looked nostalgic. "It seems very dramatic to you, and I understand why. The first time we witness the depth of another's emotions – especially love and heartbreak – they seem all-consuming. And yet, this is the very bridge that Marriel needs to walk across in order to have healthy relationships in the future. Pain is a part of that journey. That's what makes it real."

"But she went into an echo! Of her own free will!"

"As many echo chasers before her have done." Madame waved her hand as though it were the most common thing in the world for an echo chaser to willingly go into an echo in search of comfort. "You girls have more options available to you than regular girls in the world. But you also have the benefit of experience and training. As your carers, we have to trust that even if you make a choice, like Marriel did, to go into an echo, that eventually you will have the wherewithal to take yourself out of it again."

Ravlen couldn't believe her ears.

Madame laughed. "I see that my reaction has caught you off guard. And I also see that you still are not adept at hiding your emotions."

Ravlen rubbed her cheeks and took a deep breath. "Maybe you're right, but Marriel hasn't come out of her bedroom in two whole days."

"I'll have a chat with her."

"Madame, before that, I have to talk to you. About a boy at school."

Madame raised her eyebrows.

"Nothing like Marriel." Ravlen made a little gagging sound. "Yuck. No. Nothing like that. The opposite." She caught herself before saying anything more, seeing Claire leading Alison out of the house. "We need to talk about it later. It's very important."

"I can see from the look on your face how serious it is. We will make time to discuss it. Dina will come around for dinner, and hopefully Marriel will join us as well." Madame turned back to the young girls. "So, this is Alison! I have heard so much about you." She extended her hand, which Alison took. "Everyone calls me Madame, and I am very much looking forward to getting to know you."

"Madame!" Joan bounded out of the house. "How wonderful to meet you at last." Joan took Madame's hand and affectionately held it in both of hers. Ravlen watched Joan's grip tighten as she spoke. "Ever since…"

"I know."

"I have thought so much of you."

"And I of you."

"You are more than welcome in our home. Let me introduce you to Tom." Her tender gaze turned to the house where she screeched at the top of her lungs. "Tom! Get out here! It's Madame!"

Heavy footsteps rushed down the corridor and onto the small stoop as Tom practically leaped out the front door.

"Madame!"

A tour of the garden and some sweetened lemonade later, Madame excused herself and went down the hall to Marriel's room. The door was closed. Madame tapped it quietly as the conversation bubbled in the kitchen about Alison and Claire needing to pack their bags to join Madame on an island of wonders.

Ravlen wasn't listening anymore. Her attention was

focused on the conversation down the hall, behind Marriel's closed door.

"You don't have to explain it to me," Madame was saying when Ravlen finally zoned in on their hushed voices.

"I do. I owe you that much."

"You don't, Marriel."

There was a pause.

"It's okay to cry," Madame continued.

"I'm so ashamed, and I don't even know which part is worse. That I let Conrad trick me, and I fell for it, or that I went against everything I know and let myself be drawn into the falsehood of an echo."

"There is no shame in learning. I always had faith that you'd make the right decision when confronted with it. You went into the echo, and you came out of it. And what did you learn from that experience?"

"The echo closed itself quickly, before I even had a chance to explore or understand it. I know that the princes were just fairytales, but even so. It seems like "happily ever after" is impossible in love."

"I can see why it might appear that way to you, given that this was your first experience with love. The good news is that happily ever after is *absolutely* possible. Just not with four dueling princes who make you promises they cannot fulfill."

"When you put it that way…"

"Relationships – real relationships – are two-way. There's give and take, learning and testing and trying. Sometimes we get it wrong. Sometimes we put too much energy into people who aren't the right fit for us, but it's all part of life, Marriel. Even the shame you feel is part of your journey. Feel it, understand the feeling, and then recognize that there is no shame in growing up."

"Ravlen!"

"Huh?" Ravlen was snapped out of sensing the conversation by Joan's sharp cry.

"Don't eavesdrop. It's rude."

"I… uh…" She didn't want to lie. "I was just listening. In case there was something important."

"Mmmhmmm." Joan crossed her arms and pursed her lips at Ravlen.

"Look at what I drew, Ravlen." Alison passed her a page filled with swirling colors. "Marriel told me I should draw what I see in my mind and feel in my heart. Today I was feeling very confused about everything that happened in *that place*, so I tried to draw it."

"It's a great drawing." Ravlen admired it. The lines were chaotic and rough, filled with frustration and fear. "I can tell how you felt just by looking at this picture."

"It's because of Marriel." Alison smiled at her picture. "Do you think Marriel will join us for dinner tonight?"

Ravlen heard the bedroom door click open.

"I'm sure of it."

Just as Madame and Marriel reappeared in the kitchen, the front door flung open.

"Where's Madame?" Dina's voice echoed. "I'd recognize that scent of ancient lace and lilacs even if we were in the fifth dimension… Madame!" Dina threw her arms around Madame's neck as everyone shifted into the backyard for a barbeque dinner.

"What are we having?" Ravlen was practically drooling.

Tom raised the tongs like a royal staff. "Grilled veggies and trout."

Trout!

Ravlen thought back to Esmerelda and her shapeshifting trout-mermaid ways.

"You know, Tom…" Ravlen joined him at the barbecue's side. "I'm feeling kind of vegetarian today."

The yard was full. Tom, Joan, Alison, Claire, Marriel, Ravlen, Dina, and Madame used every available chair. They squeezed around the wooden table, but nobody minded. It felt like a family reunion.

Joan went to the deep freeze for ice cream, which got Alison and Claire so excited that they developed an impromptu dance in ice cream's honor, much to the amusement of everyone else in the yard. Madame took a seat beside Ravlen.

"Do you want to tell me about what you mentioned earlier?"

Ravlen had tried to put the stories from Alison and Claire out of her mind during the evening's festivities, but she only partially succeeded. She was glad Madame broached the subject. The others were consumed by a skit Alison and Claire were putting on, leaving Ravlen and Madame to discuss quietly between themselves at first.

"It's about echo masters," Ravlen began. "Do you know how someone becomes an echo master?"

Madame looked at Ravlen and then at the girls. "We have hypotheses. We do not know for sure."

"I think I know."

"Tell me more." Madame gazed intently at Ravlen, but Ravlen looked over her former carer's shoulder and gasped.

"Ravlen? What's wrong?"

Just beyond the table, Christopher Duke stood on the other side of the fence, staring at her with storms in his eyes.

Ravlen jumped up from her seat and ran toward him, but by the time she reached the gate, he was gone.

19

"Tell me everything you know about him."

Madame was all business now, every sign of the gentle visitor temporarily set aside to deal with the new and unexpected threat of Christopher Duke.

"It started in math class…"

Tom and Joan had taken Alison and Claire to the park, leaving Ravlen free to recount her run-ins with the troubled boy. His every interaction with her had gone beyond the typical behavior of a schoolyard bully. The intensity of his animosity was out of proportion, over the top.

Unless Christopher Duke really was a slip-in from the echo world. Then all possibilities were on the table.

"He might be trying to take you down, scare you out of your echo chasing." Marriel pursed her lips in thought.

"If he knows what you are, then certainly he has seen the mark of the unreal on your back," Madame said. She considered for a moment longer. "He would know to look for it."

"After our travels across the country, why here of all places?" Ravlen couldn't believe that such a coincidence was possible. Christopher Duke had arrived at the school before her. How could she end up registered in the one place where a slip-in was her classmate?

"He might be a part of a grander plan." Dina sucked on her bottom lip. "We assigned Ravlen and Marriel to this area specifically because of the increasing numbers of emerging echoes. More echoes mean more slip-ins. It makes sense there would be a few roaming around."

Silence descended as they considered Dina's point.

Marriel raised her hand. "Could it be that we have misunderstood? That maybe he's not a slip-in at all, but just a teenage boy who happens to have dark eyes? Should we consider that possibility?"

Madame put her hand on Marriel's knee. "Very pragmatic, Marriel. You are right. We cannot jump to conclusions."

"Still," Dina sucked her lip again. "The coincidences are adding up."

Madame sat back in the chair around their makeshift meeting place on the veranda. "I will consult with my mainland counterpart en route to the port with Alison and Claire. It's important to get them out of harm's way as quickly as possible, since it is possible that this has as much to do with them as it does with the two of you." She gestured to Marriel and Ravlen. "You said he was watching them closely. If his primary interest is echo chasers, or even Ravlen as our youngest and most proficient chaser, then he wouldn't have cared much about the two little ones. But he did care."

"He did," Ravlen agreed, "and he made a point of saying so."

A frown line appeared across Madame's brow and the muscles in her jaw tightened. "To go after children, it's abhorrent," Madame's voice rumbled like thunder.

"We can't let him win." Dina shot up from the table. "I won't let him. It's because of freaks of nature like him that

Julia got sucked into an echo. She was just a seven-year-old kid! Christopher Duke doesn't deserve to live. I'm going to find him and then I'll…"

Madame raised her hand, cutting Dina off.

"You'll do no such thing, Dina. Not just because we do not know the truth behind this boy, but because that wouldn't get us any closer to discovering the truth of your sister. You cannot hold this boy responsible for that."

Dina's face turned a blazing red. The vein in her neck throbbed while her hands formed tight fists. The breath coming out her nostrils was audible.

Madame stood up from her chair, moved behind Dina, and placed her hands on Dina's shoulders. Leaning forward, she whispered into her ear.

Ravlen watched Madame's lips.

"Your time will come, Dina. But it's not now. Breathe."

Dina's eyes shut, tense with creases that spread over her forehead. Ravlen and Marriel took each other's hands under the table. Dina was their mentor, they relied on her for guidance, for protection. For stability.

But Dina is being ruled by her feelings. She can't help us if she's blinded by her desire for revenge.

Madame retook her seat. "My mainland counterpart might know more. If we can make more sense of what we know so far, I'll be sure to get word to you. In the meantime," she lowered her chin, looking at Marriel and Ravlen, "you must watch him closely. Be careful of confrontation. We do not know what he is capable of. And, as Marriel said, there is always the possibility that it is not as it seems. Indeed, sometimes the easiest answers are wrong."

They made a peculiar sight, Madame, Alison, and Claire climbing onto a westbound bus. The girls rushed on board, each wanting a window seat.

"Look how tall we are!" Claire raised her arms out the window.

"Here, Marriel." Alison held out a drawing.

"This is wonderful." Marriel's face was sincere. She looked up in awe at Alison hanging out the window. "It's more than wonderful, it's incredible."

Alison's smile reached the far sides of her face. "That's what I see when I look at you. It's for you to keep."

Marriel nodded, pressing her lips tightly together. "I'll cherish it. You keep this up. Drawing out your feelings will help."

Madame clapped her hands together. "I think we're all set. Oh, I almost forgot. Imagine…" She reached into her handbag and pulled out a postcard. "I wanted to deliver this myself." She passed it to Ravlen.

Ravlen immediately recognized the scrawl and saw the signature. Her heart skipped a beat.

Daniel.

Madame took Ravlen's chin in her hand. "You are going to be just fine, you hear me, Ravlen? When you question it, remember that this is what you were born to do."

Ravlen nodded, gripping the postcard even tighter.

Madame pulled both Marriel and Ravlen in for a hug before boarding the bus and taking a seat beside Claire. "Wave goodbye, girls. It might be a while before we can all be together again."

"Bye Ravlen!" Claire grinned. "Bye Marriel!"

Alison was somber, her eight-year-old face pulled into a deep frown. She choked up when she called out, "I'll miss you!" as the bus pulled away. Ravlen saw Madame put her hand on Alison's head before the bus turned and was out of sight.

Marriel put her arm around Ravlen and led her back toward the house. "Just you and me again, Rav."

Ravlen put her arm around Marriel's waist. "Just you and me."

Echo chasing took on new meaning now that there was the possibility of someone from an echo – a slip-in – living among them. Ravlen spent all night after the girls left reviewing the lessons Janna, Madame, and Dina had taught her. Just in case. Echo masters were the ones who brought people into the echo, but slip-ins tried to change the real world to suit their own wishes. It was a dangerous proposition, especially not knowing what kind of world Christopher Duke might have come from.

Disturb. Pulling the power from within. Displacement. Calming myself so that I can rise up and see farther. Knowing my limits.

She tossed to the other side of the bed.

I've got to stay sharp. I can't become satisfied with myself or else I'll make mistakes. Like with Alison and Claire. Imagine if I hadn't sensed them at the last minute. She shuddered once more at the thought. *I have to up my game.*

She tossed back again.

Pulsing. Using all that is within me to burst forward, to fly, to float, to transform the space around me when I'm inside the echo. How could Marriel have been thinking about boys with everything we've got going on? Maybe I should quit Marching Band.

She flopped onto her back.

It's not enough to use my skills in the echo, I have to stay in practice. I have to find places in the real world to keep myself fresh, to push myself even farther. My skills are my responsibility now. Janna isn't here to push me forward. I've got to do it myself.

Someone knocked on the door. It creaked open, Joan's face appearing in the dim glow of Ravlen's nightlight.

"I can hear you tossing and turning from the next room." She sat on the edge of the bed. "Do you want to talk about what's on your mind?"

"Nothing's on my mind."

Should I talk to Joan about this? Maybe it's okay to talk about my skills. Maybe it's just the echoes I can't talk about...

"I can see the thought process across your face." Joan tapped Ravlen's knee through the bedspread. "You're not very subtle at hiding what's going on in that head of yours."

"That's what I was thinking about, in a way." Ravlen sat up. "I have to be better at what I do. I still make so many mistakes." She smacked the bed, frustration taking hold alongside her exhaustion. "I can't let myself be that way."

"What way?"

"Distracted. Scared."

"Young?" Joan smiled.

"Exactly." Ravlen flopped back, her head bouncing lightly off the pillow. "I have to be more than what I am."

Joan cocked her head. "None of us are more than we are. We can't be."

"But I *have* to be. That's the contradiction of it. And I *hate* contradictions." She smacked the bed again.

"Hey now, hey now." Joan scooted closer, smoothing the cover over Ravlen. "The frustration you're feeling, it's not unusual."

"Maybe it's not unusual, but what I'm trying to do is unusual."

"In some ways, yes. And in others, no."

"Huh?"

Joan's smile was tender. "Marriel struggled with her relationship with Conrad. You're struggling with accepting your own current limitations. You're both right on track with your developmental milestones."

"Developmental milestones? I'm not following."

"I am here to accompany you, to support you, and – when necessary – to protect you in whatever way I can. But what you're feeling now… every echo chaser goes through this stage. Do you feel like you aren't good enough to do what's being asked of you?"

"Yes!"

"And that there isn't time to waste on silly things like boyfriends or extracurricular activities, or even sleeping?"

"How did you know?"

"That's my job. And I can assure you, Ravlen, that you are right on track for where we would expect a thirteen-year-old—"

"Almost fourteen…"

"Almost-fourteen-year-old to be. You are capable of a great deal more, but all in good time. Some things can be learned quickly, others, not so much."

Ravlen considered this. If she was "on track" as Joan said, then what was she supposed to do to get to the *next* developmental milestone? She didn't want to be stuck in this place of self-doubt for very much longer. It was uncomfortable and distracting.

She had to be able to do what she had to do without her feelings getting in the way.

Joan tucked her in, the covers tight around Ravlen on the cool, humid night. "I'm not telling you to let everything go. Far from it. The responsibility that you and the others like you have is great. I respect and admire you for it. But at the same time…" Joan caressed Ravlen's hair. "Sleep, child."

The feeling of Joan's hand on her head was hypnotizing. Ravlen tried to think about what Joan had said, but her thoughts drifted, becoming gentle nothingness as she fell into dreamless slumber.

"I FORGOT MY FLUTE!" GRETA GRABBED HER HEAD. "MR. J. will kill me!"

"You run home and get it; I'll clean up here." Ravlen started arranging the notes from their science experiment on charcoal and water. "I don't mind. I've already got my trumpet."

"You're the best!" Greta slipped out before the bell. Famously short-sighted, Mr. Costello didn't even notice.

The bell rang.

"Thank you, everyone, for your care with the equipment. Glad to see you've all cleaned and sorted already. Until tomorrow, students!" Mr. Costello was walking past Ravlen when he noticed her still there. "You surprised me, Ravlen!" He grabbed at his chest and Ravlen wondered if he was having a heart attack, even though she hadn't moved.

"Just tidying up, Mr. Costello."

"Next time, tell me. No need to cause such a shock. It's not good for the blood." He walked out of the class, hand still on his chest, muttering about disrespect.

With twenty minutes before band practice, Ravlen was in no rush. She was washing the test tubes and Bunsen burners at the lab station she shared with Greta when the idea struck her.

This is the perfect place to practice!

She turned on the sink at her station.

I can slow the flow of the water...

And she did.

"Too easy," she said to the water, and she turned on every sink in the room.

Slow these waters. Disturb them in their place.

She watched as every sink, in tandem, slowed to a solid stream of water that never hit the bottom of the sink before recommencing their gush.

"Still too easy! But water always was easy…"

She reset her Bunsen burner. She'd never been a fan of the apparatus, always worried that her hair might blow in the wrong direction and catch fire, even though she wore it back in a too-tight ponytail during class for just that reason.

She snapped a spark over the gas, and it came alight. Next, she adjusted the flame to a clean blue.

"This will be a challenge." She'd never tried to accelerate a flame before. But that was the point. She had to try more, push farther, explore new limits.

Flame of fire, gas alight. I need the fuel to feed it faster.

She closed her eyes, sensing the tube of gas coming out of the countertop.

Accelerate the air, flow with new speed. Faster, faster...

A whoosh sounded and Ravlen gasped as she opened her eyes.

The flame rose a foot in the air.

"Yes!"

The reds and yellows surged out of their initial blue and remained under tight control, the flame expanding but not exploding. Ravlen nodded in satisfaction as it slowly shrank back to its original size.

She didn't hear anyone in the doorway until his voice broke her concentration.

"Playing with fire. Literally and figuratively."

Ravlen spun around, the tips of her ponytail singeing in the flame.

His voice, so full of spite and hate. And his eyes...

The storms in Christopher Duke's eyes reflected the glow of the small fire. He blew a gust between his lips, and though he stood on the other side of the science room, the flame went out.

Ravlen froze, a rabbit staring down the jaws of a wolf.

Slip-ins aren't supposed to be able to disturb, they don't have additional abilities. Or do they? What kind of slip-in is Christopher Duke?

"You have no idea what you're playing with," he spat out. "You think you're saving people, changing the world, playing superhero." He shook his head. "You're not just playing with fire, you're fanning the flames. And if you don't get out quick, you're going to get burned, *echo chaser.*" He said it as though it were disgusting. "You'd be better off chasing your own tail."

Ravlen held her breath, fearing too much what might happen if she dared to release the air in her chest.

"Don't forget to turn off the gas nozzle. Even I can't do that from across the room." He snorted a laugh that reminded Ravlen of nightmares she'd had as a child. He turned on his heel and swaggered off.

Watching him leave, Ravlen finally let out her breath. But then she caught it again, realizing what she was looking at.

An unmistakable strip of undulating shimmer escaped the collar of his leather jacket.

Ravlen snapped back into her skin and turned off the gas.

There was no doubting what she saw, and now she had to do something about it. Christopher Duke had the mark of the unreal. And he was no simple slip-in.

avlen rushed into the music room even though she was still early. Most of the other students were outside, hanging in the field between the middle and high schools, and would join only at the very last minute.

Ravlen had to talk to Marriel. She thought she might explode with what she now knew, the knowledge burning her up inside. A slip-in living among them could mean anything. She'd never come across it. Even if slip-ins weren't as dangerous as echo masters, Christopher Duke's threats had to be taken seriously. He likely knew the echo masters, and who knew what would happen then.

I should have guessed! It wasn't jail that made him so strange. Christopher Duke, a slip-in.

She scanned the field from the music room window, but couldn't spot Marriel anywhere.

"Come on, Marriel. Can you hear me? I need you," she murmured. It was a long shot – Marriel would have to be intentionally listening for Ravlen's voice in order to hear it at this distance. She'd done it before, but with the ruckus of the after-school madness, it wasn't likely now. "Please, please, hear me."

"Can I help, Ravlen?"

Ravlen spun around, her back plastered against the window.

"Mr. J."

He approached slowly, concern apparent on his face. "You're trembling. And sweating." He stopped an arm's length from her. "What's happened? You can tell me. You can trust me."

Ravlen shook her head quickly. "No, I can't. You don't know, you don't understand…"

"I do." He moved as if to take her shoulders and then thought better of it. "I know everything, Ravlen," he said, his voice low. "I've been to the echo. If it hadn't been for a chaser, I'd still be there today. Then again, maybe I wouldn't even exist anymore…" He looked over her shoulder, out the window. "We don't have long. Your bandmates will be here soon. I'll tell you what I know, and then you can decide for yourself what, if anything, you want to share."

Ravlen glanced outside, desperate for Marriel, but she was still out of sight.

Mr. Johannsen dove right in. "I know there are those like you, like Marriel, who are charged with the task of finding people in the vast labyrinth of unknown places accessed only through seemingly magical portals. You look for people like me who fell into the clutches of these tempting worlds and their promises of greatness."

That must have been what Mr. J. had wished for, greatness. She listened, trying to memorize his words so she could recount them to Marriel later.

"I watched as others in this magical place became drunk on those promises, the sense of the real world fading into the distance. A young man found me. He explained what was happening and yanked me out. I was willing to go, though I felt the absence of the place as soon as I was back in my own one-bedroom apartment."

"You were an easy-leaver."

"An easy-leaver?"

"Tell me more. Quick, Mr. J."

He glanced at the closed door. "Once I was home, I felt the sensations numbing, the sense of the place disappearing, and I questioned whether it really happened. And that's when I saw the same young man in the street. I'll be honest, I went a little crazy. I grabbed him and desperately pleaded for him to explain to me what had occurred as well as what was happening to me right then. I told him I was forgetting despite my best efforts to hold the memories close. He tried to explain, but Ravlen, the truth of it sounds like make-believe and my own mind turned over on itself. It wasn't until I met the others..."

"GET AWAY FROM HER!" Marriel jumped at Mr. Johannsen, grabbing him by the throat and pushing until his back was against the wall of boxed saxophones. They fell in a cascade of bouncing black cases.

Marriel was panting as she held Mr. Johannsen in place. "I heard you, Ravlen. I came as fast as I could."

"Marriel!" Ravlen rushed over, but Marriel's forearm was firmly pressed against Mr. J's throat. He could have fought his way out of it, but Marriel was filled with the force of adrenaline.

"It's... not... what you... think..." he managed to squeeze out through his punished windpipe.

"Marriel, it's okay, I'll explain, you have to stop..." Ravlen turned around to find the marching band students gathered inside the music room door, expressions of shock across their faces.

Marriel loosened her grip on Mr. J. "It's okay, I understand why you reacted that way," he coughed out. "I'll cover this up. But please, stay after class. Both of you. There are some people I'd like you to talk to."

Marriel looked over at Ravlen, who nodded, then stepped back, kicking a couple of saxophone cases out of their way.

Mr. Johannsen straightened his shirt, gave Mariel a weak smile, then walked to the middle of the room and addressed the group of students huddled by the door.

"Did you all see that? The saxophones fell and Marriel came to my rescue! If she—" he coughed, "—if she hadn't been there to push me out of the way, I'm sure one or more of them would have landed on my head!"

His tone was believable and most of the students' eyes grew wide in surprise while a couple of them laughed.

"Oh, she was *saving* you! That explains it!"

"I could have sworn she'd just attacked Mr. J."

"Thank goodness for Marriel!" Greta called over to Ravlen from the flute section. "I really thought something strange was happening. Just goes to show how easily rumors can start! We've got to be careful with appearances. They can be awfully deceiving..." She turned back to her flute.

The tension in the room broke as the students found their chairs and began setting up their instruments. Mr. Johannsen headed straight for the inter-classroom telephone and spoke softly into it for a moment. When he hung up, he looked over and caught Ravlen staring at him. They held their gaze until Mr. Johannsen broke it with a quick nod. He looked away and clapped his hands.

"We're starting with *Twist and Shout*, students. And then I've got good news. The new song you've all been waiting for? I'm announcing it today!"

A few kids cheered. Ravlen shook as she attached the mouthpiece to her trumpet. She looked around the room, but everything and everyone looked as normal as ever.

Greta is right. We have to be more careful.

THE STUDENTS SHUFFLED OUT OF CLASS AS MRS. BRAND strolled in, looking as standoffish and discontented as ever. She spoke with Mr. Johansson and snuck glances at Ravlen.

Be normal, just put away my trumpet, like everyone else...

"Why is that teacher staring at you like you're an alien?" Marriel stood behind Ravlen like a bodyguard.

"That happens every day."

Marriel gasped. "Every day? Why didn't you say so?"

"I thought it was normal."

"She is definitely not acting normal." Marriel shuffled to stand beside her best friend. "I hope Mr. Johansson knows what he's talking about with these other teachers."

"We're about to find out."

Miss Markham and Mr. Costello came into the music room as the last students were leaving. Mr. Johansson set up chairs, four on one side, two on the other. "Everyone, please sit down."

"I'd rather stand." Mr. Costello closed the music room door and leaned against the doorframe.

"Sit." Mr. Johannsen's tone was directive in a way Ravlen had never heard before. "The point is to put the girls at ease, but the way you're hovering even makes *me* uncomfortable."

Mr. Costello didn't take his eyes off the two girls as he swaggered to a chair. But Ravlen could see his hands shaking before he shoved them into his pants pockets.

He's scared, putting on a show. He's not nearly as brave as he's trying to look.

The four teachers sat in a row, none of them looking happy about it except Mr. Johannsen, whose cheeks were relaxed as he kicked off the conversation.

"Thank you, Marriel and Ravlen, for being willing to speak to us. I always knew a day like this was coming, but I couldn't have guessed it would be the two of you."

Marriel sat stiffly. "Shouldn't Tom and Joan be here?"

"You can feel free to tell them as much as you like, but I suspect that there are some things you keep from them, am I right? Like the nature of your missions?"

Ravlen scanned the other teachers. At the mention of the word 'mission', Miss Markham crossed her legs awkwardly while Mrs. Brand flicked a sideways glance toward Mr. Johansson.

"That's a leading question." Mrs. Brand's lips curled sourly. "You don't know what they know or don't. You shouldn't be making so many assumptions, Ron."

Mr. Johannsen looked at Ravlen. "You see? This is what I've been contending with. Therefore, Ravlen, if you could please share just enough detail so that it's clear to the others what you do, I would be most grateful. And, more importantly, that will make our conversation more productive."

Ravlen considered the options, but Marriel beat her to it. She stood, keeping one hand on Ravlen's shoulder.

"We are tasked with a duty greater than your teacher minds can imagine. Whatever story you have concocted among yourselves that has led you to treat Ravlen the way you have, you're wrong. Dead wrong. Any obstacle you throw in front of us only puts others at risk. So, Mr. J., I don't mean to be rude, but unless you have something helpful to share, I don't see why we have to subject Ravlen to any more scrutiny and mistreatment than she's already had to endure from the four of you."

Mr. Costello stood up. "Before you jump to conclusions, be more specific. Don't talk about saving lives and missions. Be clear. If not, I see no reason to believe you are who you say you are."

It was Ravlen's turn to assert herself. "Would you rather be left to the whims of an echo master?"

That silenced everyone.

The corner of Miss Markham's mouth began to bend upward. "It's true, you're chasers. Two girls."

"Don't fall for it, Maggie." Mrs. Brand's sour expression was unchanged. "Only boys are trained for such activities."

"Where on earth did you hear that?" Ravlen was offended and didn't try to hide it. "Whatever. It doesn't matter. In any case, you're wrong."

"Ravlen," Marriel urged. "Don't give too much away."

"There are hundreds of us girls," Ravlen continued. "We have abilities and, frankly, we're pretty darn good at what we do."

"Girls?" Mrs. Brand shook her head. "You get distracted, you couldn't focus on a goal if it was two feet in front of your nose."

She's testing me. Ravlen suddenly caught on to what was happening. *Pushing my buttons to see how I react. Her heart is pounding, too. This is my chance to show her I'm not what she thinks I am.*

"If that were true, then why is your heart racing?" Ravlen softened. "You've been there, Mrs. Brand, haven't you? You had to live through an echo closure. You've been hurt by that loss."

Ravlen was taking a risk making such an assumption, but it paid off. Mrs. Brand's face transformed, first losing the tense frown, then her eyebrows lifted, innocence and pain replacing cynicism.

"Yes." Her voice was barely audible, her lip quivered. "The love of my life, I lost him. I couldn't convince him. I felt the end coming, it rattled in my bones, and I knew. But Stephen... he'd finally found a place that answered his dreams, let him cast off his fears. I couldn't change his mind…"

"I'm so sorry," Ravlen knelt in front of Mrs. Brand and took her hand. "It must have been horrible."

Mrs. Brand nodded quickly. "It was."

"It's true then." Miss Markham moved closer to Ravlen. "You're not one of those who come into our world to snatch humans away."

"No, we're not." Ravlen took her seat by Marriel. "We're the opposite."

"I just didn't think girls…"

Marriel held up her hand. "You thought wrong."

"I did." Miss Markham looked at the other teachers. "We had it wrong."

"Wait a second." Ravlen crossed her arms. "All of you have been in echoes?"

The teachers nodded in unison.

"The same one?"

"No."

"You already know my story," Mr. Johansson walked to Mrs. Brand. "I found Eleanor in the teacher's lounge one day not long after I'd returned, and somehow we got discussing the fact of memories fading. Do you remember how it came about, Eleanor?"

Mrs. Brand took a deep breath. "You were in a bad way yourself. I was still grieving. A lot of our conversation was in code, and then we recognized the numbness in each other. If it weren't for you…" Her eyes teared up.

"Me too, Eleanor."

Silence hung in the group while Mrs. Brand blotted her eyes.

Mrs. Markham put her arm around Mrs. Brand. "I was a child when I wandered into one. I knew something was wrong, but I couldn't put my finger on it. I didn't stay long, but it distressed me. After I returned, I sought people who wore the same vacant look I'd seen on the humans in that other world. I eventually found them. I was working as a tutor when Ron and I crossed paths. I knew I had to find a way to join this school. Ron convinced them that French was important to complement Spanish, and here I am."

Mr. Costello spoke at last. "Let's just say I was in there, then I was yanked out. And I've never been the same since." He looked at Mr. J. "I don't want to go into the details."

"That's fine, Scott. It's your story to tell."

"I don't get it," Ravlen sized up the teachers before her, who had all been to echo worlds and had somehow managed to find each other. "Most people who come out of the echo return to their daily lives and don't speak of it again, but you became teachers at the same school and remember your experiences in the echo."

Mr. Johannsen lifted his finger. "We didn't say that."

"Quite the contrary," Mrs. Brand added.

"If it weren't for each other," Mr. Johannsen picked up, "we would have lost the memories completely by now, I'm sure of it. As it is, we only have vague recollections. Mine are all painted over, like looking through a fogged-up window."

"Mine are almost gone completely, except the sounds." Mrs. Brand shivered. "The sounds still haunt me."

"I remember a lot." Miss Markham stared off in the distance. "I was a child. The experience marked me, but it wasn't traumatic the way it was for the others."

"It's trauma that makes you forget?" Ravlen tried to keep it straight, but her understanding of the real world was changing with each passing second. What she'd thought about these teachers for the last six months was wrong. She couldn't have known they were so close to her own work. Or could she?

"The brain is a near-magical machine." Mr. Costello

clasped his hands in front of him the way he did in science class. "It protects our consciousness from the things we cannot emotionally handle."

"But you're handling it."

The teachers looked at each other.

"There is much you don't see," Mrs. Brand said, her eyes cast downward. "Many dark moments, fears, pain."

"We committed to remembering, even though it often breaks us." Mr. Johannsen looked at Ravlen straight on. "Because we committed that we will do everything in our power to prevent others from falling into the same trap. But remembering comes at a cost."

"The ones who return and forget," Mr. Costello scratched his arm obsessively, "they have it easy. There are days I wish I let myself walk among them, in blissful ignorance."

"But we committed."

"We committed." Mr. Costello dropped his hands. "*I* committed. I saw what *they* do, those from the other world who convince people to venture into the entryway—"

"The haze?"

"That's right. I've seen it. I've been there. And I can't let it happen to anyone else."

They know the haze and they know about slip-ins and echo masters, even if they don't know what they are.

Miss Markham stood. "None of us will let it happen under our watch."

"And we thought you were one of them." Mrs. Brand's voice darkened. She took a deep breath. "I felt something in you. I didn't know what, but I couldn't trust it."

Did she sense that I was born in an echo, or maybe that my father is an echo master?

Perhaps originals had more skills than Ravlen or any of the others knew.

"Here's the thing." Mr. Johansson paced between the

chairs. "We may have been wrong about Ravlen, but I believe there's someone else we *do* need to worry about."

They turned their heads to Ravlen. She took in a deep breath and found the courage to share what she'd held in for too long. They were a team now, albeit a newly-formed team, and she didn't know how far she could trust them.

But she had to try. Christopher Duke had the mark of the unreal. He knew Ravlen's mission. And he had made it very clear.

He wouldn't let her interfere.

"Let me tell you more about slip-ins and echo masters. Because I think we've got one right here at this school."

2 1

"I'm having a serious case of deja vu."

Ravlen clenched her teeth and Marriel instinctively took her hand.

"You okay?"

"I'd rather be in any other echo than this one."

They were back in her first echo. The one from the island. The same streets, the same red brick school, the same police station, the same park. Even the petting zoo had reappeared. Ravlen knew exactly what this meant.

Her father wasn't far.

"You think it's the exact same as the one from before?" Ravlen squinted into the sun. "Can we use the same logic flaw to break it?"

"I highly doubt it. The world looks the same, but it must be responding to someone else's desire."

"But *he* is here somewhere, isn't he?"

Marriel knew what she meant. "Yes, I'm sure he is."

Ravlen threw her hands up. "Why is he suddenly showing up all over the place? I thought I was rid of him."

"You were never rid of him."

Ravlen kicked the asphalt. "I wanted to be."

"Maybe… but maybe not."

Ravlen's face showed her disgust. "What's that supposed to mean?"

Marriel put her arm around Ravlen, leading her farther down the streets, into the center of town. "He's your father. He's the connection to your mother, to your history. Sure, he's an echo master. But he's also your flesh and blood." Marriel stopped. "Do echo masters *have* flesh and blood?"

"How am I supposed to know?" Ravlen dropped her head. "This is terrible. Let's figure out what's happening with this place and then get out of here. It's giving me the creeps."

"Hold up." Marriel stopped Ravlen and held her arm tightly. "You can't run just because he's here. We have to take the time it takes to understand the logic, find any originals, and safely remove them first. We don't want a repeat of the Alison and Claire episode. And now that we have Christopher Duke to worry about, we have to be extra careful."

The lump grew in Ravlen's stomach, but she remembered the teachers – teachers she'd thought hated her – and how they had completely changed their attitude once they knew she was an echo chaser and not a slip-in. They had made it very clear after their meeting in the music room that they would do anything to support Ravlen and Marriel, to protect them from whatever secrets Christopher Duke was keeping.

She was in her father's echo, but she had more friends in her corner now.

Ravlen closed her eyes and scanned her body from the inside. Her stomach was in knots, her shoulders tense, and her jaw tight. She inhaled, imagining the air reaching deep within her, releasing the muscles, slowing the blood in her veins.

When she opened her eyes, she saw the world around her differently.

Instead of fearing the familiar, she could use it to navigate faster, understand easier. And a big benefit was that she already knew her way around.

"Let's see how large the place has gotten so far." Ravlen led Marriel behind the school. "That will give us an idea of how many originals are here."

"That's the Ravlen I know." Marriel smacked her affectionately, but hard, on the back.

"And for how long they've been here. Follow me." Ravlen ran ahead, finding the neighborhood behind the school already well developed, unlike the echo from the island. "Let's try over there." Ravlen pointed to the community where Donelle had stayed. They walked purposefully but without rushing. Children, parents, walkers-by, and street cleaners began to appear around them, and the last thing they needed was to be intercepted by well-wishing echo people.

Raven paused. An unexpected sound in the distance pulled her attention away from exploring. Marriel was several paces ahead, but Ravlen had to identify the sound before she could go on.

It could be Oaken. And I am not in the mood to let him catch me by surprise again.

"What is it, Rav?"

She closed her eyes in the way she'd been taught, to gather all her energy into a single sense. Zoning in wasn't always the best option, for even though it gave her unparalleled hearing, it came at the expense of her other senses.

Losing other senses in an echo had proven dangerous, more than once.

But Ravlen knew this echo, at least she knew it enough to feel confident in the dangers she faced there.

"I think I hear it, too." Marriel quieted. "Is it an echo person? An original? I can't tell, can you?"

"Watch out for me while I focus." Ravlen did the listening equivalent of zooming in like a lens, the click-clack sound coming clearer.

"Nope, not an original, not even a person."

"What is it then?" Marriel cried, anxious and alert.

Ravlen groaned as she took her face into her hands. This was one danger she could quickly put to rest. She sighed and then took a deep breath before calling out.

"Binner! Over here!"

Marriel set her hands on her hips. "Binner? Again?"

Tongue flying out the side of his mouth, he ran with the power of the pulse, skidding to a stop and sitting obediently at Ravlen's feet.

"Did you see that?"

"He went so fast."

"Even faster than me when I pulse." Ravlen stared at the dog whose tail wagged with a loud 'whomp whomp' against the ground. "How did you do that, Binner?"

"If Binner could talk, then we'd really be in a crazy echo."

Ravlen thought about it. Being in an echo where Binner could talk would be a fascinating place indeed…

"Don't even go there!" Marriel tugged on Ravlen's sleeve. "Come on, we've been here for an hour already and haven't accomplished anything except being found by Binner."

"Binner came through the haze… after us. Oh no, Marriel…"

Marriel froze as the truth hit her in the face. "The exit point has moved."

"And we're in one of Oaken's echoes!" Ravlen dropped to sit on the curb and threw her hands toward the sky. "Why is this happening to us?"

"Don't you go getting all fatalistic on me now."

Ravlen had no idea what that meant, but she wasn't about to admit it. "I'm not getting fantalastic."

"*Fatalistic.* It means acting as though the fatal outcome is already decided. Just because we're here doesn't mean we'll see *him…*"

"It does."

"And it doesn't mean that we won't be able to figure out the logic, locate the haze, and get out of here quickly. But none of that will happen if you sit on the side of the street feeling sorry for yourself."

"Why can't one of the other echo chasers do the Oaken echoes? That would be fairer."

"Let's not get started on fairness." Marriel's voice was firm but patient. "That's an old subject on the island. Don't you remember what Carer Boria said about fairness?"

"*The only fair thing in life is waking up.* But she said it as a joke."

"Because nothing is fair."

"This is all Binner's fault."

Marriel waited with crossed arms, watching as Binner maneuvered himself under Ravlen's arm for a scratch. His tail continued to 'whomp whomp' against the sidewalk and Ravlen couldn't hold her grudge.

"Okay, I'm over it."

"You sure? Because I'd rather you get this all out of your system now than throw a tantrum again three streets away."

"Yeah, I'm done." She lifted herself from the sidewalk. She had work to do.

More people began to appear around them, lives growing into the houses and parks and playgrounds as they strolled deeper into the echo.

"Time to disturb." Marriel dropped her backpack, which Binner promptly sniffed. "Don't you dare touch the granola bars, Binner. They're my favorite, and I'm saving them in case we're stuck here for a while."

Ravlen hadn't brought any provisions. "I thought we'd be

out of here for dinner. Even if it was an established echo that we couldn't shut right away, we could always have gone home for dinner and come back to close it later."

"Sure, we could have. But now we've lost the haze, so it's a good thing I came prepared."

"Smart…" Every now and then Marriel had an idea that showed why she was still the overseer, even if Ravlen was going to be fourteen in less than two weeks.

"Here's our plan, Rav. We disturb, we get a sense of the number of originals around. Then we try to sense the haze. But given that this is an established echo, and that the echo master is who he is, I'm not banking on it being easy to find. We'll have to find somewhere to stay for the night."

"Dina is going to be worried."

Marriel tipped her head. "Maybe a little. But she knew we were in for a hard one. That's why she came to us, remember?"

"No, the other echo chaser was just tired."

"The other echo chaser," Marriel lifted her finger, "was tired from trying – unsuccessfully – to close this echo."

"How do you know that?"

"I asked."

"Smart twice in a row. You're on a roll, Marriel!" Ravlen gave her a high five. "Now if you could just find that haze we lost, thanks to Binner…"

They both looked down at the dog, who knew he was guilty of something, as he stopped panting, pinned back his ears, and lowered his chin.

"It's not your fault, Binner-boy." Ravlen patted his head.

"Tom and Joan have got to keep that back gate closed."

The girls disturbed in turns, counting four originals, at least some of whom seemed to be connected to each other given their proximity.

"There might be more than four." Marriel pointed to the

far side, past the school and police station. "The land extends a long way in that direction, farther than I can disturb."

Ravlen knew what was over there, assuming it hadn't changed since her previous trip. After strolling in the garden of her childhood, she had slept in the most incredibly stately home.

Oaken's home.

"You're right. And I wish you weren't."

I've got to stop thinking like this. It's a mission *and a mission must be done regardless of the circumstances.*

"I can see you catching yourself."

"I have to stay focused on the goal and not how I feel about it."

"Feelings are important, but you get to decide what you do beyond your feelings. How you react to what you feel is what makes adults more adult."

"Then let's go." Ravlen pointed and marched forward with stolid determination.

"Wait!" Marriel rushed to stop Ravlen as Binner jumped and grabbed her pant leg. "You can't go just like that."

"You just said I can't let my feelings hold me back!"

"That doesn't mean we run head-first into echo dangerland."

"I know this echo. I know what's over there. And I'll bet you anything, I know who is waiting for us. Let's get this over with."

"Calm down, Ravlen." Marriel softened.

Ravlen rubbed her eyes. Everything felt harder this time and she couldn't manage to clear her mind. She didn't know what the next step was supposed to be.

Not knowing created a ball of frustration in Ravlen's stomach. "I need a minute."

"Take your time, Rav. It's better that way."

She hadn't even had a chance to reflect before a voice cut through the air.

"Hey-ho, girls!"

Marriel's eyes widened at the sound of a woman's voice from down the street, but Ravlen knew right away who it was.

"Yes, you two girls over there! Can you help me with my bags?"

"Coming, referent!" Ravlen ran to her side and picked up a suitcase. "You've arrived at just the right time."

"Have I? I've been here all along, so I guess it's you who arrived at the right time."

Ravlen scrunched up her face. "Definitely not. This is the *last* place I wanted to find myself."

"I doubt that, given all the other possibilities out there. Then again, I've seen more than you have."

Ravlen had questions about that, but she wasn't sure what they were. She shook it off, as they still had their primary mission ahead of them.

And they didn't have an exit.

Binner gave a cheerful bark and spun in a circle at the referent's feet. "Ah, so we meet again… what did you say you called him?"

"Binner."

"Binner. That's right." She crouched down to pet him and her knees cracked. Binner's brow furrowed at the sound. "Don't you worry now, boy, It's the normal progression of things. I'm not like I was in the old days that you remember."

Old days that they remember?

Ravlen's jaw dropped. "Did you know Binner…"

"Oh look!" Her referent pointed. "I think you know one of those boys over there, don't you?"

A game of catch was underway farther down the street.

"There's my referent." Marriel nodded toward them. "Always playing games."

"Lawrence." Ravlen's referent whispered as she narrowed her eyes in the distance. "Ought to take this more seriously."

Marriel tipped her head. "Excuse me, did you say his name is Lawrence? I didn't think referents had names."

The referent looked around as if Marriel were talking to someone else. "I don't know what you're talking about."

"You just said Lawrence."

"Laurels. The bush over there. It's laurels." Beside the group of boys was a bush, exploding with leafy branches and large buds that seemed seconds away from bursting into blossoms.

It hadn't been there a moment before. Ravlen knew it.

She put it there, to cover up her mistake.

Ravlen observed her referent, but she seemed as calm and collected as ever. Again, Ravlen wanted to ask questions, but so far, her referent had never given a straight answer to any straight question. Ravlen needed a different approach.

"This world is still molding itself, isn't it?" she asked, but her referent's eyes remained steadily on the boys.

"Mmhmm," was her only reply.

Ravlen looked at Marriel, who motioned for Ravlen to try again.

She sought inspiration from the surroundings. *Boys playing, she appeared on cue, she has bags...*

"Have you just come back from a trip?"

"Of sorts."

"Can we carry your bags home for you?"

"That would be lovely."

They each took one of the large suitcases, lifting them without difficulty. They were the old-fashioned kind without wheels, but instead of being heavy and awkward, they were almost empty.

"Down here, to the right." Her referent pointed in a direction that Ravlen had never explored. They followed her in silence for several turns. "One more right."

Marriel and Ravlen looked at each other. If they made another right, they'd be turning back in on themselves, leading into a vortex and not down the street.

Marriel mouthed, using only breath to communicate. "Where is she taking us?"

Ravlen didn't know. She didn't want to find out, but she was going to. They made the final turn.

"Here we are!"

The black expanse of asphalt before them had a giant white squiggle painted in the middle of it.

Where have I seen this before?

The squiggle reminded her of something, something from her earlier days of echo chasing, but this was out of context and she couldn't recall where she'd seen the design before.

Marriel stepped onto the asphalt. "Is this a landing pad?"

"More like a launch pad." The referent answered Marriel's question but kept her eyes squarely on Ravlen.

Ravlen shifted, trying to put the pieces together. "And this is your home?"

"Indeed not."

"But we were taking you home…"

"It is a place of leaving and arriving, transforming and transporting."

Ravlen looked at the squiggle on the ground, unlike the "H" for hospital or the "X" of a landing pad, and yet she knew its design. She'd seen it more than once…

The tattoo on Dina's arm. It's the haze.

Finally understanding, Ravlen searched, looking around them for a sign of the haze. Marriel scratched her back absent-mindedly, still unaware of the veiled meaning behind the referent's words. Ravlen looked everywhere but saw nothing.

"I must be going, my travel awaits."

It's a riddle.

"And how will you travel, referent?"

"That? Oh, never you mind. Sometimes you have to look down to go up."

Binner barked while Ravlen followed her referent's eyes down to the paint on the ground.

"Is the haze down there?" Ravlen whispered, hoping the direct question in a whisper wouldn't shake whatever foundations they were on with the referent.

"You must look closely, and I must be going…"

Marriel and Ravlen inspected the paint but still saw nothing. When they looked back, the referent was gone.

22

"I've never seen *that* before." Ravlen's eyes were stuck on the place where a moment before her referent had stood.

Marriel looked behind a set of garbage bins. "Goes to show we still don't have this place figured out."

"She talks in riddles. Why can't she just come out and say what she means?" Ravlen walked to the spot, but there was no sign of her referent anywhere. "Do you think she's trying to make it hard for us on purpose?"

Marriel shook her head. "Look at how helpful your referent has been. Mine only hangs around. He doesn't ever talk to me. He's just there."

A baseball bounced high along the road toward them, a boy – not just any boy – trailing behind it.

"Sorry about that," the boy-referent said to Marriel as he captured the ball in midair. "Sometimes things around here get out of control! And you might soon be in the middle of our game…" He stopped, staring Marriel in the eye with a look that communicated more than the risk of bouncing balls.

Without another word, he turned and ran in the other direction. Marriel's mouth hung open while Ravlen did a double take.

"We should go." Ravlen pulled on Marriel's arm. "Let's take your referent's hint to heart."

"Yes... yes..." Marriel stumbled, watching the boy disappear from view while walking in the other direction. "He's never said anything to me before. Why now?"

"Because something in this echo isn't right, and they know it."

Ravlen tugged harder on Marriel's hand and got her moving. She knew where they had to go, and she would lose her nerve if they waited too long.

Marriel hesitated when she saw the direction they were heading. "This is the way to your father's house."

Ravlen took a deep breath and clenched her fists. "It sure is."

Binner growled.

The stately home rose in the distance, the house and its surroundings unchanged. They crossed land faster than walking speed, the ground shifting under them like a moving sidewalk. The wrought iron gate was open a crack, inviting them in.

Does he know we're coming?

Binner stood in front of the gate and barked.

"I don't think he wants us to go in." Marriel crouched. "We don't have a choice, buddy."

Binner looked again at the house and his lip curled, but he stepped aside to let Ravlen and Marriel enter.

Ravlen saw the window of the bedroom in which she had stayed, the one where Mrs. Smuthen had waited on her and her father had read her a bedtime story. Where she'd been haunted by wonderful dreams that threatened to pull her into the echo's grasp.

A shiver ran down her spine.

I thought I'd never have to come back here again.

"I'm here." Marriel put her hand on Ravlen's shoulder. "Now let's go find this father of yours." Marriel leaned over, whispering breath in Ravlen's ear. "Can they hear us?"

"Probably," Ravlen breathed back.

"Do you know what you're going to say to him?"

"I'll know when I see him."

They approached the mansion. Marriel squeezed her shoulder and Ravlen climbed the steps alone to the front door. Beside it was a rope with an ornate wood handle that was shiny from use. The wood was cold and smooth in Ravlen's palm. She pulled it downward and a great bell rang, echoing through the house.

A curtain far down the east wing shook. Binner growled at it.

"What's over there?" Marriel asked with her breath.

"I don't know. I never went that way."

The front door creaked open.

"Ravlen." Her father smiled, genuine and warm. "I was hoping you would come."

Mrs. Smuthen set out tea and cookies, which Ravlen and Marriel pretended to enjoy while sitting on elegant furniture that looked like it belonged in a museum. Marriel bit off a corner of the cookie, but then spit it into her hand and stuffed it in her pocket.

"I've seen to it that my business for this afternoon is cleared up." Oaken reentered the room. "We can be uninterrupted for as long as necessary."

"Necessary for what?" Ravlen's voice was sharp.

"What she meant to say is," Marriel shot Ravlen a glance, "what is there for us to do?"

Oaken took a seat in an ornate armchair, the wooden armrests carved with gargoyles like Ravlen had seen in textbooks about medieval Europe.

"You came to me. I can only assume there is a reason, given that as much as I wish my daughter would visit me for the pure enjoyment of our family connection, I know better. There is always purpose to her movements." He turned to Ravlen. "I don't blame you, daughter. Seems you get that from your father."

Ravlen opened her mouth, but nothing came out.

"And you." He turned to the older of the girls. "Marriel, is it?"

Marriel nodded.

"Yes, I remember seeing you on the island when I first gained access to it."

Marriel stood from her fancy chair, composed, but with a firm look on her face. "You mean when you opened an entry where you shouldn't have."

She's so good! Where did she come up with that?

Ravlen admired Marriel's stance, her feet wide and her arms crossed as though Oaken couldn't do anything to hurt her.

Ravlen stood and did the same. She didn't feel as strong as Marriel looked, but it was better than shrinking into the corner.

Oaken was unfazed.

"You are both welcome here. Ravlen can attest to my hospitality. She stayed overnight and was no worse off for it, nor did she experience any hostility. Isn't that right, Ravlen?"

Ravlen looked at Marriel and back to Oaken. She was suspicious of the leading question. "That's true. At least it was true last time, but hostility isn't the issue here. It's about the fake world that you try to draw originals into."

"Adolescent girls." Oaken lifted his hands and let them drop back to his armrests. "I've heard many things about adolescent girls, witnessed it myself even, but it's never the same when it's your own daughter."

"You have to stop saying that." Ravlen's head throbbed every time he said the word 'daughter.'

"It's the truth."

"I've never been a daughter to you."

"And yet you cannot deny your own heritage. You've only just begun to learn about it. I always knew it would be challenging for you to accept your birthright, but I am a very patient man. Hundreds of years, if that's what it takes."

"He's exaggerating," Marriel stepped closer to Ravlen.

"I'm not. There is much that neither of you know about the rules of our world. I forgive you for that."

Ravlen scowled. "*Forgive* us?"

"Marriel," he gestured toward a window where there had not been a table before, but now there was a small wooden desk with a chair at its side, "on that table is a photo album that will be meaningful for you. Ravlen has already seen its contents, through her own eyes, that is. It will be different for you."

Marriel looked to Ravlen for guidance.

She has to make her own judgments on what she sees in the album. I can't take that opportunity away from her.

Ravlen nodded.

Oaken strode to the desk and pulled out the chair. "When you're ready. In the meantime, I will show Ravlen to the east wing of the house."

"Binner, you stay with Marriel." Ravlen pointed to the desk and Binner took his spot by the table.

"Come with me, daughter."

They left Marriel on her own as she opened the album to the first page.

Ravlen swallowed hard. *The east wing. What's so special about the east wing?* She looked out the window from the hallway as she followed Oaken deeper into the house. The sky was darkening, though Ravlen couldn't see a sunset. No reds or oranges or purples. Just the coming night.

"This way."

Oaken's eyes caught the light of the ending daytime, glowing gray and deep.

Just like Christopher Duke, Ravlen shuddered. The pieces were starting to come together.

"It's best if you stay close behind me. Parts will be familiar to you, but others will be new."

"Parts of the east wing? You mean it's like the west wing?"

"That's not what I mean at all."

Ravlen stopped, refusing to go another step with him. She couldn't let him stomp all over her like she was a doll he could play with or a puppet he could pull the strings on.

"I said it's this way."

"And I say I'm not moving until you tell me what is going on."

She crossed her arms and set her stance the way Marriel had done. She felt more confident this time.

"I'm trying to explain it to you."

"It *what*? What is '*it*'? Explain rather than leading me around. I'm not a toy."

He pursed his lips, considering. "That's fair." He set his stance in response to hers, his feet wide, his arms crossed and his eyes darker than she'd seen before. "You have received a substantial degree of special treatment, daughter, specifically because you are my daughter. This is not the case for others like you, and you should know that. All of this is easier for you than it is for anyone else, and you take it for granted."

"All of this *what*?"

She said it, but she was losing her nerve. His dark eyes swirled. Ravlen was beginning to understand who her father was – or more accurately – who he wasn't. He wasn't like her. He wasn't like the carers or Madame. He wasn't like any original. He was a different thing altogether.

Ravlen had to know, even though she felt her resolve shaking the way her hands shook pressed against her hips.

Her voice broke. "Who are you?"

"You know who I am. I'm your father."

"That's *not enough*," Ravlen paused, finally finding the words she'd spent nights planning, the right thing to say to Oaken to make him see her for who she really was. "There's more, so much more that you're not telling me. And I won't let you keep stringing me along."

He tilted his head, studying her. "Maybe when you're older."

"I won't give you that chance if you don't start telling me what this is all about *right now*."

Oaken stood, assessing the veracity of her claim, but Ravlen meant every word.

"And what if you don't like what I have to tell you?"

"Then I'll have to live with that."

"But so will I. What I share with you will impact us both. You for the knowledge you gain, and me for what you choose to do with that knowledge. It's not the knowledge that I wish to hold back from you, but the decision you might take from it. I won't let anything come between us the way it did when you were small."

"How can you say that?" Ravlen shook her head at his arrogance. "There's so much you've done already. The way you bring originals into these worlds, the way you try to keep them here…"

"This is exactly what I'm trying to show you." He stepped forward and placed his hands on her shoulders, and though Ravlen felt a tingle running off his fingertips, she also felt his sincerity. "What you see as my actions are part of a much bigger and complex movement of people through time, place, and presence."

"Presence?"

He released her. "If you must see it, then I will show you. But I will not let you stay long and you may have more questions than I am willing to answer. Do you accept that?"

"Yes."

"Then follow me."

Down one corridor, and then another, they twisted and turned, Ravlen again sure that they were turning back on themselves, and yet every hallway looked different.

"How do you move the walls?"

Oaken didn't turn around. He pounded forward in a thundering rhythm of steps. "This house has existed for a very long time. It's bedrooms, hallways, corners, and closets turn in undulating harmony with the worlds between them."

Ravlen felt like she was supposed to know what that meant. Something in this wing of the house was calling to her, like a home she once lived in. As she stepped deeper, she tried to place the sensation.

Could this have been my home with my mother? Is that why I feel like I know it? I'm sure I've never seen this place on the mainland, so that can't be it.

Paintings on the walls, faces and landscapes, and still images ignited memories at the core of her being, even though she was sure she'd never seen them before.

Oaken picked up his pace; Ravlen had to jog to keep up with him. He was down the hall and around the corner before her eyes saw him move ahead. She turned and he was gone, only an open door in front of her. She stepped through it.

Her foot caught on an invisible door jam and she skidded, dropping to her knee. When she righted herself, she turned around, looking in every direction, but she was in a grassy field with a single tree and the door she'd just walked through was gone.

"Where am I?"

"Welcome," Oaken appeared from behind the large oak tree. "You have just jumped your first echo presence. And you did it very well, I must say. Most echo masters do much worse than skin their knee."

23

"I did *what?*" Ravlen's mind ran a mile a minute, trying to figure out where she was and how to get back to the stately house where Marriel was waiting for her.

But the access point was gone, or at least it was invisible, and there was nothing she could do.

She had to depend on her father.

He crossed his arms and lifted his chin. "You said you wanted to know. There aren't enough words to explain to you what just happened, but you've experienced it yourself. This is the way echo masters have done it for generations."

Her jaw clenched, she shot daggers with her eyes. "Take me back."

"I will. Don't worry, daughter." His tone was sincere. "I have no intention of holding you anywhere you don't want to stay."

Ravlen felt like she could breathe again. She wasn't trapped, she just didn't know where she was. Her chest still felt tight. Too many unknowns. It was too different.

"Come out of the way now." Oaken gestured for her to join him. "Behind the tree is safer."

"Safer? There's no one here."

"Come *now*."

Ravlen obeyed. She reached the tree just in time, as a stampede of hooves resounded over the countryside. Voices bellowed, commanding the horses faster, driving them forward. Ravlen peeked around the tree as the creatures flew by, some towing chariots with men in armor holding swords, spears, and shields.

"Where are we?" Ravlen shouted over the thundering hooves and commanding voices.

"More like *when* are we – and the answer is ancient Rome."

"Who would wish for ancient Rome?" Ravlen peeked around the tree in time to see the last horses with their whip-cracking master go by. "And how did you know the horses were coming?"

"To answer your latter question, it's my job to know. To the former, the desires written on the human heart remain a mystery to me. My job isn't to tell them what to wish, just to make sure that it can be so."

"But *why?*"

At last, Ravlen was getting closer to knowing what was behind these worlds and the masters who moved within them. She tried to tame her impatience, to focus on the question. She'd have to recount every last detail to Dina. The origin of echoes was the holy grail of echo chaser intelligence.

"Why..." Oaken started to walk away from her. Ravlen quickened her pace to remain in step with him. "I can answer many questions, but I don't think that 'why' is one of them. Instead, let me explain what you're looking at. This is one of many echoes to which I am bound. I move between them, assuring their health, their stability, their viability. As much as I can, that is. There are some which seem to have been created only to die, and there is little I can do to preserve them."

Ravlen thought about the echo where she'd met Oliver and Clara, and the great big bubble that had lifted her into the sky.

"Humanity has greatness within its beating heart. The ability to overcome and persevere and create where there had been nothing. That is what breathes life into the worlds behind every door."

"The doors in the hallway?"

He ignored her question. "But when I open a door, there is nothing I can do to change the foundation of that world. I only add color. I mean that in the figurative sense. I am a servant to the place, bound to its trajectory as I am bound to my own immortality. And that is what allows me to love those who come through the haze as my own kin, even if I don't know who they are."

It was too much to digest. Ravlen tried to untangle the words, keep them as clear and crisp in her head as she could. So long she had yearned to know how this all worked, and now that she was being given the answers, she felt them slipping away like sand through her fingers.

"But the people…" If she could get back to her most basic question, she thought she might be able to hold more in. "Why do you lure people into the echo?"

Oaken's face fell. "I do no such thing. I can only represent what is within the echo world's invisible walls, the beauty and strength of the human spirit that they represent. It is always the choice of the earth-walker to come and then to go or stay. Don't you understand, Ravlen?" He met her gaze and held it. "I read the wishes that are written on their hearts."

His eyes churned with the gray of a great storm, and Ravlen believed him. At least, she believed that he believed what he said.

And for now, she was in another world with no way of getting back to Marriel. She had to trust him.

He took a step back, tilting his head and touching her cheek with the tenderness of the father Ravlen always wished she'd had.

"You want to go back."

"You can see the wishes in *my* heart, too?" The thought terrified Ravlen.

He smiled. "No. But you're not hard to read."

He led her to the edge of the field where the stately home stood. The exact same home, but in a completely different environment. She headed for the front of the house.

"Come around the back." Oaken pointed with his head. "Going through the front door might be confusing."

Confusing? Ravlen looked at the front door. *What happens if I go through there?*

"It's best that you get to know how things work before you find yourself in an uncomfortable situation."

He responded to her every question before she asked. Was she that easy to predict? Or did he have powers that he had not yet revealed? Ravlen vowed to be more veiled in her thoughts when she was around him.

He led her through a rickety old wooden door in the back of the house that delivered them directly into one of the many hallways they'd walked through before. From the inside, that same door was a lacquered dark wood, nothing like its appearance from the outside. They walked quietly now, Ravlen's mind overflowing. She figured they must be close to the salon where Marriel awaited them when Oaken stopped.

"This is just the beginning of your legacy. I know that what you've seen will keep you awake nights, even though it was only a glimpse of the many worlds behind these doors. It did the same to me. Let my words comfort you when questions arise that seem to have no answer. You know more of me than you think you do. In time you'll come to recognize it in yourself."

A growl followed by full-on barking reverberated down the hallways, and Ravlen knew exactly who was coming their way. Oaken sighed.

"After all this time, you'd think he'd recognize my scent."

Ravlen was about to ask what he meant when a furry blur flew through the air, catching her in the belly and knocking her backward. Her face was in the process of being licked to excess when Marriel called out.

"Binner? Where'd you go? Ravlen? Is that you?"

Ravlen sat up and wiped at her face. Marriel helped her up as Binner jumped at her sides, but Oaken was gone.

"Ravlen, you've got to see what's in this photo album. It's incredible."

"I'm sure it is."

"Where did the echo master go?"

Ravlen knew it was futile, but she looked up and down the hall anyway. "I have no idea."

RAVLEN HADN'T BEEN SURPRISED WHEN THE PHOTOS MARRIEL had seen in the album disappeared when she looked at it. Ravlen tried to explain to Marriel how the book operated, but Marriel was too upset to listen. Ravlen understood; she had been upset as well when she'd looked at it the previous year when the echo master had first shown it to her.

"My parents, I saw them. I swear it to you," Marriel said. "They were *there*. Now there's only spilled tea." Marriel slammed the photo album closed. "I wanted to show them to you. I have such good memories of them from the time before... before..."

She didn't have to finish her sentence. Ravlen knew Marriel's story because it was the same story of most of the girls on the island. Whole families that had found themselves in the grip of an echo, children who were separated from their parents but saved from the echo, and became wards of the island school under Madame's watchful eye.

Ravlen wanted to comfort her, but Marriel's grief was palpable. Ravlen knew too well that any words she could offer wouldn't begin to heal that wound. Only Marriel could do that.

She let Marriel stare at the page for another few minutes before delicately touching her shoulder.

"It's time to go."

Marriel nodded and walked out of the house. She sat on the front stoop. "I thought I'd dealt with all those old feelings. I thought I was done with them."

Binner nuzzled himself under her hand.

Ravlen twirled Marriel's hair between her fingers. "I get the sense that we are never done with them. They are part of our story. But it will get easier."

"How do you know that?"

Marriel couldn't hide her longing, her voice dripping with the need to be consoled. Even though Marriel was her overseer, right now it was Marriel who needed Ravlen.

"I've seen it in every echo." Ravlen looked back, but the house was dark now, as though there was no one inside. "People escaping what's hard, choosing an easy way out. But in the end, they don't stay in the echo because they want to, they stay because they've grown numb to real feelings." She sat beside Marriel, their shoulders brushing. The warmth exchanged between them was a timely comfort. "What you're feeling now is real. And that's why it hurts. Don't push it away."

"What do I do with it then?" Her voice was barely more

than a breath. "It sits so heavy in me. My past is like a block of concrete in the middle of my stomach. I bet I would drown if I fell in water, that's how heavy it is."

"It's there because this matters to you. And it's important to have memories of people and history and relationships that matter. You're not numb, Marriel. You've seen the stories that an echo will play out to make those feelings go away. You can defy it." Ravlen leaned in close. "You can welcome the feeling."

"Welcome it?"

"Don't push it away, but don't drown under it either. Welcome it because it comes from places and experiences that no one else in the world has except you. Those experiences are treasures, pearls threaded together to make up your whole life."

Marriel looked at the horizon, the garden of Ravlen's childhood just beyond the fence.

"Pearls. My life is a string of pearls..."

Bells rang in the distance.

Ravlen remembered the force of those bells in previous closures, no doubt their ringing would grow with time as the echo began to collapse. How long it would take for the echo to fall, she didn't know, but something was underway and they still had to find the originals, and the haze.

Marriel looked back at the house. "Can I bring the album?"

"Best that you don't."

"Yes, you're probably right. Do you hear those bells?"

"I do."

"I've got a bad feeling this place is going to close up on us soon."

"Me, too."

They left the stately home behind. The window shutters slammed shut, though Ravlen didn't see anyone pull them in.

They now faced the difficult decision of what to do first: find the originals or locate the exit.

Marriel marched ahead. "There's no point in finding the originals if we have nowhere to take them."

"You're right. Haze first." Ravlen looked at Binner. "And if you've got any ideas on where we find it, boy, I'm all ears."

Binner cocked his head with canine curiosity.

"That's what I thought. Let's start with the place my referent took us. There must be something more there. She wouldn't have taken us to a specific place with the mark of the haze on the ground if it hadn't meant something."

They wove through the streets, staying in the shadows, offering a simple hello when greeted by people who appeared to be living their normal routines. No one tried to intercept them. Binner woofed at a fellow mongrel, and Ravlen could have sworn the two held a conversation in rumbles while passing each other on the street.

"Here we are," Marriel stood on the very spot at the center of the haze markings, "and I still don't see anything. What are we missing?"

Ravlen walked over to stand with Marriel. The scribbles on the ground were a perfect copy of Dina's tattoo, but the paint on the asphalt was white. The tattoo was black, and the haze was a blend of all colors except black and white.

"It's the haze, but it's not *the* haze," Ravlen murmured. She touched the lines painted on the ground. "Marriel, what did we learn in science class about light?"

"Huh?"

Ravlen looked at her wrist. The white on the ground was now on her wrist.

It's not paint. It's light projecting onto us.

Ravlen looked up. "What did we learn about what happens when we mix colors of light?"

"When all colors come together, they make white light. But I really don't see…"

"That's what I thought. Look."

Marriel followed Ravlen's gaze. The haze was larger than any they'd seen before. That's how they missed it. From where they stood between buildings, it looked like the sky was clear. In fact, they were standing below the haze, its entry suspended in midair. The colors emanating from it blended to form its own white light projection.

Ravlen pointed. "It's facing the ground. We need a ladder."

"It's three stories up. We're not going to find a ladder that high, not without alerting the people of the echo to our plan."

"Let's find the originals. We can figure it out from there. Something will come to us."

"Wait, Rav. I don't think that's a good idea. If we round them up but can't get them out, then what?"

A bell tolled.

"We find the originals first. Time is ticking." Ravlen was already down the street, but she could hear Marriel shaking her head in that doubtful way she did.

"This isn't getting easier."

Fortunately, it did get easier.

The originals were a mother with three children who had all come in together and were ready to leave. There were dark circles under the mother's eyes. She had been fighting the numbing effect of the echo since they had arrived.

"Something in this place isn't right," she recounted, holding her three small children of equal height close. "I wanted us to turn around and head home, but then I couldn't find the way out."

"That's our fault," Marriel whispered to Ravlen.

Ravlen took the hand of one of the girls. "I'm sorry for that, but we're here and we'll help you."

"What about my kids?"

Two girls and a boy looked up with wide eyes at Ravlen. They weren't even of school-going age. Triplets with the same chin, same broad-set shoulders, and same piercing honey-colored eyes.

"We're all going together," Marriel reassured, leading the family forward.

They arrived at the spot between the buildings as the sky began to cloud over. The wind sent Ravlen's hair flying. The growing storm was the sign they had to get out and quick.

"Thank goodness for easy-leavers."

"But now what?" Marriel tried to hide the worry in her voice, but her arm shook as she pointed to the haze. "It's still hanging in midair."

"Let me think." Ravlen bumped her head with a fist as if trying to shake an idea loose.

"We don't have time."

"Then what do we do?" Ravlen asked. "We need a plan."

Marriel set her hands on her hips. "Could your plan include moving the haze?"

Binner barked. Marriel and Ravlen looked at him. His mouth was closed and for once, his tail wasn't wagging.

"Binner was the last one through the haze." Ravlen bent to be at the dog's height. "How did you do it, Binner? Did you just fall through?"

Binner jumped.

He jumped two stories in the air.

"That's it!" Ravlen clapped her hands. "We have to pulse. We can take a running jump and then force ourselves up higher, just enough to reach the haze!"

"I don't mean to burst your bubble, Ravlen, but that's three stories high. You might be able to pulse that high, but I can't, and certainly these originals won't get close."

"Maybe I could hold them, one at a time. Carry them up

with me." Ravlen assessed the height. It was far up, even for her, but they had to try.

Thunder cracked.

"Why is it closing?" Marriel cried out. "We didn't do anything to break the logic!"

"Maybe it was them," Ravlen looked at the mother. "Excuse me, did you say you've been fighting the effects of this place?"

"I sure have. And today someone offered to take our family in, to have us join their crazy compound of strange people who did nothing but smile. I didn't trust them for a second."

"You're the one who broke it." Marriel touched her shoulder. "You are a strong lady."

"Raising three kids by myself, I have no choice. Now, can we get out of here?"

Ravlen evaluated her trajectory. "I'm going to give it a shot. I'm going to jump higher than anyone you've ever seen, so don't be surprised."

"Don't worry about that." The mother hugged her children closer. "After what we've seen here, a leaping girl pales in comparison."

Ravlen prepared herself, seeking out that place from deep within, knowing she was demanding something new of the energy inside her.

I can do this. For sure I can. I just have to go farther than I have before.

She ran. She leaped.

"PULSE!"

She reached the second floor, softening her landing back on the white light of the haze below.

"Not bad." Marriel admired. "Try again."

She did, and she made it to two and a half floors, nearly reaching the haze.

"Again, Rav."

She did, and this time, Binner was beside her, flying through the air like it was the most natural thing for a dog to be three floors off the ground.

Ravlen landed awkwardly, her ankle twisting a little too far to the right. Marriel ran to her.

"You hurt yourself! Don't pretend you didn't, I saw you roll over it. What are we going to do now?"

Ravlen rubbed her ankle. It was her bad one, the one she'd hurt in her first echo. But she hardly noticed. She had an idea.

"Binner."

"What about Binner?"

Ravlen limped to the spot where Binner sat with his eyes turned up to the haze.

"Binner, can you reach the exit?" Ravlen pointed to the spot. "Go on, good boy." She put on her excited voice and the dog animated in return. Go on, show us what you can do!" She kept her finger pointed, so the dog had no question what she was asking from him.

Binner reversed a few steps and took the stance of a beast ready to pounce.

He launched himself. Up, up he went, reaching the first story of the building to the right. He re-launched himself off the wall and reached the second story of the building on his left.

"It's like he has suction cups on his feet." The mother gawked.

He flew, away and off the wall, grabbing at the edge of the haze with his strong jaws. He hung there, holding the light fabric as it stretched under his weight, lowering him a few feet.

"Good boy!"

"Look," Marriel leaned into Ravlen, "he's pulling the haze."

Little by little, a foot at a time, the side of the haze pulled downward as Binner tugged. The bells rang ominously. Too close. Thunder rolled.

"Good boy, Binner!" Ravlen cried out. "Bring it here, boy, bring it here!"

"Come." Marriel gathered the originals. "As soon as it is close enough, we'll have to climb in."

One of the children tapped Marriel's leg. "We won't fall?"

"You won't fall. Once we're in, it will twist us back to the right side up." Marriel glanced at Ravlen and mouthed, "I hope."

In they went, mother and children first, followed by Marriel. Ravlen pulled herself in, just to the edge, and looked back at Binner. There were new wrinkles around his eyes. She hadn't realized the effort it was taking him to hold the haze. And still, he didn't give up.

"Come, Binner," she choked up. "You're such a good boy. Extra treats for you tonight."

Binner waited until Ravlen was safely inside the haze before releasing it and launching himself in. Through the exit point below her, Ravlen could just make out the light turning dark in the echo world. Not daring a second look, she headed home with Binner at her side.

Under the covers, and with a flashlight, Ravlen read through the longest letter Daniel had ever sent her. The unmarked envelope had been on her bed when she and Marriel had arrived home.

It was, in fact, the *only* letter she'd ever received from him. He'd gone from a few scribbled words on the back of a postcard to a five-page epistle of everything going through his mind.

It was revealing and confusing all at once.

She re-read it for the third time even though her body was desperate for sleep. She fought her eyelids to focus on the adolescent boy scrawl.

"I don't know why I felt I couldn't tell you all of this before. A part of me thought you've become too important to care about what petty troubles or minor adventures I've had since I joined the boy's commune. But after the day I had yesterday, I know I was wrong to hold back."

Ravlen had gone through the letter backward and forward and couldn't find any hint of 'the day he'd had'.

Why couldn't he just tell me what happened 'yesterday'! Was it his first voyage into an echo? Did something bad happen to him or someone else?

She adjusted the flashlight so that it was nuzzled between her shoulder and chin. This way she could bring the letter closer, examine its meaning, the loops and slashes of rushed penmanship.

"You must have had these days, too. Days when you wonder how this came to be, and how it was us, of all people, who were cosmically selected to know the difference between the real and unreal. Don't you ever wonder what it would be like to not know any of it at all? What if we could be ignorant, living our lives like normal people? Having breakfast. Going to school. Learning to ride a skateboard. (I've decided to do that, by the way. You can say I'm trying to rebel, but I actually just want to do it.)"

She tried to imagine Daniel on a skateboard, but every scene ended with it flying out from under his feet and Ravlen rushing to tend to his wounds.

She read several paragraphs that covered the mundane daily life at the boy's commune. It sounded familiar. Most of their education, regulations, and schedules were the same as at the girls' encampment on the island. Whoever had set up the boys' curriculum had taken a page from Madame's book. Or did the boy's commune come first?

She knew so little about how everything came to be. Madame had only offered her a glimpse of the history behind their separate society. She'd spoken of times before the encampment had been in place, how girls like Ravlen had been ostracized, set aside for their talk of parallel worlds existing among the rest of civilization. Ravlen realized this was likely true for the boys as well.

Unlike Daniel, Ravlen had never considered why she'd been chosen to be separate from the rest of society. She'd only lamented that she was even *more* different from the others on the island. The way her emotions could overtake her rational mind. Memories that weren't her own. A sense of always being in more than one place at once and the instability that brought with it.

Now that her fourteenth birthday was on the horizon, Ravlen knew the path she had been given wasn't an easy one. But it was the only option she'd ever had. No, she didn't wonder why others could be ignorant to the happenings of the world around them. She only wondered one thing now.

How to put an end to it all.

She fell asleep with Daniel's letter clutched in her hand.

"Up and at 'em, Ravlen m'dear!" Tom's sing-song at the break of dawn intruded into Ravlen's consciousness, but wasn't quite enough to pull Ravlen all the way out of her half-awake state. A hundred different possibilities, ways to close echoes forever, had played out in her imagination all night long as she'd fluttered between stages of sleep.

Find echoes before they open.

Unlock the secret of established echoes.

Tap into the heart of the echo masters and change their will, their essence, their very...

"Up, up, up! The daaaaaay awaaaaaaits!"

Ravlen groaned. "I'm trying to think through something important here."

Tom crouched down beside her bed. "In the chaos of your adventures yesterday with Marriel, did you forget what's happening today?" He glanced at the letter in her hand. "Or did a certain young man whose name starts with a capital D invade your dreams, hmmm?"

Ravlen playfully threw her pillow at the face looming over her. "Quit it! What's today?"

"The school trip..."

"The fair!" Ravlen jumped out of the opposite side of the bed, tripping over her pajamas, and crashing into her closet door.

"Slow down there!" Tom delivered one of his big belly laughs. "No need to break a leg over it, you've got a solid… seven minutes before you have to leave to catch the bus."

"Seven minutes!" Ravlen became a flurry of activity.

She was the last one to join the line in front of the school, but she made it, barely. Greta was waiting for her.

"I thought you were going to miss it. And your shirt is on backward, by the way."

"Ack! Cover me." Still breathless, Ravlen tugged her arms out of the sleeves and twisted her shirt right-side-forward. "It was a hectic morning. What about *him*?" Ravlen tried to scan the bus, but she was too short to see inside properly.

"You mean 'C.D.'? He's already in there."

"Shoot. I thought we might be free of him for a day."

"Did you learn anything more about his prison history?"

Ravlen caught herself from saying more than she should. Greta was becoming a better friend and stronger ally than she'd expected, but that didn't mean Ravlen could – or should – share her secrets.

She thought of Daniel's letter, how lucky he thought some people were to not know anything about their missions, the dangers, and the wild ride that was the life of an echo chaser.

There are some things it's better Greta doesn't know.

"Nope." She shrugged as innocently as she could. "Not a thing."

Greta pulled Ravlen closer as they climbed the steps of the bus. "I got some intern."

"Intern?"

"Yeah, you know, internal information. About C.D."

"I think it's called *intel*."

"No, the expression is intern, because it's only for us to know." Her explanation made sense, even though Ravlen was sure it was wrong. Greta lowered her thick, wire rim glasses, looking at Ravlen over the top of them. "He lives with an uncle. A really rich, really sick uncle, so no one ever sees him. I wonder if C.D. poisoned him."

"Whoa, you just went from him being weird to being a murderer. That's a big jump."

"Just a little poison, you know? Enough to make the frail uncle sick, but not enough to do him over."

"Do him in."

"The expression is do him—"

"Never mind. Why would you think that?"

Ravlen reached the top of the stairs and immediately saw Christopher Duke sitting near the back of the bus on a bench by himself. No one else dared to sit beside him and he seemed perfectly content to be on his own. He raised his eyes, latching onto Ravlen's gaze.

"Look at his eyes, Ravlen. Those aren't the eyes of an eighth grader. He's done stuff. He's seen stuff. I just don't know what."

Greta and Ravlen couldn't get a seat together, being the last to board the bus, but they sat in adjacent aisle seats. Neither of them dared to speak about Christopher Duke, who was sitting only six rows away. Not that it mattered. If he was anything like Ravlen suspected, he'd probably heard everything they'd said anyway.

When they arrived at the fair, Christopher Duke stomped to the front before the bus came to a full stop. Miss Markham blocked the way.

"I appreciate your enthusiasm, Christopher, but no one moves until the bus is sufficiently parked." He glowered at her, but lowered himself to the edge of an occupied seat, ignoring the students who crowded together to avoid being sat on.

Miss Markham shook her head, then turned her attention back to the rest of the students. "Remember everyone, stay in groups of at least two at all times. Bus leaves sharply at three o'clock. Be there or be left behind – figuratively that is, I don't mean it. But I'll be ticked if I miss my yoga class because someone is having too much fun at ring toss."

Miss Markham winked at the busload of students, and Ravlen saw why Greta liked her so much. Her attitude toward Ravlen had completely changed since the conversation in the music room. Her words now were gentle and encouraging, vague enough that others wouldn't know what she meant, but Ravlen always got her point.

"Watch your step now, Christopher, and remember, in twos!" She then looked directly at Ravlen. "In *twos*, Ravlen. The fair is a great escape, but you never know what might happen."

The fair was a mix of traditional games and rides, with other unusual fixings like a video game center and performers working in the alleys between stands. There were people covered in paint who stood still as a statue, a snake charmer, a magician, and a contortionist dressed in a shimmery blue-green skintight cat suit.

"Check it out. Candy floss!" Greta rushed for the food stands, so Ravlen followed, but the contortionist had caught her attention.

The way she moves, it's animal-like. Maybe she's just really well trained? Or could she be...

Ravlen shook her head.

I can't start seeing signs of the echo everywhere, I'll go crazy. She's just a contortionist. They're supposed to look super weird.

"Want some?" Greta dove face-first into the pink cloud.

"I can see you're enjoying your first minutes at the fair." Miss Markham walked alongside them.

Greta's stained-pink nose emerged from the fluffy cloud. "I love this stuff."

"Me, too. When I was a girl…" Miss Markham led Greta down a laneway of games a few paces ahead of Ravlen. Mr. Costello, Mrs. Brand, and Mr. Johansson fell into step with Ravlen.

"We missed you at school yesterday." Mr. Costello looked around to see if anyone was listening. "We thought that you might have been… busy."

"I was… busy. It was a more complicated assignment than I had expected."

"That was my guess," Mrs. Brand said. She added, "Didn't I say that, Ron?"

Mr. Johannsen stepped closer to Ravlen, ignoring Mrs. Brand's question. "We did some research. There is little to no paper trail on your… *classmate*." Ravlen looked around but she didn't see Christopher Duke anywhere. "He appeared out of thin air, and someone found a loophole to get him into the school system without an official guardian, though an uncle is mentioned in the paperwork."

"None of us have ever seen this uncle." Mrs. Brand crossed her arms and raised her eyebrows with righteous suspicion.

"You really should speak lower," Ravlen whispered. "You underestimate what he might be capable of."

"A slip-in. That's what he is." Mr. Costello hissed. "Don't look at me like that, Ron. I know a slip-in when I see one and it's time we called a spade, a spade. No more tiptoeing around like he's just a troubled kid. He's troubled alright, because he is in the wrong place, the wrong world!"

"I'm serious," Ravlen hissed again. "You've got to lower your voices!"

Even though all signs pointed to Christopher Duke being a slip-in, Ravlen couldn't help wondering. She knew there was more to him than just a relocated echo person roaming the halls of their middle school.

How can I tell the teachers without setting them off? Mrs. Brand is so high strung, she might go find Christopher Duke and let the cat out of the bag.

Mrs. Brand took a step and then searched left and right as if a tiger might jump out and attack her at any second.

"What have you seen, Ravlen?" Mr. Johannsen walked close to her but kept enough space that they didn't look strange, a teacher and student whispering in the middle of a fair.

"I don't want to jump to conclusions, but I think he might be more powerful than your average slip-in."

Mr. Johannsen leaned in so only Ravlen could hear. "Echo master?"

Ravlen shrugged.

He tapped her shoulder. "I see why you're hesitating. Hey, Eleanor, why don't you go see if anything is happening down that alley to the right, in case there's something untoward underway."

"Oh my, yes, I'll check."

"I'm coming with you." Mr. Costello hurried to catch up to her.

"What can you tell me?" Mr. Johannsen directed Ravlen to the side of a water pistol game, where they could be seen, but not heard.

"I learned a lot yesterday, and I'm still trying to piece it all together. Here's the thing," she spoke slowly, in case the revelation shocked Mr. Johannsen. "Echo masters run many echoes at once and can move between them."

Mr. Johannsen didn't react.

"Did you hear me?"

"Yes, but I already knew that."

Ravlen's jaw dropped. "You knew that, and you didn't tell me?"

"I thought you knew it, too."

"What else have you been keeping from me?" Ravlen's temper rose.

"Quiet down now. I haven't kept anything. Given all you know, I thought this was self-evident."

Ravlen bit her tongue. "All right. Tell me everything you know about echo masters."

Mr. Johannsen scratched his lip. "Echo mastery isn't a permanent state."

"Huh?"

"They can join the real world, live among us like anyone else. If they choose to."

"They can *do* that?"

"It happened to the echo I was in. A new leader took over, explaining the unfortunate migration of the former president back to a sad land. After returning and talking with the others, we pieced together that both echo masters and slip-ins can move seamlessly through both types of worlds. But the conscious choice to leave echo mastery means relinquishing the power that comes with it."

"Whoa."

This gave a whole new dimension to the echo masters. She'd learned on the island that slip-ins often joined the real world with the purpose of changing it to fit their own vision. And she knew echo people were the reflection of real people. She'd heard of 'doppelgangers' before. A slip-in who decided to remain permanently in the real world would be exactly that. A perfect replica of an original.

But echo masters were supposed to keep echoes alive, not leave them behind. They were servants, like Claire had heard them say.

"What else do you know?" Ravlen was hungry for knowledge now. If only she'd thought to ask Mr. Johannsen sooner. Maybe he had the answer to who, or what, Christopher Duke was.

Mr. Johannsen thought about it and then shouted, "Down from there, Carl! I see you climbing the roller coaster grid. Not happening. If you do it again, I'm sending you back on the bus right away." He sighed. "Where were we?"

"More information on the echo masters."

"Oh yes. When they enter into the real world from a new echo, they have to learn the language, just like slip-ins. There's a language barrier when they come through the haze from a new echo, even if they've spoken that language before."

"Yes, I know." That wasn't entirely true. She knew most of that, having witnessed it when Oaken arrived at the pond. She didn't know it happened every time they came into the real world.

"In that case, the only other information that I know, which might be useful, is that like royalty, echo masters follow a lineage."

"So only children of echo masters can become one?"

"I'm not sure it's that straightforward, but I know there's some kind of connection. It may be that echo masters can convert someone into their ranks, or change their blood to adapt to the echo world."

"Like a vampire? Yikes."

"I don't think it's like that, but the truth is I don't really know," Mr. Johannsen said. "I've pieced this together through stories from people who have returned and the other teachers. It's not scientifically proven."

That almost made Ravlen laugh. She tried to imagine doing science experiments on her echo master father. Sprinkling him with baking soda and vinegar to see what would happen. The vision was almost domestic, a twist on the family scene she'd always imagined.

But her daydream was swiftly interrupted by Mrs. Brand's near-breathless arrival.

"Come, quick. I can't find Christopher Duke anywhere."

Mr. Johannsen joined the others, leaving Ravlen on her own by the water pistols. She set out to find Greta, but on her first turn, she was standing directly in front of the blue-green contortionist whose legs were flipped backward over her shoulders.

How does the human body do that? It looks painful. And unnatural. But I can't stop watching...

The woman danced, her feet light as she twisted limbs in opposite directions and turned her body more than a hundred and eighty degrees while keeping her feet in place.

The crowd around her swayed, captivated and silent.

"Imagine if we could do that," someone behind her whispered.

"It's like she's from another world."

It's not just me who thinks she's more than human. That's a relief.

But Ravlen's relief was short-lived. The woman bent forward, and though her jumpsuit ran the full length of her body from ankle to the base of her neck, the collar pulled down a touch, revealing the top of her spine.

It shimmered.

slip-in.

Ravlen couldn't move. She watched the woman's body fold on itself, the human form evolving into new shapes, the iridescence of her costume rolling like waves catching sunshine. Ravlen felt at once blinded and hyper-conscious.

She's so beautiful, she's captivated everyone who walks past. And yet they don't know the truth.

The woman shifted her eyes, saw Ravlen watching her.

She isn't real.

The contortionist's gaze was hardened, that of a combatant more than an entertainer. A shiver ran through Ravlen, but she wouldn't break her stare. The woman smirked as though secretly amused. She balanced herself on one hand, her legs stretched out straight in front of her, while her other hand reached out, beckoning Ravlen forward with her finger.

"She's calling you," a woman behind Ravlen said. "You have to go."

"Go on," another bystander coaxed.

Ravlen approached the woman, who was shifting positions. As she twisted, pointing her legs upward, she gestured with her free hand for Ravlen to come even closer. Ravlen swallowed hard and did so.

"Hasswanuwa?" the inverted woman asked with big blue eyes and an innocent expression. Anyone else would think she was speaking a different language, but Ravlen knew better.

A new slip-in, her language was still being formed. She started with the first word that they all began with, the same one that her father had uttered at the pond's edge. The word sounded something between foreign and nonsense, but Ravlen knew its meaning.

Have what you want.

Ravlen kept a straight face. "Who do you take me for?" she hissed. "I know who you are. I know *what* you are."

She was shaking inside, but her voice didn't waver.

The woman's face changed. She slowly lowered her feet to retake a normal standing position. After so many minutes of seeing her twisted into geometric shapes, Ravlen found it strange to see her standing as any other woman, on her own two feet with her arms dangling at her sides. She wasn't much taller than Ravlen.

Her face twisted into an odd smile, one that cajoled while it taunted, as though she wasn't sure what Ravlen wanted. Her lips moved silently for a moment before her next word came out in a breathy whisper.

"Adventure?"

It was an offer. Her eyebrows rose and her wide smile broke into a hysterical laugh.

"More!" someone from the crowd shouted. "Don't stop now!"

"You're wonderful!" another joined in. "Please continue!"

"We need more!"

Ravlen looked at the crowd, whose heads were tilted in the way of the people who had been touched in the echo. They were more than captivated; they were under her spell.

But it's not magic. She's using her own body to allure them.

The woman strode, her gait like a horse, her legs stretching out in front of her before she transferred her weight. The woman was new to the original world, but not new to her craft of aerobatics and contortions. Ravlen watched her every move, the way she lifted her finger and every person in the audience looked up. Meanwhile, the woman looked back at Ravlen.

"Adventure? Now."

She twisted herself into a tiny ball on the ground.

What on earth is she doing? Inviting me to adventure and then curling up like a snail?

But then the woman burst up and out, her body retaking its shape as she flipped and somersaulted through the crowd. The crowd parted for her, applauding with cheers of "Bravo!" and "Encore!" as she moved through them.

Ravlen followed at a run.

She had to catch up with her. Already the woman was an alley ahead of her, maneuvering herself between and around stands.

Ravlen lost sight of her. She'd lost the teachers. She'd lost Greta.

The sun beat down on Ravlen's sweaty forehead as she came to a stop. She closed her eyes and listened. She wasn't going to find the woman by running. She wasn't fast or agile enough. But she could hear better than anyone she knew.

Quiet, my heart. Slow your beating so I can listen.

She took a deep, trained breath, calming the rush of blood through her veins. She listened.

Conversations, trivial. Car rides and games and hamburgers. A mother shouting at a child. A teacher scolding.

Then she heard low voices, whispering in a corner. A voice she recognized right away.

Christopher Duke.

He wasn't far. And though his words were few, they were sharp and accusing.

"No," he hissed. "Your ways don't work with me. I'm not going, and you can't make me. Pass that message along."

"Ravlen?" Miss Markham's voice interrupted her. The teacher stood beside Ravlen, their arms brushing. Ravlen took a step away, the heat of her touch too distracting.

"Don't talk, Miss M. I have to focus."

"I'm so sick of this chase," Christopher was saying. "Leave me alone!"

"Shhhh," the other voice hushed and then replied to him in tones too low even for Ravlen to hear.

"Is it Christopher? What's happening?" Mr. Johannsen joined Ravlen's side.

"That's what I'm trying to find out!" Ravlen snapped. "Hush!"

Christopher laughed. "Just try it. I dare you," he said to the unseen offender.

Ravlen walked forward, following the sound, knowing the teachers were following her.

"Give me some space," Ravlen told them, lifting her hand. "I need to ask him some questions, and he won't talk if you're hanging over us."

"We'll stay a few paces behind. But we're here, Ravlen. And we won't hesitate to intervene if we must."

"Fine. But stay out of sight."

They were just around the next corner. Ravlen steeled her nerves, then made the last turn.

Before her stood Christopher Duke and the contortionist slip-in. Their heads snapped to her. The three stood in a triangle of silence charged with fury and confusion.

"You again?" Christopher's words came out in a half-growl.

The woman inhaled, sucking in air loudly through her nostrils as she flashed Ravlen eyes full of enchantment. "Come! The invitation…"

Without finishing, the woman ran.

Christopher raised his hand to stop Ravlen. "Don't do it. Why will no one listen to me? Don't do it, don't run after her. She's—"

"I know what she is. And I know what you are, too!"

She ran after the woman.

She didn't even make it to the next alley. Christopher tackled her, knocking her to the ground. He flipped her over and sat on her chest.

"You're not going. You can't. You'll ruin everything."

"Get off of me!"

"Promise you won't run."

"I won't promise you anything."

"Then I'm not getting off. You've gone too far this time. I know what's through there. You don't."

"I sure do. Don't you try to tell me any different, you *slip-in*."

The words hit Christopher like a slap in the face. He sat back, his black jeans and black t-shirt with chains hanging off jingled as he moved. Ravlen struggled to get out from under him, but he was much bigger than her.

Christopher regained his composure and leaned forward, pinning her hands to the ground.

"Why don't you listen to me? You're like all the rest, hell-bent on some mission when really you're all being used. You call me slip-in. What do you know? You run around left and right, but do you know what these echo masters are capable of? When you rush through those other worlds, your actions don't only have an effect on that one place. Or did you know that already? From the look on your face, I'm guessing not."

"I've been to a lot of echoes."

"Not as many as me. And not from my point of view." He snorted. "'Slip-in.' Who's sending a child like you into these jungles? Didn't your referent warn you?"

Ravlen eagerly sought through her memories. She didn't know what her referent was supposed to have warned her about, but wasn't about to say that to Christopher Duke.

"I've got to go in there. People might be at risk – their lives are on the line. Don't you get *that*? I do this for them."

"If that's what you think, then you really have to change your tactics, kid." He pressed harder against her wrists.

"You're in my class, bozo. Don't call me a kid. I have to do what I've been created to do, and find anyone who might be stuck in that bendy lady's world. Now get off me before I scream and they throw you in jail again."

"What do you mean, again?"

Ravlen didn't have a chance to answer, before a voice called out, over the sound of footsteps hurtling in their direction.

"GET OFF OF HER, YOU MISCREANT!"

Ravlen barely made out the transformed, furious face of Miss Markham as she leapt, flying through the air on a collision course with Christopher Duke. She took him out at the shoulders, knocking him several feet to the side, the two of them rolling as Ravlen lay, stunned, trying to make out what had just happened.

"Run, Ravlen!" Miss Markham shouted.

Mr. Johannsen appeared and helped pin Christopher down. The lanky boy fought, legs kicking and body bucking.

"You're walking straight into the lion's lair!" he cried from the ground, his eyes on Ravlen. "I'm not what you think!"

"Ravlen, *run!*" Miss Markham shouted again.

Ravlen ran.

Christopher's voice faded as she tore through the fair, seeking out the slip-in woman, but his words stayed with her as she went.

"You've got it all wrong. You're only going to make it worse."

She tried to shake it off, to ignore the repeated warning but it wouldn't leave her.

"You're only going to make it worse..."

She skidded around the coin flip game, the water pistol horse race, and the fortune teller until she reached the back of the fairgrounds, the place where the trucks parked and the shine of the fair was left behind.

A swatch of blue-green shimmered as it wove between trailers.

"Adventure," the woman whispered.

Ravlen followed the sound of her breath.

In the few trees behind the trucks, the woman only half-hid, clearly having every intention of letting Ravlen find her. When she saw Ravlen following, she spun and walked deeper into the small woods. Ravlen kept her distance.

Ravlen's skin was prickling from head to toe. She didn't need the woman to lead her forward. The way was clear.

The woman dove into the haze, unconcerned about what would be on the other side. Ravlen was not so quick to leap. She had learned that lesson. As she set her first foot through the swirl of colored light, Christopher's voice rang in her ears.

"You're only going to make it worse..."

Ravlen took the next step. She didn't have a choice. And she wasn't about to trust Christopher Duke. Not for a second.

She landed in the dark, on sand. Heavy packed sand, not like the sand of the Atlantic beaches behind Joan and Tom's place, and not the white sands of the island. This was dark, moist, and heavy.

A single spotlight turned on with a whoosh, the sound of electrics hissing in the air. The light blinded her, but she could hear breathing amongst the heartbeats around her.

There are people here. Lots and lots of people. Hiding in the dark. Why? What is going on in this place?

Ravlen shielded her eyes, but with the others still in the shadows, the impressions she picked up from her senses blended.

Whispering, tense breath and tapping feet. Heavy steps on the sand, a cage rattling. I'm surrounded by sounds and the smell of... of fur? Of straw and raw meat.

Speakers came alive around her, someone tapping on a microphone.

"Ladies and gentlemen! You have seen wonders from around the world, the 'ooohs' and 'ahhhhs' that have traversed time and space to delight your eyes and feed your weary souls. Acrobats dangled above your heads from ropes of spider-silk, the flames licked at the limbs of the bravest, and now... now, ladies and gentlemen, we move from civilized to savage, from tame to wild, from beauty to beast!"

I have a really bad feeling about this.

"Only in the face of death can the true meaning of life be cast in the light!"

More lights turned on, spotlights that blinded Ravlen in every direction she turned.

The audience gasped.

Where am I? Is this indoors? I can't pulse without seeing where I'm headed. I'll leap into a wall... or off a cliff!

Ravlen crouched, her body at the ready, but without seeing the limits of her location, she did not have many options.

"What wonders of life might this child share with us when she looks into the eyes of death? Release the beast!"

Heavy footsteps headed in her direction as the voices of thousands of spectators rumbled around her. She was breathing too fast, on the cusp of hyperventilating, fear paralyzing her limbs. She blinked, relieved that her eyes still followed her instruction. She needed them more than anything right now.

Into the light strode the largest tiger Ravlen had ever seen. The size of a car, its crystal eyes latched onto her, its steps sure and steady while Ravlen trembled. In a few steps, it stood only inches away, hot breath from its nose steaming Ravlen's t-shirt.

The tiger opened its jaws, revealing sharp white teeth as shiny as new daggers. As Ravlen's knees shook, it let out a roar that reverberated against Ravlen's collarbone.

"What will the child do, ladies and gentlemen? What secrets will she tell in the face of violent death?"

R avlen stared down the throat of the beast. In the blaze of the spotlight, she could count its teeth.

What's the logic? I've got to break it, and fast!

"Only when we face our own demise do we see the truth of our souls," the voice carried on. "This moment will be the greatest in this child's life. Or else it will be her last… which will it be ladies and gentlemen? Can you show her some support?"

Deafening applause surrounded Ravlen, making it impossible for her to think.

The echo wants me to be happy... someone wished for this. Someone wished to face death in order to find truth... there must be something in that, but what?

The tiger exhaled, sending Ravlen's hair straight out behind her. The audience gasped.

"The big moment is coming. Watch the animal's movements. He has not been fed for days. Tender, young meat is a great temptation to him."

Ravlen heard the tiger's heartbeat racing, but she'd never tried to understand the emotions of a wild animal before. He lowered his head coming eye to eye with her. The audience was going crazy.

"Look at what it's doing. It's staring her in the eye!" He paused for dramatic effect. "Intimidating his meal before he takes his first bite. Will the girl escape?"

The crowd noise dropped to a low murmur. From somewhere nearby, Ravlen heard a child's voice cry out.

"Daddy, look! She's just standing there! Why doesn't she move?"

"Let this be a lesson to you, my girl," a man's voice replied. He spoke in soothing tones, calming the child, but it seemed to Ravlen as though he was speaking as much to her as to the child. "When the time comes, do what must be done."

Do what must be done. Ravlen rolled the thought over as the tiger tilted his head. A stream of drool dripped from his mouth. *Do what must be done.*

But she didn't know what that was. She needed more time, but as the gleaming white teeth inched closer, time was the one thing she did not have.

If this echo was built out of someone's desires, then at its core is something someone wants. To change their life. Or is it to change someone else's life?

"Ladies and gentlemen, watch closely now – the deciding moment is nearly upon us."

Ravlen thought back to the established echo where the man was attached to a tree. An echo where the desire was to make someone suffer, to hold them to account for the terrible things they had done.

Human desires were not always altruistic.

Is this for people who have wasted their lives, who need to face death to start living? Or is this to teach a lesson to people who haven't learned to appreciate their lives?

The tiger circled her now, moist breath brushing past her legs, her arms, her neck.

She didn't have time. She felt it running out in front of her.

"Why doesn't she *do* anything?" a voice cried from the audience.

"She has to *do* something!"

Do something. Is that the message? Don't be a victim waiting for a tiger to eat you, do something?

Again, the tiger faced her. The crystal shards of color caught the light and nearly blinded Ravlen.

I have to do something!

Her hands shook. Her knees would give out on her any second now.

The tiger roared, the sound shaking the clothes on her body, filling the massive tent. Ravlen's ears rang. She clutched at them but kept her eyes firmly on the beast.

"Now!" the voice on the microphone shouted. The tiger obeyed. He pulled back on his haunches, opened his jaws in a wide roar, and pounced toward Ravlen.

There was no time to think about tapping into the place of energy. Ravlen reacted on pure instinct. She thrust her arms out, the cry flying from her lips.

"PULSE!"

The phantom, a black and white ghost of the tiger, hovered, frozen, directly over her head.

Ravlen's chest heaved from the intensity of the moment. So close to death, but she had done something. She'd pulsed, but what now? If she released the pulse, the tiger would devour her whole.

A slow clap from a single pair of hands resounded through the non-space of the former circus tent.

"Took you longer than I might have expected, on all counts."

The man was dressed in tight black pants, high shiny boots, and a red coat with tails. His top hat tilted left but he straightened it with gloved hands.

"What are you talking about?" Ravlen barely glanced his way. She didn't dare release the pulse.

He pursed his lips, his head swaying side to side. "Some give in to their fear right away, and the tiger slinks off. Others fight the beast and win. But you? You had to see it through to the very end. He is a direct reflection of your will." He gestured to the form suspended in midair. "And from the looks of it, your will is iron clad."

"What would have happened if I hadn't pulsed?"

"Let's not imagine that, hmm?"

Ravlen knew who she was talking to. She adjusted her body and began the gentle release of the pulse, enough so that she could carry on a conversation but not so much that the tiger would come tumbling down on her head. "Ringmaster. Not a very subtle guise for an echo master."

He shrugged. "We each have our personal fixations. I always loved the circus."

He led her to the entry of the tent, the tiger still suspended over the empty sand, though without Ravlen's intentional hold, it wouldn't last long.

She surveyed the space around them. Other circus tents rose in the distance with echo people moving between them like phantoms through molasses. She thought she saw the form of an original, but too far away to be sure. "This place is huge."

"It's been around for a long time, so it rarely needs my intervention anymore. We've had some long-term residents."

Originals. I have to find them.

"I see that look on your face. Don't even bother. It's been years. She won't go."

She? He said residents in plural, but now it's only she...

"As for you," he continued, tapping his circus cane on the ground, "the logic of this echo is strong. Time has that effect.

It irons out the kinks, creates powerful bonds between the logics of desire. Come, step over here, and then release this silly pulse. It's giving me a headache."

"But the tiger—"

"Don't worry about him. His moment has passed, just like your will to face him. He'll be sweet as a kitten."

Ravlen narrowed her eyes. She didn't trust him, but based on all she knew from previous pulses, he was probably telling the truth. *Probably.*

She let her arms drift gently to her sides. Winding up like a toy, the echo world retook its shape, color dancing like paint across the black and white expanse. The circus became a circus again, and the people within moved on. She watched the ring closely, in case the echo master had been lying and the tiger was coming for her.

The tiger dropped to the sand, landing on its four feet. He looked at Ravlen with black eyes, which filled in with emerald green as she held his stare. Then he blinked, licked his paw, wiped his face, and walked away from the circus ring.

"I told you." The echo master winked. "Now follow me. I think it's best you see things from a different perspective."

They burst into the main square of the circus, night having descended. The place wasn't so different from the fair she'd been at just minutes earlier. The audience filed out of the tent declaring, "Wasn't that wonderful?" and "What a treat!"

The contortionist was in the middle of a laneway, high up on a stand that was carefully balanced below. She was folded in three but managed to wave to Ravlen.

"I had a feeling Azizi would be successful out there. She has a way with people, wouldn't you say?"

"You sent her for me?" There were moving pieces to this

echo master's story, and Ravlen couldn't keep up. Why would this echo master want her in his world?

"No, not you."

Not me, but someone. Someone specific from the sounds of it.

Ravlen swallowed, trying to hide what she'd just figured out.

It's Christopher. He wanted Christopher.

"If you are who you say you are," Ravlen said, hoping he would take the bait, "then my father might have something to say about this."

"Oaken? Please. He should have kept a better eye on you from the start. It's one thing when children run off on their own accord. It's another to let them be taken from you."

"He didn't want me to be taken."

"No? That's what he says, but any alternative explanation would have been punished, so what would he ever say to the contrary? Don't go in there," he interrupted himself to point at a tent. "Not unless you want to be lost in the labyrinth of time and space, exposed to every whim of human desire."

It took her a moment to realize what he was talking about. "This tent is where you move between echoes?"

"I prefer to call it home."

The tent was mid-size, nothing like the mansion in which her father lived. "But it's so small. There are no doors."

He waved his hand dismissively. "Doors are overrated. Curtains work just fine and take up less space. But don't try telling that to Oaken. Him and his taste for the refined." He rolled his eyes. "Puts a bad image on us all, but he always was above the law."

"What law?"

"More like 'who's law'."

Ravlen sighed. Every bit of information he gave was shrouded. "Okay, who's law?"

His eye took a glint. "That's the great question of life, isn't it?"

Ravlen sighed again. Always riddles. Whether it was her father, or her referent, or now this echo master. She'd try another angle.

"How many of you are there, out there, managing these worlds?"

"Enough of us."

"I had a feeling you were going to say that. And I bet if I ask you what your name is, you're going say, 'whatever you want it to be'."

He laughed. "I've been called many things throughout the ages. And yet, the one name I am most deserving of is the one I hear the least."

"Which one is that?"

Footsteps approached behind Ravlen.

"Hello, Father."

Ravlen whipped around. Christopher Duke stood with his hands on his hips and his piercing eyes set on the echo master.

"Christopher?" Ravlen felt the anxiety of their changed dynamic. They were two. She was only one. If they ganged up on her, she wouldn't stand a chance.

He didn't look at her, instead his eyes remained fixed on the man he'd called father.

The echo master smiled. "Good to see you, son. I'd been hoping you would visit. So, you're calling yourself Christopher now?"

"Don't play dumb. I know you sent your pretzel-twisting crony to the fair."

"The fair seemed the best chance to catch you. She wouldn't have fit in well at the middle school, don't you think?"

Christopher's lips were tense. "I don't know why you

didn't listen to me last time. I don't want to be here. I've said it over and over. Why won't you just let it go?"

"Because I don't believe you."

"Don't believe me? What's not to believe? You act as if you know better when you've never made a single effort to find out what I want."

Ravlen looked back and forth like watching a ping pong game. They were equally set in stance, in the intensity of their gaze, and in the sharpness of their tone.

The echo master pointed his finger. "Nobody walks away from the opportunity you were lucky enough to be born into."

Christopher took a step closer. "*I* did. And you can't do anything about it."

The echo master stepped closer. Ravlen was nearly sandwiched between them, though they seemed to have forgotten she was there.

"I'm your father."

"You're a fraud. Ever since you threw me into the training with the others, you couldn't care less about what I wanted. As long as I didn't embarrass you while serving among the other sons."

Serving among others. Is he one of the prince-servants that Alison and Claire talked about?

Christopher's face grew red. "This was never about you and me. It was about keeping this vicious cycle going. Well, father, I'm stepping out of it."

"Just because you can't understand the value of what we've been doing since the dawn of time…"

"Just because it's been done for a long time doesn't make it right."

"Right, wrong, good, bad, black, white." The echo master paced, waving his hands in the air. "Not that tired argument again. A circle has no ends. That's all this world is, a circle that turns itself round and round—"

"I'm going to stop you there, dear old dad, I'm not here for a lesson in metaphysics. You clearly have misunderstood the purpose of my visit today." Christopher turned to Ravlen. "Come on, Ravlen. We have to go."

Ravlen had felt invisible during the verbal chess match and now she was being tossed into the middle of it. And worse, by the boy who had tormented her for months.

"Me? After everything you've put me through, you think I'd trust you for a second? No way, I'm not going anywhere with you."

Christopher rubbed his forehead the way a parent did when handling a belligerent child.

"You heard the girl," the echo master piped up. "She's not going anywhere with you. Best you stay with me, Ravlen. Your father would prefer that."

"Trust me or don't," Christopher hissed into her face. "But I can tell you that you'd be better off trusting me than that weaselly, manipulative, power-hungry immortal."

Immortal. Of course! That's how my father has been around for generations. And Christopher Duke is an echo master's son, not just a regular slip-in. I knew it. If he's an echo master's son, then he's immortal, too. But wait... I'm the daughter of an echo master...

Christopher laid his hand gently on her arm, effectively wiping every thought from her mind with an electric touch. He lowered his voice and spoke with a gentleness she'd never thought him capable of.

"I'll explain everything to you. I promise. But we have to go. Please."

Ravlen looked at the echo master, a smug grin on his face. Her heart was sure that he was not on her side. Echo masters were singular in their goals, and Ravlen's mission was the exact opposite of everything they stood for.

But go with Christopher Duke? Am I crazy to even consider it?

"Look here, girl," the echo master goaded, leaning in close enough that Ravlen could smell his rancid breath. "Try what you might, the story will always end the same way. Where one world closes, another may open. It is the natural order of things. It's you who is against the ways of the world. Consider that as you run around trying to *break logic.*" He mockingly fluttered his hand in the air.

Where one closes, another may open. Those are the exact words of my referent.

Ravlen looked around her. Could her referent be nearby? Could she offer the insight Ravlen needed to decide what to do next?

Christopher's turbulent gray eyes implored her, and her referent was nowhere to be found. She was between a rock and a hard place, and she had to make a choice. Going with the echo master wasn't an option.

She reached out her quivering hand to the boy she'd known as Christopher.

He took it.

The next moment they were running, leaping, hurtling through the vast expanse as the circus sang out around them.

Ravlen pushed through pulses to keep up with Christopher. He gripped her hand tightly, but his legs were longer and he was more adept than her at shifting the fabric of the ground.

She'd never felt so much like a novice.

Then again, she'd never been in the presence of someone more capable than she was of navigating metaphysics.

"Stop," Ravlen dared to whisper. "We need to talk."

Still, he pulled her forward.

"Christopher, you have to stop."

"We aren't in a safe place yet, he can still hear us. Sometimes I wonder if he can hear my thoughts. Genetics and mysticism combined can be a real pain in the neck."

So she let him drag her, doing everything she could to match his pace. But eventually she couldn't take it any longer. She released his hand.

"Stop!"

He did, whirling on her and speaking through clenched teeth. "I'm not sure you understand the kind of danger we're in here."

"I understand perfectly well the danger I'm in by continuing ahead with you."

"I'm not the enemy."

"I'm not convinced that's true." She crossed her arms and assumed the stance Marriel had taken, her feet wide and her spine tall. "We're far enough now for you to explain yourself."

He let out a clipped sigh. "What do you want to know?"

"Who are you?"

"Christopher Duke, eighth grader in the dullest middle school on the east coast."

"Lies." She knew he was using a false name. She knew he had associations with the echoes, and she wouldn't let him treat her like an idiot. "Let's start with this. What's your real name?"

He visibly weighed his options, then his shoulders relaxed. "My birth name is Meridian. Can we go now?"

It was the first time anyone had given her a straight answer. She wasn't going to stop now.

"Are you an echo master?"

"I was supposed to be." He shifted his weight. "That's what sons of echo masters do."

"You take his place?"

"No."

Ravlen pointed her finger in his face. "I'm not sure if you've noticed the kind of day I've had. I chased a slip-in, was tackled by you, nearly eaten by a tiger, and confronted a new echo master. I've been spoken to in riddles all year long, and I'm sick of it. I'm going to ask you direct questions and you're going to give me direct answers, or else I promise I'll do everything I can to make this as difficult for you as possible."

She stared at him and he stared back, but ultimately he wasn't going to win and he knew it.

"I don't take his place. I was to take the place of one who defected."

"Echo masters defect?" She remembered what Mr. Johannsen had said about them joining the real world.

"They do, but not easily and not without consequence."

"Namely?"

"Joining the real world comes with one sacred rule."

A long pause passed between them as Ravlen waited for him to reveal the sacred rule. She wasn't going to beg him for it. She lifted her chin even higher.

Christopher softened, his voice barely above a whisper. "Death."

"Echo masters die in the real world?" She tried to make sense of this. Her father had come to the real world, so did the slip-ins, and they didn't die.

"Everyone dies in the real world, Ravlen. It's the only thing certain in life. When they make the choice to abandon their echoes, when they defect, they lose their immortality." Christopher took her arm, firmly but without force. "I can't stay here, Ravlen. My every move is tracked."

"And I can't go until I understand its logic."

"You intend to shut it down?"

"That's what I do."

Christopher released her and rubbed his head. "It's futile, don't you get that? You close this echo down, another one opens. Just like my father said. Only then it's worse because you don't know where it is or who might be sucked into it. I've been trying to tell you this all along, but you won't let it sink into your hard head. *You're not helping*. You're making everything worse!"

"You're only saying that because you're an echo master yourself!"

"I'm *not* like them," he spat out. "I've always known what lies at the heart of echo mastery, especially at this level."

"At this level?"

"It's selfishness. A selfish desire to live in the greatest of circumstances. To rule one's own independent kingdom. The echo masters are bottom feeders, the catfish of the double universe. They wouldn't dare to make the sacrifices of those at the top of the food chain. They willingly sacrifice their own offspring under the auspices of heritage, when it's really out of their own desire to advance."

Ravlen was completely lost. She tried to hold onto the many threads that Christopher – Meridian – tossed out, but she was beginning to realize how limited her own understanding was of the echo world structure.

And she realized something else about Christopher – Meridian – too.

"How old are you?" Ravlen asked.

Meridian blinked, caught off guard by the question. He stared at her before answering.

"Older than I look. And don't ask me to say more than that." He read the look of shock on her face. "I'm not *that* old. While in training we don't age. It's part of the gift of immortality, even if we haven't yet accepted our heritage."

The prince-servants. He's one of the ones that Alison and Claire witnessed. I knew it.

"Will you?" Ravlen wrung her hands.

"Accept my heritage? I'm doing everything I can to prevent it."

"Can't you just say no?"

He let out a tense laugh. "No. It's not that simple. And that's also why I haven't slept properly in years. Not since I managed to nestle myself away at the middle school with my own kind of referent…"

"Your uncle?"

"He's not my uncle, but that's the easiest answer for earth-walkers – you call them originals – who can't understand the kinship of the double universe."

Ravlen nodded. Sharing her own history with people like Joan and Tom was hard enough. She couldn't imagine what it was like for Meridian to explain that he was an immortal sent to earth to propagate the wishes of originals.

Immortal.

"Christopher, I mean, Meridian…"

"I prefer Christopher, please."

"Christopher," she gulped. "Am I immortal, too?"

He tipped his head to the side, taking her in. His stare lasted longer than was reasonable. Ravlen squirmed.

When he finally spoke, his words were gentle, as though he was addressing the most fragile creature on earth.

"Don't you know what you are?"

Ravlen bit her lip. "I've never known who or what I am. Every day I discover something new."

He stepped slowly toward her, like she was a bird who might flutter away at the slightest movement. He pulled her hair away from her face, tucking it behind her ear.

"You, Ravlen, you are—"

"ENOUGH!"

Christopher was on the ground, his father standing over him. Ravlen hadn't seen how it had happened. She'd been too focused on his words and lost track of the physical world around them.

And that was dangerous.

The echo master's voice was aflame with fury. "Too far, my son, you stray too far!"

"She has a right to know!" Christopher screamed.

His father stood, lifting him by the neck and holding him in midair. "You abuse your position." He looked at Ravlen. "It's always those who have been given the most who are most ungrateful for their legacy."

Ravlen had to do something, but she didn't know what. "Christopher!"

He looked down at her, suspended in his father's clutch. "Don't worry, Ravlen. You don't need me. You were born for—"

The echo master tightened his grip, cutting off Christopher's words.

"Children." He shook his head and was gone, with Christopher still in his grasp.

Ravlen was left alone in the middle of the circus, life springing up as new acts rolled along the sandy ground.

But Ravlen couldn't breathe. Around her, there wasn't a single familiar face. The crowd grew, activity bursting as a monkey danced and a clown walked by on his hands. Ravlen was frozen in place.

She was more alone now than she'd ever been, and the enemy could be standing behind any tent.

Worst of all, she didn't know who the enemy was.

I've got to figure out its logic and get out of here with the original.

Christopher would be safe; he had the ability of the masters. He could move between echoes seamlessly. Or so she hoped. She forced herself to put him out of her mind and began her analysis of the world, the intellectual exercise calming her frayed nerves.

She inspected performers, vendors, animals, and ticket takers. Every face held a secret, every movement of every performer hid the meaning of the echo, but the language of their bodies, their voices, and enchanting songs were unknown to Ravlen.

Nothing made sense, and yet it all worked together perfectly.

She didn't know how many hours had passed, her watch having stopped on her arrival in the first tent, as if even time couldn't bear to face the tiger. She didn't know the hour, but she knew she was tired. And hungry. And far from safe.

For all she knew, the echo master could be around any corner. He had taken Christopher just when he was to reveal what he knew about Ravlen's destiny.

Ravlen couldn't be distracted by that now.

How many times have I let myself be sidetracked while trying to close echoes? Lots.

She slid under the bleachers in a tent full of acrobatics.

And how many times has it gone wrong for me? One hundred percent.

Spying between the feet of spectators, more bodies than Ravlen could count flipped in the air. Wrists clasped at ankles as the acrobats rivaled a crowd of students rushing to get into school after lunch break. They twisted and tucked, a constellation of bodies moving like a Celtic knot, weaving on itself in an infinite cycle. But not a single one fell. It was just as well.

There was no safety net below.

What logic is there? None of it has logic to start with. A circus is a place of magic, by its definition it is illogical. So how do I break it?

She heard wood snap, a trapeze broken in two and a body tumbled through the air to the gasping horror of the audience.

Ravlen held her breath. Things weren't supposed to go wrong in the echo. This must have some meaning, but what good could come from a performer's broken neck?

The acrobat twisted his body as he tumbled, a cloud of sand rising through the bleachers as he hit the ground. Everyone stood to see what had happened. Ravlen shuffled on her stomach to the bleacher's edge, her chin grazing the ground.

From there she could see the acrobat in a crouch. He lifted his chin and met Ravlen's eyes.

He winked.

Arms wide, he stood victorious, and the crowd went wild. Screams and shouts filled the air, along with sobs of joy and "Bravo!" as the acrobat climbed the pole to rejoin his flying comrades.

And the show went on.

It was late. Ravlen's eyelids started to close and her chin nodded, smacking into the sand below.

That woke her up.

I need sleep. I can't continue like this. It must be the middle of the night. But where could I possibly be safe enough to rest?

She snuck toward the exit, slipping out through two panels of the tent walls so no one would catch her, and walked straight into someone.

"Sorry, sorry," the person said.

In the dark, Ravlen couldn't see the woman's face, but she didn't need to. Ravlen knew who she was, or rather, *what* she was, right away.

The original!

"It was my fault," Ravlen said, hoping to keep the woman near enough to assess if she would be an easy-leaver or not.

"I have to go." The woman's voice sounded younger than Ravlen first thought, and she was only a little taller than Ravlen. She shuffled backward, the whites of her eyes gleaming in the overhead light of the nighttime circus. With her face silhouetted, Ravlen couldn't make out any details.

"Please, wait…"

"I know what you are," the girl hissed before turning and running away.

"Not an easy-leaver, I guess," Ravlen said to herself before clapping her hand over her mouth. Anyone might be listening.

She knows what I am? She knows I'm an original? Or an echo chaser? And what difference does that make?

Ravlen was once again taken back to the mermaid-turned-trout world where the man had convinced himself that the echo was real. The way he fought to go back into it, even as it was collapsing on itself.

This girl had been in the echo circus for years. Who knew what she had become? The circus, full of its performers and acrobats and creatures of wonder had warped everything the woman could know of the real world.

On top of that, it had been nighttime ever since Ravlen arrived.

Time is wrong here. Could that be part of the misplaced logic? Is that the foundation of the lies the echo master created?

Ravlen tried to imagine what it must be like to live years alone, the only original in a never-ending nighttime circus. No sunshine to replenish, no moment of calm to rest. As it was, Ravlen was exhausted, and she'd only been there for a few hours. Her body was heavy and her knees threatened to give out with each step she took.

But every time she thought she'd found a safe corner hidden away, someone appeared, casting light, as if to intentionally prevent her from every wink of sleep.

"I can't go much farther," Ravlen whispered into the starless, moonless sky. "I need somewhere to lie down. Please," she implored without knowing whose ears might perceive it, "just for a little while."

She tripped on an unseen obstacle, falling forward into an echo person wearing a massive skirt that broke her fall with a cottony bounce.

A whisper from the darkness soothed her.

"Hush now, child. You're safe." A strong arm scooped her up by the waist, holding her steady while bringing a shawl over her head, hiding her from peering eyes. The shawl created perfect blackness. Ravlen's heart skipped a beat just as the voice said, "You feel fear? Don't fear me. Perhaps the secrets I reveal to you, yes, fear those. But never fear me."

"Referent?"

"Shh. I'll take you to the far edge. That will buy you a few hours to rest."

Silent tears of relief streamed down Ravlen's face as the sounds of the circus faded into the distance.

RAVLEN'S EYES OPENED INTO DARKNESS. ONLY THE CARESS OF A finger on her forehead told her she was awake. Her head was lost in the sweet scent of lilacs and summer days that clung to the cotton of her referent's skirts.

"Best you wake now, child. I could see you were struggling. This is not a good place to be. But as it is, I have surpassed my allotment."

Ravlen rubbed her eyes, willing the sleepiness away. "What allotment?"

Her referent brushed an errant strand of hair from Ravlen's forehead. "I've gone this far, I suppose a little further can't do more harm than I've done already. I'm talking about my allotment of energy for you. I surpass it, and I pass the energy along to those most undeserving of it."

There was only one type of person Ravlen thought undeserving of any more power.

"You mean the echo masters?"

The referent took in a deep, wheezy breath. "Please don't ask more of me than is absolutely necessary."

Ravlen thought hard about her next words. She had to pose her questions in a way that didn't even broach the subject. Her referent continued to wheeze, a high-pitched whistle with each breath.

"Carer Killian used to say that energy cannot be created or destroyed. It only ever transfers."

"That is an excellent way to describe a very difficult concept."

"Like a yin-yang. Total opposites."

The referent touched her shoulder. "Yes and no. Even yin and yang are two parts of a whole. Duality exists within us all, but also in the world around us. To upset one part is to upset the whole."

Even in the near-black of night, Ravlen's eyes adjusted to look her referent in the eye. "I understand. You don't have to say any more."

Ravlen looked up, the sound of footsteps coming closer, the beginning of new life in this part of the echo.

"I have already said too much. He will have grown stronger for it, I'm sorry to say. I have created an imbalance that twists in his favor. The unity of opposites demands it."

"Oh, the unity of opposites, that old friend." The echo master hung off a lamp post. He turned the light directly into Ravlen's face. "And how does our visitor enjoy our show? Is it not the greatest show you've ever seen?"

"Give it up, Ramos." The referent stood.

The echo master slid down the pole. "Big words for a woman who has defied her own rules. And I thought you were the upright one."

"The girl is on to you. My role was rather less than you let on, as I'm sure you've noticed. Your abilities are not so inflated as you might want to think. By the way, where's that son of yours? Your shining glory, your pinnacle of pride?"

"A boy is a slippery thing."

"Like your integrity."

The echo master smirked at the insult. "You say that, but look at what I'm about to do." He cracked his neck to the left and then the right before setting his eyes on Ravlen. "You feel that over there?" He leaned on his knees as if speaking to a five-year-old. "I bet even you can sense what is just down that lane, what was before you all the while you slept in the streets when you could have been home in a comfortable bed."

Ravlen turned her head. A shimmer caught the light of a single lamp post.

The haze.

"Go on home, girl." The echo master caressed her cheek with his middle finger. "I opened that one just for you. This is not a place for you to play. Years have established a coherency that even your divinely charmed little—"

"Ramos!"

He paused. "Finger. I was going to say 'finger.' Even your charmed little finger can't undo the logic here. Head home. Come back later if you must. Maybe my son will greet you instead of the tiger, but I make no promises there. Boys... slippery..." He shook his head before glaring at her. "So, what do you say?"

Ravlen looked at her referent. Any advice would help.

But her referent raised her hands. "This is all about you, and the consequences of every decision you make."

Ravlen walked toward the haze, telling herself she would only check it out to see if it was real or a trick. But the truth was that she wanted to go home. She *needed* to go home. She had nothing left, no energy, no ideas. She was empty. She observed the haze which looked as real as any other she'd ever seen.

An original who has been here for this long will last a few more days. Or weeks, even. She'll be fine...

She looked for excuses to make it okay to give up. She was overpowered. Defeated.

Maybe she would even find her own way out. Maybe she doesn't need me at all.

Ravlen heard whimpering. In the sea of circus voices, it cut through, grabbing at her ears, reverberating in her head. Her body told her to listen, and she obeyed.

"Could it be true? I'm not the only one anymore? And a girl, just like me. I saw her eyes." The original sobbed and Ravlen's heart twisted. "She was so real, the touch of her skin… finally, I remember. I remember. I remember…"

Ravlen couldn't leave. The choice was no longer hers to make. Someone needed her more than Ravlen needed to recover.

"PULSE!"

She leapt, leaving the echo master and her referent in a cloud of circus dust.

"Go get her," the referent's voice reached her in mid-leap. "She's been here for way too long."

Ravlen approached the place of the original's cry, but the crowds were packed in dense groups. She wove through alleyways with performers scattered about, blocking her way. Ravlen didn't want to scare the girl, so pulsing to reveal the echo's falsehood wasn't an option. Not yet anyway.

She'd have to use a different tactic to find her.

An accordion sang out over the crowd accompanied by a man's voice, growly and deep. At first, Ravlen couldn't make out the words over the din of chatter, but little by little the masses turned and listened. The accordionist stepped forward, tipping his head to his adoring public as he went. A few people joined in the song, the words now clearer.

"Into this wondrous world of enchantment
Ahead we march with reckless disdain
For we are the protected ones
The loved ones, the joyous ones
We march into adventure, the adventure of every day"

The melody repeated, the words varying but always in the same theme. A life of magical wonders, of sights to amaze, of ever-changing illusions. The accordionist's song rang out through the ever-night sky.

Ravlen climbed the base of a lamppost to get a better look. As far as she could see, every voice was singing, the song as familiar to them as an anthem. A clarinet joined, playing out the tune in hypnotizing tones.

"Join in!" a boy standing below her called out. "It's our time of union!"

"I don't know the words."

"Neither do I."

"But you're singing them."

"Everyone knows them in their heart. You have to sing from your heart."

Ravlen hazarded a try, herself being pulled into the song, but her lips couldn't make the words. She didn't know them. She couldn't sense them. She was the only one not singing at the top of her lungs.

The other original might know the song already, but there's a chance... if I don't know it, maybe she doesn't either...

Ravlen scoured the alley, but the clouds of sand rose up between the stomping circus people, their song now accompanied by a stepping rhythm that they all knew. Even the boy below her joined in.

"I'm guessing you don't know the dance steps either?" she called down.

"Nope, not a single one. It's in the blood, don't you know?"

Ravlen raised an eyebrow and continued searching for the one person who might be still and silent among the crowd of hundreds, swiftly becoming thousands. Everyone was headed in the same direction, new instruments joining into the compelling song. Hands smacked backs and the stepping evolved into a jig. Toes tapped and hands clapped as the flurry of the mass moved as one.

There she is!

On the outskirts of the crowd, a girl a bit older than Ravlen wore a muted smile, watching the singers and dancers go by.

The words of the song captured Ravlen's attention, even as she kept close watch on the girl.

"Join in, all lonesome, all lonely, all sad
Come sing with the splendor of the beauty we've had
No lonesome, no lonely, no sad here these days
For we become one in the circus of strays"

The words of this chorus finished out the lyrics. Voices continued with 'la la la' and lips whistled in tune. Ravlen saw more meaning in the chorus than its simple words.

The circus of strays. Could that be at the heart of this logic? A place where all are accepted and loved for whoever they are?

It wasn't a bad idea at all. That was the thing about the circus that had always drawn Ravlen in. The circus, where everyone had their own special talent.

When everyone is unique, no one is alone.

It was a spellbinding thought, and an anthem for everyone in this echo. They all sang the same tune. It was comforting on the one hand, and a bit creepy on the other. Ravlen was sure it would be useful for finding a way to close this place out once they were safely on the other side of the haze. It might even help her to connect with the girl.

One step at a time, Ravlen reminded herself. *If she hasn't seen an original in years, this might not be as straightforward as that.*

Ravlen jumped down from the lamppost and ran in the direction where she'd seen the girl. She wasn't tall enough to see over the heads of the singing-dancing crowd.

Ravlen jumped on a performer's box that had been liberated in the march. She scanned the crowd, but the girl had moved. The light was not on her side. A lamp glared directly in her eyes.

Where did she go? She was right here...

"Are you looking for me?"

Startled, Ravlen jumped and fell off the box.

She landed sideways on her hip, a sharp pain piercing her torso. She moved gingerly. Testing. Nothing seemed broken, but she was surely going to have a nasty bruise.

The outline of a girl standing over her shifted left and right, observing Ravlen on the ground, but not offering to help. Ravlen shielded her eyes from the light and could see the shape of the original's face, a young woman with white-blonde hair.

Why does she look familiar?

Ravlen stood awkwardly, still getting no help from the girl who looked at her as though she was some kind of alien.

"You're not like them," she accused.

I've got to be careful. She's suspicious. Maybe rightfully so from her perspective...

"That's true."

"Why are you here? And what do you want from me?" Still accusing.

Ravlen was beginning to feel like she was being interrogated. She looked around; the chaos of the dance was dying down, but there were still too many people around. "Let's go somewhere to talk."

"Just to talk?"

"Just to talk. I promise."

They hadn't taken more than a few steps when the girl stopped.

"What's your name?"

"Ravlen."

"Did you just make that up?"

"No, why would I?"

The girl looked around. "No one here has names until I ask them for one."

"I'm not from here. I'm from…" How to explain it? "The other place." Ravlen winced. Would that be good enough for her to understand?

She didn't have a chance to find out.

"Girls, girls!" A man turning a handle on a music-making box approached them. "It's time, don't you know? She's taking the stage in tent number two! *You can't miss this.*"

"Oh," the girl said to Ravlen, "we absolutely can't miss this." Her eyes had taken on a glassy look, and she ran ahead in the direction of a massive tent, the same size as the one where Ravlen had first arrived. Ravlen shook off the memory of the tiger and ran to keep up.

Hundreds of people filed into the tent, and Ravlen was pressed against the girl as well as the bodies of the echo people around her. Her skin shook with the electrical charges coming off of them, but she was able to resist.

The girl, however, was a different story.

Squished within the crowd, the girl's face changed. Her expression melted into an expressionless lull, her head tipping to the side. She walked forward in a directionless shuffle, the crowd moving her like a sheep in the middle of a pack of wolves.

No wonder she's stayed so long. Being touched every day in such quantities, the effects are deeply ingrained in her.

Eyes now empty, the girl marched forward, the light in the tent bright enough that Ravlen could finally see more detail in the girl's face. Under the mass of her white-blonde hair, her nose and cheekbones were angular, her shoulders and hips narrow. Her brow had the shape of someone perpetually concentrating, even if she wasn't.

Ravlen gasped.

She'd seen that brow before.

And then all the pieces fell into place. The angles of her face, the narrowness of her body, the look of disdain and mistrust that Ravlen knew so well. She was just about the right age, eighteen or so.

Dina's sister. It's got to be her.

The stakes had suddenly gotten a whole lot higher.

"Let's sit over here," Ravlen suggested and the girl followed without reply.

Her skin is so white, I can see the veins in her neck. Even her face is nearly translucent. If she were to come into the light of day, she'd be blinded.

This was one extraction she was going to have to think through carefully, but no matter what, she had to make it happen.

The girl sat down, and Ravlen realized she didn't remember Dina's sister's name. There was no way for her to verify it, or was there?

"Who's that?" Ravlen pointed to the woman preparing to perform in the center of the tent floor.

"Maia the Allegorist."

The girl's eyes remained wide, unblinking, staring at the woman. It was as though she'd forgotten Ravlen was sitting beside her.

Ravlen had an idea. "She looks a lot like someone I know. Her name is *Dina*."

Ravlen watched carefully. The girl's eyes blinked three times and her lips moved silently, "Dina. Dina. Dina."

"Ladies and gentlemen, welcome!" Ravlen's stomach dropped. She knew that voice. Ramos. She'd hoped she was rid of him for now, but the echo master had taken his place in the circus ring with a microphone in hand.

Ravlen slumped down in the hopes she blended in with the other captivated circus-goers. The lights on the crowd dimmed while brightening on the ring. So far, Ravlen felt safe. The echo master-turned-ringmaster looked right past her as he announced the coming act.

"What you shall see today is a feast for the eyes, a song in movement, a soliloquy in dance, an oration in physical sacredness," Ramos called out to the mesmerized crowd. "You too shall play your part in the show, but I do not dare speak more than that! You must experience it yourself, connect with the divinity that lives in the heart of us all."

The woman strode into the center as the echo master retreated, his arm inviting her to take her place. All eyes were on the woman, but Ravlen didn't dare let Ramos out of her sight. As soon as he was out of the spotlight, his face changed from delighted ringmaster to calculating sentinel.

He must be looking for the original. And if he sees her, he's likely to see me...

Ravlen slumped deeper in her seat.

"So beautiful," the girl commented.

Ravlen turned her eyes back to the ring as the echo master slipped out of sight. A relieved sigh escaped her lips.

"Shhh," the girl chastised, her eyes still fixed on the woman below.

The woman's face was void of all emotion, and Ravlen wondered what it was that was keeping a tent of hundreds focused on her.

But then she clicked to life.

Her jaw locked and tightened, the lighting of the tent angled so that every muscle in the woman's face cast a shadow. Each step she took was hesitant, as though she expected the crowd to turn on her any moment.

But it didn't. The crowd sat in mesmerized silence, absorbing the visual story.

The woman found someone in the crowd and locked eyes. She stepped closer to the division between stage and audience, her arm reaching out in front of her.

The woman's eyes passed from one spectator to another as she chanted words from a language Ravlen didn't know. A soothing, rhythmic incantation, her body pulsated in time with her words. It was like she glowed, the light not coming from above but from within her, a story growing in momentum. The woman's arms lifted slowly, beckoning further.

Ravlen tore her eyes away from the sight, but it was harder than she expected.

She's putting a spell on us.

Ravlen refused to look at the woman, even though her chin kept leading her in that direction. The woman's speed accelerated, words rolling faster in a joyful bounce. Ravlen saw Dina's sister sitting on the edge of her seat, a gentle smile across her face.

"A-ha!" the woman cried from below.

"A-ha!" the enthusiastic crowd replied, all except Ravlen who nearly jumped from her seat.

Dina's sister grew more enthralled, her eyes tearing from lack of blinking, a bit of drool threatening to fall from the corner of her mouth.

Ravlen did not like where this was heading.

"Watch friends," the echo master's voice rose like thunder from the ground. Ravlen looked around, but in the blackness of the tent and the disjointed rumbling of the microphone, she couldn't find him. "She tells a story that belongs to us all. The story that brings us and keeps us together. It is your story, too. Join in the glory of its unity as your soul moves you."

A man on the far side of the tent stood calling out words but Ravlen couldn't make sense of them. The woman's body responded with a flourish and her head rolled heavily to one side. She lifted her hand up, inviting more.

A woman near Ravlen was the next voice to join in. She spoke in regular tones, with words that didn't fit together.

"Any in someness the lightness my being together we wishing…"

More voices called out in the blackness. Words, sounds, cries, laughter. The cacophony grew. The person in front of Ravlen stood, and others stood, everyone then standing as the sounds whisked higher and stronger, hundreds or even thousands, Ravlen couldn't tell.

She covered her ears.

"Me," Dina's sister spoke. "It was what I always wanted, always thought I wanted, with you, I thought, but I… no… I must want it, I've lived it so long…"

The energy was mounting, voices joining in common tones that grew louder, stronger in their unity.

"We should go now," Ravlen said to Dina's sister. "This is the best chance we're going to get."

The girl's eyes didn't budge from the woman.

Ravlen tried again. "Can you hear me?"

"What I always wanted. Always wanted. Always wanted."

Ravlen waved her hand in front of the teenager's face, but she didn't react.

Oh boy. Never mind easy-leaver… she's in a trance!

Meanwhile, the crowd was getting rowdy. Their bodies moved left and right, thousands shifting, stepping, arms shooting up to the sky and out toward the woman. Their voices grew to shouting, ear-splitting cries so high-pitched that Ravlen could barely endure.

What now? Where are you, referent? What do I do?

Someone grabbed Ravlen's arm.

"Referent?" Ravlen squinted but the crowd was in an ever-darker shadow. "You heard me?"

"It's me," Christopher whispered into her ear, his hot breath casting shivers down her spine.

"What's happening? They're going crazy for this woman!"

"It's only going to get worse. Keep your voice to a whisper. Just before they break into madness, I'm going to lead you to the exit. It's the only moment when my father won't notice our departure. Got that?"

"Yes, but there's also Dina's sis—"

A bloodcurdling scream tore through the tent as the woman collapsed in the center of the circus ring.

"NOW!"

Ravlen had just enough time to grab the girl's hand before Christopher had them out of their seats. Tripping down steps and tumbling toward the exit, they maneuvered through the crowd who sobbed and cheered in mad screams. The mass of people fell into and over each other just as Christopher, Ravlen, and the girl reached the clear night air.

"Run!" Christopher screamed, but try as she did, Ravlen couldn't pull Dina's sister into a fast enough pace. She barely strode one foot in front of the other for three steps. "Get her to move!" Christopher pointed his finger in the girl's face.

"Look at me," Ravlen stood in front of her, gently patting her cheeks. "I know your sister."

"Sister?" Still, she didn't make eye contact with Ravlen.

"Dina."

"Dina?" She blinked and looked at Ravlen. "Dina?"

"Dina, your sister. She's waiting for you. I'll bet anything she's waiting on the other side of the haze for you now."

Suddenly the girl was animated, as if an on-switch had just been struck. "Dina? Where? She's here? You have to take me to her! I have to see her!"

"Come!" Christopher led them through the nearly-empty alleys and quickly arrived at the haze.

Dina's sister stopped dead in front of it.

"She's not here."

Ravlen coaxed her forward, a hand on her shoulder. "I'll take you to her. She's waiting for you, just through there."

"No… no…" The girl looked deep into Ravlen's eyes, her

own eyes brimming with tears. "I can't go through there. I've been gone so long. No one out there remembers me, no one cares. Or if they do, they'll hate me. I didn't know what I was doing, I was just a child. But I never wanted to go back. They'll blame me."

Ravlen kept her hands on the girl's cheeks. "What's your name?"

"Julia."

"Julia, what happened to you is unfair, but the way you feel is normal. And I promise you, people have been searching for you for a long time, wishing you'd come home."

"I can't… I can't…"

"Now!" Christopher screamed. "No more playing around! You have to decide." He stood nose to nose with Julia.

"Then I'm staying."

"Fine." Christopher turned.

"No!" Ravlen took Julia's hands. "Please. Dina needs you. Her heart is breaking for you."

Julia's eyes overflowed. "Dina…"

Ravlen was sure they'd waited too long, that the echo master was going to appear at any second. Christopher already had one foot in the haze, and he wouldn't hesitate to leave without them, Ravlen was sure of it.

"Dina…" Julia took a step. Only one, but it was enough. She reached out her hand and Christopher took it, violently yanking her into the haze. Ravlen jumped in after them.

They were moving through the colored air when Christopher pushed Julia ahead, shoving her out into the real world. But he blocked the exit for Ravlen.

Ravlen's heart jumped into her throat. "What are you doing?"

Visions passed in her mind of all the things that could go wrong.

I should have known he wanted to keep me here! He's going to bring me into the lair of echo masters and then he'll...

"I can't come with you," Christopher's eyes were earnest and clear, the undulating storms calmed to a near-normal gray. "I'm not safe out there."

She sighed in relief. This was about him, not her.

"But you're not safe in here either."

He looked back and forth between the direction of all that was real and the fantasy that had been created those many years ago. "I'll figure something out. In here, I sense better, I react faster. And here I can keep track of the false gods who've grown too full of their own self-importance. Nothing will get any better until they are put to an end, stuck back into their own mortality." His spine straightened. "And I'm going to be the one to do it."

Ravlen stared at him. She still didn't know what to make of the schoolyard bully turned echo master in training turned defector and enemy of his kind.

But she had to go. Not just back to the real world, not to Joan and Tom's. No, she had to go back to the beginning. Her referent's words circled in her mind as she nodded goodbye to Christopher, though she was sure she would see him again.

"Go well, Ravlen," he whispered as Ravlen stepped out of the haze and into the real world.

Julia was wrapped in Dina's arms, both of them in breathy silent sobs, eyes closed tightly. The family resemblance was even stronger than Ravlen realized, now that they were together in the light of day in a back alley of the fair.

Dina's wet eyes blinked open on Ravlen's arrival. "Thank you," she mouthed, embracing Julia tighter.

Ravlen had only seen Julia and Dina, but now she realized they were surrounded. Everyone was there.

Mrs. Brand, Miss Markham, and Mr. Costello waited in a

group behind Mr. Johannsen to the right. To the left were Marriel, Joan, and Tom.

All eyes were on her, waiting to hear what happened with Christopher and eager to hear how she'd found Dina's sister.

But Ravlen was far off, back in the words of her referent. Those words blended now with others. The riddle was untangling and becoming a map.

"You can only end it with the very beginning," her referent had said.

Ravlen turned to Marriel. "The beginning isn't where I thought it was."

Marriel cocked her head. "Then where is it?"

Ravlen wasn't ready to announce it to the others. She might have been wrong… She might have misunderstood…

But her instincts told her otherwise, and this last year had taught her one great lesson among the many others. She had to trust her instincts.

"Marriel, we're going back to the island." She disregarded Marriel's look of shock. "What I know now changes everything."

29

To anyone walking by, it would have looked like a normal Saturday afternoon garden party.

But as Ravlen watched plates of potato salad and grilled chicken pass by with Binner's eager nose pointed toward the table, she knew their gathering was anything but normal.

She was saying goodbye.

The teachers were going to cover for Marriel and Ravlen at school. Mr. Johannsen had connections with the child welfare authority and the principal was Miss Markham's cousin. This would leave all possibilities open should they need to come back one day to resume the facade of regular, school-going girls.

Mrs. Brand, never one to show emotions other than cynicism and doubt, dabbed at her eyes. Ravlen tried not to stare, but the teacher's vulnerable state forced Ravlen to think differently about her. Words like hard-headed and narrow-minded were quickly transforming into fragile, sensitive, and loyal.

"Before I met you two, I thought this task was impossible.

Moving mountains. I don't know how many times I told Ron – Mr. Johansson – that what he imagined was impossible. Children couldn't possibly take on the wicked, the powerful, and the persuasive rulers we had witnessed." She reached out, letting her soft hand rest on top of Ravlen's. "How grateful I am to have been wrong."

"We're all counting on you," Mr. Costello added.

"More than that," Miss Markham said, jostling in front of Mr. Costello, "we know you can do it. Just look what you've done already…" She gestured across the patio where Dina and Julia were in an intimate, quiet conversation, contented looks on their faces.

Mr. Johannsen clapped Ravlen on the shoulder. "You made this moment a reality. You found someone lost to the world, and you brought her back."

The adults continued their conversation, sharing tales of those brought back and of their own lost loved ones, but Ravlen was hypnotized by the sight of the two sisters reunited.

That is what echo chasing is about. Rediscovering those lost along the way.

She thought of the years the two had missed together, the shared experiences of going to school, of playing hopscotch or Go Fish, or attending each other's dance recitals. So much time, missed.

And that's why closing the echoes forever is the only possible answer.

"What are you most looking forward to when you're back on the island?" Joan leaned her chin on her hands, ever the supportive and dedicated carer. But Ravlen had seen the sadness in her eyes when she'd first told her that she and Marriel had to leave. Joan hid her heartache well, putting on a good show for everyone's benefit.

"Madame's berry tea!" Marriel cried out and everyone laughed.

"It'll be nice to see my friends," Ravlen said faintly, only just realizing how eager she was to see Madame, Janna, Donelle, and Yuna. "But I will really miss you all. Especially you, Tom and Joan." Her voice cracked but she forced herself to go on. "Without carers like you, Marriel and I couldn't do what we do. We'd be lost. We'd be…"

"Miserable." Marriel finished when Ravlen couldn't go on. "You've made it so easy for us. Even when we weren't easy to be around…" Marriel lowered her chin. "I'm sorry for every time I made things hard for you."

Joan got up and wedged herself between the girls, an arm around each of their shoulders in a big embrace.

"It was never hard. We are the lucky ones."

"Hear, hear!" Tom stood up. "A toast!"

Dina and Julia hurried over to join the festivities.

"To Marriel and Ravlen," Tom raised his glass, "without whom we never would have known anything about marching band," he nodded at Mr. J. "We never would have met Claire and Alison – by the way, this garden has never been so well wormed as when they came through – and we'd never have heard about student parliament." He winked at Marriel, who could finally laugh at all that had happened with Conrad.

"To Marriel and Ravlen!" everyone chorused, and orange juice splashed as glasses clinked.

A knock on the garden gate interrupted their festivities. Everyone fell silent. No one else had been invited, and a stranger at the gate had never been a good sign.

Binner, however, didn't seem to notice. That alone soothed Ravlen's nerves.

"I'll go." Joan stood.

"No," Ravlen jumped in front of her. "It's better if it's me. Just in case."

Joan nodded, but Ravlen knew she would follow her. That's how Joan was.

But within a few steps, Ravlen saw the head of blonde hair and let out her breath.

"It's Greta!"

"Greta, of course!" This from Joan.

"Greta, what a relief," said Marriel.

"Who's Greta, and why is she making our barbeque so tense?" That was Dina, because that's how *she* was.

Ravlen laughed as she opened the creaky gate to her friend. "Your timing could have been better, but it's great to see you."

Greta slinked in, as much as a five-foot-ten thirteen-year-old could slink. "I hope I'm not interrupting, but I wanted to say goodbye."

"I'm glad you came."

"I made you something." She fished in her backpack, sending everything in it flying. Water bottle, socks, sunscreen.

Ravlen picked it up. "Sunscreen? Are you going to the beach?"

Greta shyly took the bottle. "I live far. And with a complexion like mine, I can't be too careful. Still, I wish I could go with you. Living on an island would be so great."

"It's not *that* great."

It really was, but she didn't want to make Greta feel bad.

"Maybe you can send me pictures?" Her blue eyes perked up.

There was nowhere to print pictures on the island. They were lucky they had lights and fully-functional plumbing. "Maybe I can write you really descriptive letters."

"Yeah, that would be good, too."

Greta tore out a page from her notebook and scribbled her address, adding a heart and a smiley face.

"And this is for you. I saw how you like to carry around the shell good luck charm, so I made this."

Ravlen unwrapped the tissue paper to find an acorn that had been dipped in silver. It hung on a strip of black leather that downplayed its beauty.

"It's very pretty."

"Where my parents come from, acorns provide protection. They used to put them in the window to keep the bad gods out."

Ravlen held it tighter. "This just might come in handy."

Greta hugged Ravlen awkwardly given the difference in height between them, then left without saying goodbye. Ravlen liked it that way. When Greta turned to wave at the end of the driveway, Ravlen waved back until Greta was out of sight.

Everyone else pretended they were chatting as usual, but Ravlen knew they'd been waiting for her to come back to the table.

"Let's see the gift," Marriel coaxed.

Ravlen held up the necklace.

"From a little acorn, the mighty oak grows," Joan recited, not realizing the impact of her words.

Ravlen looked at the charm with new eyes.

An acorn from an oak. Oaken. May this charm protect me from him and all the others. As Greta said, let's put those bad gods on notice.

She held it up into the afternoon sun.

I won't let them get away with this anymore.

Charged silence fell over the group, as they watched the acorn dangle from Ravlen's fingers.

Ravlen held tight to Binner as Dina's car banged over the rough lane, having securely taken them on the long drive across the country. The dust settled to reveal Georgie standing on the veranda with her arms open wide. Binner was out and spinning at Georgie's feet before Ravlen had fully opened the door. Ravlen followed him, rushing into the waiting embrace.

"Look at you, doll! You have changed so much! And Marriel, I could have mistaken you for a woman. How mature and settled you look. I'm guessing it was hard-won."

The unusual blush in Marriel's cheeks betrayed her embarrassment. "You could say that. It's a story best told over hot chocolates around the campfire."

"Deal." Georgie winked.

The garden was unchanged since their landing a year earlier. A wave of comfort and nostalgia warmed Ravlen from the inside. Her world had been changing every day. It was nice to know that some things stayed the same.

"I've only come for the pancakes," Dina called out, grabbing the bags from the trunk. "After all this driving, I need them soaked in maple syrup. And a cup of coffee." She dropped the first load of bags and walked to the passenger side of the car. Her voice whispered gently through the window.

"It's okay, Georgie is safe. She's one of our most trusted carers. And she's accustomed to people like... like you. People unfamiliar with the mechanics of the mainland. It's a great place for us to stay a few days."

Julia had a long way to go in readapting to the real world, but Ravlen was amazed at how quickly she picked things up. It was natural she was suspicious of, well, just about everyone. The man at the gas station, the waitress, the lady behind the counter at the pharmacy. It was only awkward when they got pulled over for speeding ten miles over the limit. Ravlen was worried that Julia was hyperventilating at the sight of the police officer. After that, Julia only rode in the front seat. It gave her a sense of control.

"A trustworthy person?" Julia's reply was hesitant as she checked out the larger-than-life personality on the veranda.

"Very. She's the one who welcomes the girls who have just arrived from the island where Ravlen and Marriel grew up, girls who know next to nothing about how the real world works."

Ravlen almost objected, but she held her tongue. Dina was right.

A year ago, Ravlen had no idea how many echoes were opening every week. She didn't know that echo masters concentrated them in places where people were most vulnerable. She didn't know there were people in the world ready to help her, nor that there were people eager to stay within the grasp of the echo's fake promises.

And she certainly didn't know how to close them down forever.

But now she had an idea, and that's why she had to go back to the island.

Julia took a tentative step out of the car. Everything she did was tentative. Her eyes were sensitive to the light, so she wore sunglasses most hours of the day and she trembled when the silence stretched out too long. Silence had never been a part of life in the circus. Sleep was caught in brief moments between acts, always with singing and laughing and declarations of belonging somewhere nearby.

Julia strode to the veranda, removed her sunglasses, and squinting slightly in the bright sunshine, held out her hand to shake Georgie's.

"Pleasure to meet you, Miss Georgie. And I do hope you can teach me everything I need to know."

Ravlen admired Julia's bravery.

Georgie took her hand. "Consider this your home, child. You are welcome here any time, any day. I am certain we will become good friends."

Georgie always knew the right thing to say.

Dina and Julia finished unpacking the car, and Ravlen thought she caught Georgie motioning to Marriel. Marriel slipped into the house.

"Now Ravlen," Georgie began, wrapping her arm around Ravlen's shoulder and leading her forward. "We have many things to discuss. Very serious things. And I must say we cannot waste any time…"

Ravlen pouted in spite of herself. The drive across the country had been exhausting and she wanted nothing more than to eat some yummy food, nap in the hammock in the garden, and listen to Georgie tell silly stories from her youth. That had been her wish the whole trip.

After all, today was Ravlen's fourteenth birthday.

She wasn't going to make a big deal about it. So many people had already done so much for her. But it would have been nice…

Georgie cleared her throat and spoke louder, as though shouting it to someone in the next room, "I said, we *cannot waste any time…*"

The sizzle of a sparkler on top of a cake cleared Ravlen's mind of every thought she'd had a moment before.

"You remembered!"

"How could we not!" Marriel laughed.

Dina and Julia had slipped in behind, and the song rang out in disjointed but enthusiastic melodies.

"Happy birthday to you, happy birthday to you…"

Ravlen had never felt so loved before. She got her afternoon in the hammock while Dina and Julia discussed their plans with Georgie. Ravlen knew she shouldn't eavesdrop, but they weren't making any effort to keep their conversation private. Snippets reached her in the hammock as she drifted in and out of sleep.

"Much to learn."

"Hard to know what's normal or not."

"I'll do what it takes."

"I'm here for you."

"Best you see Madame."

"Yes, the island might do her good."

So Julia would come with them to the island. It made sense; no one knew better than Madame what Julia needed after all she'd been through.

Madame has seen so many girls come and go… she's seen us at our weakest and helped us become our strongest. Julia will be in good hands…

She slipped into a deep sleep then, swaying in the breeze under the shadow of the cedar trees. When she woke, a fire was crackling nearby. She rolled out of the hammock, rubbing her eyes to find everyone else whispering around the fire.

"Good evening, sleeping beauty!" Georgie declared.

"How long have I been out?"

Georgie tapped her watch. "Three hours. And you can have this back now."

Ravlen eyed her own watch with awe, the seconds once again ticking by on the face. "You fixed it! How'd you do it?"

Georgie crossed her arms and gave a knowing smile. "It's a trick well-known in the sphere of watch repairers the world over. I changed the battery."

Ravlen smacked her head. "The battery!"

They shared a good laugh as Georgie dropped potatoes wrapped in foil into the fire. "If you're good girls then once you've eaten your stuffed potatoes, there just might be s'more makings in the kitchen."

"S'mores!" Ravlen lifted her fists in victory. "Greatest birthday ever!"

Her hands were still in the air to the unbridled laughter of her companions when she was hit by an overpowering sense of being watched. She glanced left and right, hoping not to alert her friends to the sensation. This moment was too precious to break if she was just being oversensitive.

But the feeling rolled over her like a wave and she knew.

Someone's here. Watching us. Watching me.

The potatoes sizzled in the fire and Ravlen excused herself, muttering something about being thirsty. She headed toward the back door, then looked around to see if anyone was watching her. When she saw no one was, she slipped around the side of the house, surveying the bushes, the trees, the brush. Whoever it was had to be there somewhere. The feeling was getting stronger.

The moon had risen, a bright sliver that cast shadows through the wild garden and its natural surroundings.

Ravlen's eyes settled on a tree. She was drawn to it, a magnetic pull without explanation, but she listened to her instinct and walked toward it. Branches cracked under her steps. If someone was there, they knew she was coming. But Ravlen had a better read on the sensation now. It was curious, not malicious. Watching her with avid interest.

Is it the tree itself?

The tree was not remarkable, a wide oak. Ravlen held onto the silver-dipped acorn dangling from her neck.

Then she saw the eyes. Gray eyes reflecting the moon perfectly in their pupils, the gray rolling over itself like storm clouds though the sky itself was clear.

"Christopher."

He stepped out from behind the tree. "I didn't want to scare you in front of the others."

"I'm not scared."

"I had to see you before you left."

"Why?"

Christopher took a deep breath. "I sense that our paths have not finished crossing."

Ravlen put her hands on her hips. "And I sense that if you really mean what you said about putting an end to this, then our paths might be the same one."

He stepped close, the moon shining off his skin and his breath warm on her cheek. "I don't want to do this alone, but I will if I have to. No one else has ever been willing to do what it takes to break the power of the masters. But then I'd never met someone like you."

Ravlen's stomach fluttered. His breath caressed her cheek and she felt her own breathing grow shallow. He was so close, but she didn't fear him, not anymore.

He was her ally.

"Fly, little bird." He stepped back into the shadows. "Go back to the nest and prepare yourself. The next time we meet, it will be under different circumstances." He backed into the brush, but Ravlen kept focused on his eyes. Eyes with storms in them, eyes which betrayed an age greater than the smoothness of his cheek. "I'll be waiting for you."

She didn't see him leave but she sensed it when he was gone, leaving Ravlen feeling emptier than she expected. She memorized the place, the position of the moon, the gleam in his eyes, and the feeling of his breath on her cheek. On days when she felt like she couldn't endure chasing echoes, she would remember this moment – she promised herself – and that would keep her going.

She rejoined her friends at the campfire. No one seemed to have noticed her absence. Georgie was in mid-story, a misadventure in her youth involving a lame horse and a traveling rodeo. Marriel was in stitches, Julia had a broad smile that shone in the light of the fire, and Dina was smiling at Julia. All felt right in the world.

"The 'taters must be about ready. I'll prepare the bits that go with. Ravlen, can you help me in the kitchen?" Georgie's tone hinted there was more in the kitchen than shredded cheese and chives.

Once inside, Georgie headed straight for the table in the entryway of the house. Sliding open the top drawer, she used her fingertips to pull out an envelope that was crumpled and dirty. No postage.

"This has been waiting for you for a few days."

Is it from Daniel?

"A few days?" Ravlen laughed as she smoothed it against her knee. "It looks like a few years."

Georgie narrowed her eyes. "Inter-carer postal service does its best, but we're not a professional operation. This was stuffed amongst a backpack of preserves, dried fruit, and candied sardines."

Ravlen was about to ask what someone would be doing with candied sardines in their bag, but the scrawl on the outside of the envelope confirmed right away who had penned the letter.

She glanced up at Georgie with a smile on her face. "It's from Daniel." She continued inspecting the words without actually reading them. She wasn't ready for that yet. "His handwriting has improved."

Georgie looked briefly, without spying. "Improved? I can barely make it out."

"You didn't see it before." She ran her fingers over the ink. "Can I read it later?"

"Sugar, it's your birthday. You can do whatever you like."

She refolded the envelope gingerly, worried she might damage the letter inside, though it had already survived much worse. "Then I'll read it later."

"After s'mores, perhaps?"

"Definitely after s'mores!"

The potatoes were mouth-wateringly good and the s'mores surpassed Ravlen's memory of them. The group of five laughed and told stories of funny times over the past year. No one mentioned the echoes, nor their upcoming departure in three days' time. There would be other opportunities to discuss those things. For now, it was all birthday and all about the good times. Embers crackled and sparks shot into the star-filled sky.

MARRIEL WAS IN A HEAVY SLEEP WHEN RAVLEN OPENED THE letter. She shuffled under the covers with a small flashlight Georgie had snuck under her pillow at bedtime. The letter was short, but its meaning was as important as ever.

"Ravlen," he'd written in artistic swirls. *"I now know why you struggled to tell me about your experience in the echo. I find I have no words to share what I've seen. Instead, the images spin inside me, invading my dreams whether I'm awake or asleep. I wish I could tell you about them. I wish you were here so we could talk about it deep into the night, sharing stories only we could understand. I hope we can see each other again. Soon. Your friend now and always. Love, Daniel"*

30

Dawn was about to break into the pink sky as Dina hung off the edge of the boat, having enjoyed seasickness the entire trip. Ravlen brought her a bottle of fresh water.

"I hated this ride on the way out from the island, too."

"How long ago was that?" Julia appeared from the sleeping quarters below.

"I left at fourteen," Dina said, "more because I was a troublemaker than because I was ready. But Madame had faith in me. She figured the mainland would do me good, and she was right." Dina looked at the tattoos that ran up and down her arms. "She wasn't thrilled about the tats. But, hey. I did better than many others when it came to chasing."

"Girls," Captain Elaine's voice pierced through the hull. "Head to the front of the boat. It's a striking sight to see."

They were heading west. Straight ahead the night sky was slowly slipping under the water. Dark blues gave way, revealing the outline of land on the horizon.

"The island!" Ravlen pointed.

A horn rang out loud enough that they could hear it

across the calm waters. All the girls and carers on the island would be heading toward the beach to welcome their arrival.

The boat moved quickly, yet now that the island was in sight, it seemed to take forever to reach it. Anticipation hung like electricity in the air.

Finally, the boat pulled into the shallow waters, and Ravlen could start to make out individuals among the crowd of people on the shore, awaiting their arrival. The horn rang again, this time followed by cheers. It was just like every other time a boat came back from the mainland. Except that this time she wasn't waiting for the boat to arrive, she was *on* it. She scanned the water's edge, trying to recognize individuals among the crowd.

A black dress. *Madame!*

Red hair, seeming to float though there was no wind. *Janna!*

"You are home," Madame said loud enough for everyone to hear. "And your voyage has not been in vain. Word of your deeds precedes you. Congratulations."

"Welcome home!" several voices cried out.

"We're so proud of you!"

"You're the best!"

The applause and cheers continued until Madame raised her hands for silence.

When the boat docked, Binner rushed down the plank, disappearing into the trees. Ravlen knew he'd be back for dinner. The girls waited their turn to be called upon by Madame.

Dina was first. Madame whispered into her ear. Dina nodded, then stepped forward on the beach. She and Janna nodded to each other, and Ravlen couldn't help thinking it had something to do with her. After all, these were the two people most responsible for developing Ravlen's ability to chase echoes.

Dina scanned the crowd to identify one girl who caught her attention in a special way – the girl Dina would select to hear her stories from the mainland, as was their tradition. She walked up to a scrawny teenage girl and put her hand on the girl's shoulder.

"I select you."

Ravlen thought the girl might faint. Sure enough, the girl held tightly to Dina's arm for balance as they waited for the others to disembark.

Julia went next.

"In a beautiful twist of fate," Madame began, "we are able to welcome Julia among us. Julia is Dina's sister. We will find a fitting role for her, but in the meantime, I ask you all to make her feel at home. Welcome, Julia!"

Applause broke out anew, and Julia's shy grin broadened on seeing the sea of girls and carers celebrating her arrival. She stepped out and moved to stand next to her sister.

"Come forward, Marriel." Madame stretched out her hand. "Many of you remember Marriel. She returns to us now with more experience, more insight, and more wisdom, but still with a true heart for her friends."

"Marriel, Marriel! Over here!" Alison beamed as her hands waved wildly. Her overseer, a girl of about eleven, quickly swooped in and spoke in Alison's ear. Ravlen was certain her overseer was explaining the seriousness of the occasion, for Alison nodded with a furrowed brow. When her overseer stepped back, Alison waved meekly with a coy smile. She couldn't help herself.

Madame leaned in, whispering in Marriel's ear. Marriel's face grew serious. She stood with a straighter spine, her lips tight, and she looked Madame in the eye.

"I will, Madame. Always." Marriel then scanned over the masses, looking for the girl she would select. She walked through the crowd, the bodies parting in front of her, making way. "I select you," she said to a well-dressed, put-together girl of Ravlen's age. The girl nodded her acceptance.

It was Ravlen's turn. Madame reached out her hand, which Ravlen took with a full heart.

"We have much to discuss," the head carer said.

"Much," Ravlen agreed. "As in, a whole lot."

Madame's face relaxed. "Tonight we will return to serious matters, but for now, take the time to enjoy your contemporaries." Madame leaned in, cradling Ravlen's head as she whispered in her ear. "You have been so very missed, Ravlen dear."

She had to select a girl now. Ravlen was taken back to the time when she had always waited with eager anticipation, but no one had ever picked her. Not until Janna had come along, and then Ravlen's world had changed forever.

Several faces were keen, excited, and caught her eye. But she was waiting for something more.

A small girl with a crooked brown-haired ponytail stood hunched off to the side. She was alone, no overseer in sight. Another girl bustled to stand in front of her, making the girl trip backward, landing on the ground.

Ravlen ran over and offered her hand to help her up. The girl's eyes widened, and she smiled shyly as she silently took Ravlen's hand.

"Hi. I'm Ravlen. And I select you."

"Me?" the girl squeaked. "Are you sure?"

Ravlen squeezed her hand. "I'm sure."

The girl swallowed hard but nodded quickly. She stood taller now than she had before.

The ceremony ended and girls scattered in excited anticipation of the evening's festivities.

"Ravlen! Ravlen!"

Alison and Claire ran toward her at full tilt. They nearly

crashed into her waist and encircled her with a strong embrace. Ravlen giggled as she struggled to stay upright.

"It's so good to see you both!" She rubbed Alison's back with one hand and wiped the bangs out of Claire's eyes with the other. "Have you been doing well here?"

"Ravlen," Claire said in her serious voice, "do you have any idea how many worms are on this island? They are everywhere! Not only that, but beetles, dune bugs, cockroaches…"

"I hate the cockroaches," Alison added.

Claire huffed. "I already promised I won't bring one into your dorm again."

"It sounds like you've settled in."

"You should see my marks in metaphysics," Alison beamed. "Carer Shannon says I'm at the top of my class."

"I don't doubt it for a second." Ravlen looked up from the girls to find Janna, Donelle, and Yuna patiently waiting for her to be released from the girls' grasp. "I'll tell you what, I've got to see some other people now, but tomorrow we'll play a great game of Memory together, just like old times, okay?"

"Yay!" The girls ran off the beach, skipping and tripping over logs.

Ravlen fell into the arms of her friends. They didn't exchange a word; they didn't have to. They breathed into each other in their shared hug, and Ravlen felt their emotions wash over her.

"Welcome home," Donelle whispered.

"We've missed you so much." Yuna squeezed her tighter.

Janna smoothed Ravlen's hair. "We know it has been hard for you. Madame didn't have to say it, we saw it written on her face when she returned with Alison and Claire."

Ravlen swallowed. It had been hard. Only now was it starting to catch up with her, now that she was in the most familiar and safe place she knew. She didn't have words to describe it, nor did she want those experiences to invade her first moments back.

"You don't have to tell us." Janna read her thoughts. "But we're here for you, however you need us."

The girls walked slowly through the forest, back to the main encampment, as stories of all that had taken place on the island came swift and unending.

"So many newcomers, there's a lot of faces you won't recognize."

Donelle jumped in. "Madame says some places are getting out of control, echoes around every corner."

"She said that?" Ravlen asked Donelle. "Around every corner?"

"Not exactly, that's just how it sounded."

Ravlen was relieved. For those on the island didn't know that finding an echo around every corner just might be their future.

Unless Ravlen did something to stop it.

The afternoon flew by in flurries of 'welcome home' and joyful reunions with the carers and her classmates. But Ravlen wouldn't be able to rest until she'd had the talk with Madame. With every passing second, she felt the weight ever greater. She had come back to the island to come up with a plan, but her body was eager to be back on the mainland, back doing what had to be done.

Yuna appeared at her dorm door as Ravlen was unpacking.

"Some quiet reflection time?"

She didn't have to ask twice. Ravlen took in a deep breath as Yuna led the way, just the two of them walking arm in arm with Binner circling at their feet, back to the place where their friendship had begun.

The land was arid and the ground cracked, though they

kept their distance from the crevice that had nearly ended Ravlen's echo chasing days before they'd begun.

They sat quietly, looking blankly into the distance. The only sounds breaking the stillness were the wind swaying the grasses and the pattering of Binner's feet as he explored the area.

"I understand better what you went through," Ravlen said after several minutes. "I see why it was so hard for you to come back to this world after that."

Yuna nodded, her eyes still fixed in the distance.

"Julia is going to need you. She was in there so long, and that world ran by its own rules. She has to learn the rules of this place again."

"Metaphysical rules or societal rules?"

"Both."

Yuna nodded. "I'll help her."

The two friends sat in comfortable silence, knowing the evening's celebrations back at the encampment would soon fill the air and mark the end of any quiet reflections.

Music struck up as they approached the edge of bonfire field. Yuna nodded to Ravlen, then disappeared into the crowd. Ravlen knew she was going to find Julia, and she was thankful for it. Ravlen, too, was eager to spend time with the girl she had chosen. She knew how much that would mean to the young girl, for she had once been that girl herself.

But she had to turn her mind to other subjects now. One subject in particular.

Echo masters.

Ravlen scanned the crowd as the skies grew darker and evening fell. Torches were lit, flames making the shadows dance as the girls huddled in excited groups, dancing or tapping to the rhythm of the music pouring out from the mainland instruments.

Ravlen saw Madame as Madame saw her. They walked

the edge of the crowd to find each other in a small clearing, just out of earshot but within reach of the celebrations.

"Ravlen."

"Madame."

She cocked her head. "You're not the same as you were when you left."

"I'm not. We have to talk about the echo masters."

"Indeed." Madame nodded knowingly. "You wear the body of a young woman, but your soul has taken on the weight of the world."

"This isn't about me anymore."

"That's how I know you've changed."

Ravlen got right to it. "We can't keep chasing echoes." Ravlen watched for Madame's reaction.

The older woman blinked, looking out to the crowd of girls who were being trained for that very purpose. "Perhaps you are right. Perhaps I've always known this was coming." She looked back at Ravlen. "But I don't know what else we can do."

Ravlen took a deep breath.

"The secret lies with the echo masters. It is with them that an echo begins and ends. We have to go to the very beginning, not to the echo, but to those who are the origin."

"Echo masters." Madame's brow furrowed. "But Ravlen, they are the supreme authority. In the echo, they have unequaled power."

Ravlen smiled, the torches illuminating her face like a beacon of hope in the black of night.

"Not anymore."

THE END

The fate of humanity could not be contained in this single volume. Please leave a review on this book because all those stars look great and help others decide if they'll enjoy this book as much as you have. We appreciate the feedback and support. Reviews buoy our spirits and stoke the fires of creativity.

Ready for Book 3 – Echo Ender?
Grab it on Amazon now!

Don't stop! Keep turning the pages as we talk about our thoughts on this book and the overall project called *Not Enough.*

You can always join Craig's newsletter – https://craigmartelle.com or follow him on Amazon at http://author.to/CraigMartelle so you are informed when the next book comes out. You won't be disappointed.

…Consider joining Eden Wolfe's reader's club to hang out and chat about life, books, dogs, and such. Get some sneak peeks of Ravlen's upcoming adventures and follow her on Amazon! http://author.to/EdenWolfe

Written October 2021

Why hello! You're still here, and that makes me happy!

One of my worst kept secrets is that I am a huge extrovert. I love going into a room of strangers and figuring out who is going to be my new friend. Indeed, I was a golden retriever in a past life (and my dog, Missy, totally concurs. Just ask her).

This penchant for all things people-oriented meant that becoming a writer had new challenges. "Wait, so I have to be alone for hours on end, not speaking a word, while I write these stories down? No conversation? No witty banter except the ones I invent on the page?"

It was tough.

But the story kept me going. And this book took me to a special place.

Eighth grade.

I don't know about you, but eighth grade was tough for me. All the trappings of adolescence kicked off, and I always looked younger than my age. I desperately wanted to be like the older girls, the high school girls. I had close friends, but not many at school, because somehow I was different.

Ravlen took me back to those days and I even came to terms with some really old feelings thanks to this fictional teenager and her middle school antics.

In fact, I became a high school teacher specifically because I wanted to know that it could be done differently (though eventually I realized it wasn't necessarily the best thing to base a career decision on spite, but when you force an 18-year-old to make a career decision, that's what happens). I also was drawn to teaching teenagers because I did – and still do – believe that the only way to change the world is through young people.

I worked with at-risk adolescents in state care. Kids that the system had long ago written off. They were aged 12-17, mostly boys, and all they knew was that people in authority tried to control them.

Not the easiest place to start an educational relationship.

But what I learned was that those kids had superpowers, starting with survival. All they had lived through, everything they were up against, it was a miracle they had made it that far in their lives and were still pleasant to be around. More than pleasant, we became a classroom family. They were with me and a social worker from 9-4, every day. They taught me about life, about resilience, and about trusting instincts.

I wonder what happened to many of those kids; they enter into my thoughts often.

This book is dedicated to them. I hope if you ever read this, you know that you all made a real difference in my life, and I hope I did the same for you.

Finally, I have to say a monster-sized thank you to members of my readers club who helped me out when I was stuck for character names. Being the extrovert I am, the readers club is the closest I can get to making writing a social event. So, I have to thank these people for character names which made it into this very book!

Crissy C.

Abyala E.

Shannon S.C.

Amy S.

Susan C.

Thank you for staying on this journey with me.

~Eden

Eden Wolfe on Amazon—http://author.to/EdenWolfe

Facebook—

www.facebook.com/edenwolfeauthor

BookBub—

https://www.bookbub.com/authors/eden-wolfe

My web page—

https://edenwolfe.com/

Also by Eden Wolfe:

Lower Earth Rising – a dystopian sci-fi adventure series with strong women running the world

AUTHOR NOTES – CRAIG MARTELLE

Written October 2021

And this draws the second book to a close. I hope you enjoyed it and are jonesing hard for the third one. Echo Ender will hit the shelves less than a month after this book is published and who knows, it might already be out there.

This book went from concept to final product a lot more quickly than the first book and the third book, even faster. When a story flows, it's a magical feeling. When it's finished, we look back and see a great book. That's what you're getting with the Not Enough series.

We started this project last winter, but in central Alaska, that's not a great time reference since we have six to seven months of winter each year. It starts in earnest in October and ends in April, maybe lingering into May. One year, the last of the snow melted the first week in June. This year wasn't too bad. April was Spring and took care of most of the snow.

Eden Wolfe has a big dog at her home in France. We have a pitbull who is a little smaller, only sixty-two pounds, and he is the most gentle dog I've ever had. He loves the woods behind our house. It's like he has a nature trail all to himself and it covers about ten acres. He may be a little spoiled with the amount of room he has to roam.

But that's Alaska with a population density of one person per square mile. I saw an article on trees per person by country and Canada had some ten thousand while the UK had forty-seven. I tried to count the trees on our property once and the number was in excess of ten thousand. We have a lot of trees. It's probably why the air almost always smells fresh.

It's good to get outside a bunch of times a day, something I wouldn't do without Stanley around. He's good for me. I lost a bunch of weight because I walk two and a half to three miles a day.

And with a clear mind comes better words, a better flowing story, and all the good things that come from those who create. Imagination is a wondrous thing. It helps us escape whatever trials and tribulations are going on in our lives. I read to escape, and I write to escape.

A dreamworld where your fantasies come true, but they aren't real. Reality is a cup of cold coffee, but it doesn't have to be. Like a vacation, come back from the dreamworld refreshed. It makes it easier to be patient and positive.

So that's what we do. We create for ourselves, and we turn that into something for you, too. Hopefully you've found the first two books in the Not Enough series to help you through something that didn't sit well. It's always easier with your book friends walking beside you.

Keep reading and keep dreaming. Both can be great places to spend time.

Peace, fellow humans.

Craig

If you liked this story, you might like some of my other books. You can join my mailing list by dropping by my website craigmartelle.com or if you have any comments, shoot me a note at craig@craigmartelle.com. I am always happy to hear from people who've read my work. I try to answer every email I receive.

If you liked the story, please write a short review for me on Amazon. I greatly appreciate any kind words; even one or two sentences go a long way. The number of reviews an ebook receives greatly improves how well it does on Amazon.

Craig Martelle on Amazon—
http://author.to/CraigMartelle
Facebook—
www.facebook.com/authorcraigmartelle
BookBub—https://www.bookbub.com/authors/craig-martelle
My web page—
https://craigmartelle.com
Thank you for joining me on this incredible journey.

Other series by Craig Martelle:

<u># – available in audio, too</u>
Terry Henry Walton Chronicles (#) (co-written with Michael Anderle)—a post-apocalyptic paranormal adventure

Gateway to the Universe (#) (co-written with Justin Sloan & Michael Anderle)—this book transitions the characters from the Terry Henry Walton Chronicles to The Bad Company

The Bad Company (#) (co-written with Michael Anderle)—a military science fiction space opera

Judge, Jury, & Executioner (#)—a space opera adventure legal thriller

Shadow Vanguard—a Tom Dublin space adventure series

Superdreadnought (#)—an AI military space opera

Metal Legion (#)—a military space opera

Battleship: Leviathan—military science fiction

The Free Trader (#)—a young adult science fiction action-adventure

Cygnus Space Opera (#)—a young adult space opera (set in the Free Trader universe)

Darklanding (#) (co-written with Scott Moon)—a space western

Mystically Engineered (co-written with Valerie Emerson)—mystics, dragons, & spaceships

Metamorphosis Alpha—stories from the world's first science fiction RPG

<u>**The Expanding Universe**</u>—science fiction anthologies

Krimson Empire (co-written with Julia Huni)—a galactic race for justice

Zenophobia (#)—a space archaeological adventure

End Times Alaska (#)—a Permuted Press publication—a post-apocalyptic survivalist adventure

Nightwalker (a Frank Roderus series)—A post-apocalyptic western adventure

End Days (#) (co-written with E.E. Isherwood)—a post-apocalyptic adventure

Successful Indie Author (#)—a non-fiction series to help self-published authors

Monster Case Files (co-written with Kathryn Hearst)—a Warner twins mystery adventure

Rick Banik (#)—spy & terrorism action adventure

Ian Bragg Thrillers (#)—a hitman with a conscience

Not Enough (co-written with Eden Wolfe)—a coming of age contemporary fantasy

Published exclusively by Craig Martelle, Inc

The Dragon's Call by Angelique Anderson & Craig A. Price, Jr.—an epic fantasy quest

A Couples Travels—a non-fiction travel series

Mischief Maker by Bruce Nesmith—A Norse Mythology Contemporary Fantasy (not superhero)

Love & Haight by Jean Rabe and Donald R. Bingle—a courtroom drama with the undead, humor, horror, and the law.